Something I'm Supposed to Do

An "almost-but-not-quite-true" story

Patricia J. Parsons

MOONLIGHT PRESS | TORONTO

Copyright © 2022 Patricia J. Parsons

ISBN   978-1-7779032-1-3

For information or permissions:

Visit www.moonlightpresstoronto.com

Or email moonlightpressinfo@gmail.com

For Art & Ian

SOME OTHER BOOKS BY PATRICIA J. PARSONS

The "almost-but-not-quite-true stories"

The Inscrutable Life of Frannie Phillips (Book 3)
Kat's Kosmic Blues (Book 2)
The Year I Made Twelve Dresses (Book 1)

"Lit-for-Intelligent-Chicks"

Plan B
Confessions of a Failed Yuppie

Historical Fiction

Something More Than Love
Grace Note: In Hildegard's Shadow

Memoir

Another 'Pointe' of View: The Life & Times of a Ballet Mom

Differing Perspectives

"The purpose of life is not to be happy. It is to be useful, to be honourable, to be compassionate, to have it make some difference that you have lived and lived well."
— Ralph Waldo Emerson

"The purpose of life is to live it, to taste experience to the utmost, to reach out eagerly and without fear for newer and richer experience."
— Eleanor Roosevelt

ONE

CHARLIE, PRESENT DAY

"WELL, LITTLE SISTER, I HAVE TO ADMIT YOU WERE RIGHT about the dress. Charlie, you look beautiful."

Evelyn had been banging so frantically on the bathroom door that I finally had to emerge and put on the dress. I had just been trying to have a moment of peace before the festivities began. Now, Evelyn was walking around me as I stood there in the middle of the hotel suite where I was getting ready for my wedding. It was scheduled to start in—I checked my new Cartier watch that Tom had given me as a wedding present—exactly twenty-seven minutes. But since the wedding would be taking place only a few stories below me in a ballroom overlooking the harbour, it wouldn't take much time to get there.

I put my hands on my hips as I often did when we were little girls. "Say it, Evelyn," I said. "Just once. Say it." I knew that while Evelyn might have finally agreed that I was right about making my own wedding dress—I believe she had mentioned something about it being an archaic thing to do—she would have difficulty saying what I so wanted to hear.

"Okay, Charlie. I give up. I was wrong. You were right. Happy now?"

I was almost embarrassed at how happy I was to hear that my perfect sister, with her perfect fuchsia-coloured Chanel suit, her perfectly coiffed hair, her perfect baby girl, her perfect husband, and her perfect, successful career as a litigator in Toronto, wasn't so perfect.

"Yes, Evelyn, I am happy." Just then, the sun streaming in through the sheer drapes seemed to have been blocked out by a passing cloud. I felt a slight chill crawl up my spine and settle into

1

the back of my neck. Nothing startling—just a tiny thing. But still. "I wish Mom were here to see her dress." I felt a tear sting my eye. "I just wish she were here."

Evelyn nodded, her eyes crinkling just slightly. "You know, Charlie, you probably think it's odd for me to say this since I didn't see Mom very often in the years before she died, but I miss her. I miss our weekly phone calls and just knowing she was there. I really miss that she didn't live to see her first granddaughter—and to see you at your wedding. You know, I think she would have loved Tom."

I nodded. I stared at myself in the three-way mirror the hotel staff had placed in the suite and sighed. "Mom would have looked stunning if she'd finished this dress and worn it herself as she had planned."

I remembered the moment I found the pieces of the dress. They had been buried away in the attic for decades. It was only after Mom died two years earlier that I discovered so many of her secrets—chief among them was that she had been an avid dressmaker and so much more. This dress had been cut out in the mid-1960s and never finished until I decided it would be perfect for my own wedding. Inspired by Mom's love for sewing—a passion that had been entirely unknown to me before that—I had spent a year teaching myself to sew, and in her honour, I finished the dress. Now, on New Year's Eve, I felt like a princess on the way to meet her prince. That thought made me smile. "She's here with us, Evelyn," I said quietly, my hand over my heart. "I can feel her."

Evelyn looked over at the bottle of Veuve Clicquot champagne chilling in the silver ice bucket beside the electric fireplace we'd switched on for ambience. "A glass of bubbly before the throngs descend, perhaps?"

I smiled and nodded. I liked nothing better than a glass of Veuve (except maybe Evelyn's killer martinis), and I knew that my big sister was an expert at removing champagne corks—one of her many well-honed skills. Evelyn had the bottle angled perfectly and was encouraging the cork on its way out of the bottle's neck when something on the coffee table distracted her.

"What the hell—" The cork burst forth, struck the corner of the room, and then bounced back, hitting a lamp on its way to where it finally rested on the floor in front of my feet.

Evelyn put the now foaming bottle on the marble-topped table, something she would never do if she had been thinking about what she was doing and the damage it might wreak. I pulled my dress up around me and dived for a linen napkin to keep the champagne from marking the table. Who was I kidding? I didn't want to lose any more of it should Evelyn decide to turn around quickly, knocking the bottle to the floor.

She was now standing in front of me, holding the object of her distraction. A book. My book. *Kat's Kosmic Blues*.

"What the hell, Charlie? When were you going to tell me this was out? I thought it wasn't due to be published until the spring."

"It isn't really out," I said. "It's an advance copy." I took the book from her and looked at the cover. I was prouder of this accomplishment than I could ever express. After so many years of struggling even to finish a manuscript, I was finally an author. And it was all because of Mom. *Kat's Kosmic Blues*—although seriously fictionalized—was loosely based on Mom's life as a struggling fashion designer in the 1960s. The first publisher I had approached with the manuscript had snapped it up, and it was due to be released in April.

Just then, more loud knocking began. This time, it was coming from outside the suite, and I could hear Michael's frenzied voice. "Ladies, do you know what time it is?"

Evelyn looked at me and winked. "What do you suppose has Michael so frantic? Your wedding or the fact that he's been on baby duty for the past two hours?"

I stifled a laugh. I don't think Evelyn's husband, Michael, had been forced into baby duty alone even once since darling little Katherine's birth four months earlier. Just thinking about Katherine gave me a warm feeling since she was named after our mother—her grandmother. I wondered if Evelyn would ever call her Kat, as our mother had been known.

Evelyn opened the door, and Michael, bow tie askew—a situation I'd never seen before—fell into the room, practically buried under a tsunami of baby paraphernalia. And there, in the middle of the pile, smiling up at us from her gigantic baby carrier (why were today's baby things so big when babies were so small? A minor modern enigma, I guess), was baby Katherine. My hand flew to my face, and I began to laugh. I wasn't sure which of the tableaus was funnier. It was either Michael's state of disarray or the billowy white chiffon dress that made Katherine resemble a tiny cherub sitting in the middle of a cumulus cloud. And the picture was made especially perfect by the ludicrous headband festooned with a large red blob of fabric wound around the tiny head. I only hoped Evelyn would have the sense not to post that one on her Instagram account. Katherine would not thank her for it when she got older.

"Whatever is that thing on her head?" I said when I finally gained control of myself.

"What?" Evelyn looked at me, then at Katherine. "What thing?"

I pointed, laughing again. "That thing. It looks like a giant pimple." I could barely get the words out.

Evelyn looked horrified. "I'll have you know I bought that at a designer shop in Yorkville."

"I hope it wasn't expensive," I said, knowing full well that if it came from a designer shop in Yorkville, one of the toniest (and most expensive) neighbourhoods in Toronto—the city where Michael and Evelyn called home—it wasn't just expensive, it was eye-wateringly expensive.

Evelyn looked daggers at me as Michael adjusted himself. "I told you it looked daft," he said. "At least you gave up the idea of wearing that fascinator you wanted to wear."

Oh-oh, I thought, *I hope this isn't the first family wedding squabble about to erupt. But a fascinator? Really Evelyn, what were you thinking?*

I thought it, but I didn't say it. A fascinator? Who wore those? Anyway, I had never been to a wedding where there wasn't at least one family drama. I had hoped mine would be the one to break the tradition.

"Will you look at the time," I said, reaching for my bouquet of white roses and baby's breath. "Time to meet the photographer."

"Isn't he coming up here to take getting-ready photos?" Evelyn said.

"Nope," I said. "*She's* not. *She* wants to try some outdoor shots on the deck overlooking the water."

"But it's freezing outside."

I couldn't argue with that.

~

Two hours later, I was a married woman. At the age of thirty-four, I had occasionally wondered if this would ever happen to me—if I would ever meet someone I liked well enough to share my life with. I fully expected to fall in love. But to *like* the person, too? Well, I had thought my parents had broken that mould years ago. But here I was, standing in front of the floor-to-ceiling ballroom window, watching tiny snowflakes dance in the pools of light that dotted the boardwalk just outside. Guests milled around me, and my newly minted husband, Tom, had just peeled off in search of more champagne, yet I felt entirely alone with my thoughts.

What do brides think about at their weddings? Have you ever thought about that? Even if you were a bride once, you probably can't remember. And if you're a man who will never be a bride, you can never know. I'm telling all soon-to-be brides to pay attention because someday, you'll sit back and wonder what *was* going through your head. (I only hope it isn't along the lines of, "What in the world was I thinking?")

The bride always seems to be the centre of attention at a wedding. It must be something about that wedding dress. It seems to attract the guests, like magnets picking up pins from the floor under a sewing machine. The image seems appropriate since, as I mentioned, I'd made the dress I was now wearing. As I had laboured at my sewing machine and the dress emerged, I had picked up innumerable pins off the floor. Now, I didn't want to be that magnet. What I really wanted to do at that moment was to melt into the draperies to observe the guests. Just for a moment, I wanted to be the writer that I was and just watch.

I could see several of my teaching colleagues chatting with Devin O'Brian, the headmaster of the private high school where I taught creative writing and played the part of writer-in-residence. Next to them was another tight little knot consisting of the four other members of the writing group I'd been attending for years and their plus-ones—assorted spouses and partners.

I first noticed Miriam, the unofficial leader of our little band of writers. How could I not notice her? Miriam, whose passion was serious literature, was wearing what I could only describe as her uniform—albeit her dressy one. It was a purple and red caftan festooned with several rows of red sequins along the hemline. I smiled behind my now-empty champagne glass. Miriam was a tough cookie who always shot from the hip, as they say. She was never one to mince words, always saying what was on her mind and your feelings be damned. But I remembered that she had been the only one who had liked my first attempt at making a piece of clothing. I believe she had called it "artistic." Given her penchant for over-the-top billowy garments, I wasn't sure this was a good thing.

Miriam was chatting with Joseph, who looked especially dapper in his green-checked bowtie. I remembered Joseph had been less than complimentary about my "artistic" dress. He had told me it resembled a shower curtain—and why not? I had, in fact, repurposed a shower curtain. I smiled at my audacity in appearing in public in a shower curtain. Joseph had brought along his new partner, Darius, who looked equally debonair in his classic black tuxedo. I had met Darius only twice before today when Joseph hosted the writers' group in his apartment. I had been struck by the apparent differences in their styles at the time and noticed it again today. Yet, it seemed to work for them.

Also in the group were Karl, the truck-driver-turned-best-selling-romance-author and his adorable wife, a nutritionist. Karl was a man of many talents who had helped me with some of the heavy lifting (literally) when I cleaned out my mom's house after she died. He'd become a good friend whose subtle wisdom I'd come to cherish. Karl and his lovely wife were chatting animatedly with the perpetually frazzled Wendy, who wrote children's books and her husband, the picture of serenity—another couple whose differences seemed to work. I loved them all.

I looked over to the other side of the room. I spied Elizabeth (whom I had known as Miss Davies), my junior high school home economics teacher. Unbeknownst to me at the time, she had once been a close friend of my mother's back in the 1960s. My mother had never once mentioned that she and my sewing teacher had once been friends, much less close friends. It was only after I read Mom's diary that I understood why she would have chosen to keep that part of her past a secret. But when I met Elizabeth just after Mom died, she became something of a mentor to me. Elizabeth was now deep in what appeared to be a serious conversation with Peter and his wife, Fatima. Peter. I could hardly believe he was here.

Dr. Peter Taylor-Jackson III was my half-brother whose existence had been unknown to me up until this past year. To say Evelyn and I had been stunned to find out we had a brother would be a serious understatement. Peter was the head of pediatric oncology at Boston Children's Hospital, and I couldn't figure out how he did it. How did someone work every day of his life with sick and dying children yet maintain the positive perspective that Peter exuded? And his wife, Fatima? I had met her for the first time this week and had fallen in love with her already. Who wouldn't?

Fatima was an obstetrician-gynecologist who worked almost exclusively with refugee women in desperate need of medical care.

She was the founder of an organization called The Tara Group. At dinner the evening before, I had asked her about what Tara meant.

"Tara," she had said, "is a Buddhist deity. A female deity, but what's even more important is that she is considered a Boddhisattva. You've heard of this?"

"I think it has something to do with enlightenment, doesn't it?"

Fatima nodded. "Yes. A Boddhisattva is one who has reached enlightenment. An enlightened woman. How wonderful is that?" She smiled, and her beautifully even, white teeth lit up her face. "She is a beacon of light for our clients."

I wished I'd had more time to find out about the organization. It seemed like something I should get to know. I was deep in thought about Fatima and her work when I felt a gentle nudge. Tom was standing beside me, holding two champagne flutes.

"Penny for your thoughts," he said, passing me a fresh glass of champagne.

"More than a penny," I said.

"Uh-oh," he said. "Does that mean you're still brooding about what to do with your money?"

I nodded and sipped my champagne. I mean, who wouldn't be perplexed? I wasn't like Evelyn, who found out she'd inherited money from our great-grandmother and immediately bought a five-million-dollar house in an old-money neighbourhood in Toronto, set up a trust fund for baby Katherine, added a Hermès Birkin crocodile handbag to her collection, and still had millions to spare.

I had no idea what I'd do with fifteen million dollars. No idea at all.

Two

MY PARENTS MARRIED IN 1976 and spent their honeymoon in the Bahamas. When Tom asked me where I'd like to go for our honeymoon, I told him that I'd like to go to Nassau in the Bahamas to see what drew my parents there. Neither Tom nor I had ever been there, so it seemed like the place to go on the first of January in the middle of a cold Canadian winter.

"You do know that it's not that hot in the Bahamas at this time of year?" Tom said as I poured over online brochures two months earlier. "We could go to Barbados. It's farther south and warmer."

I shook my head. "I think that twenty-one degrees Celsius is just fine. We can go to Barbados another time. "

And that's how we found ourselves reclining on two incredibly comfortable beach lounges under a shared blue sun umbrella, sipping the most incredible rum punch from crystal glasses while gazing out into the azure blue beyond the gentle waves lapping the shore. The moment I placed my empty glass on the table between our two chaises and lay back, sighing in ecstasy, the beach attendant materialized out of nowhere and quietly asked if I'd like another. I smiled up at him and said, "Please." The handsome attendant, resplendent in impeccable white shorts and polo shirt, slipped away quietly as if not to disturb our repose.

"I could get used to this," I said.

"Well, we can certainly afford to get used to this," Tom said. "But I suspect neither of us could do this relaxation thing for more than a week or two without going stark-raving mad."

I laughed. Tom knew me so well, and we were alike in so many ways. He was right. We had decided to spend our honeymoon at The Ocean Club, which had pride of place on a five-kilometre stretch of the most amazing white sand beach on Paradise Island, which was connected to downtown Nassau via two modern bridges. My parents, too, had honeymooned on Paradise Island, but they had stayed at the more budget-friendly Holiday Inn that no longer exists, razed in the 1980s to make way for the behemoth resort Atlantis. Tom and I had considerably more disposable income than they did at this point in our lives, and I did have to admit that it was, in fact, money that seemed to be swallowing up a lot of my psychic energy these days. Specifically, my rumination still focused on what to do with it.

"You know, I've been thinking about all that money," I said as the attendant quietly slipped another drink into my hand and once again disappeared after we assured him that we didn't need a cool cloth just then.

"You don't say?" Tom said, laughing. My preoccupation with all that money seemed to be a recurring theme for us lately.

"I know, I know. I can't seem to get it out of my head." I placed the straw between my lips and sipped. The delicious taste slid over my tongue and down my throat, cooling and warming me at the same time. "I have a thought."

Tom put his drink down on the table and sat up, facing me. "Okay, Charlie. I'm all ears."

"I've been thinking about opening a writers' haven." I sat up and threw my legs over the side of my chaise, burrowing my feet into the warm softness of the sand. "I was thinking about buying an old house close to downtown and turning it into a place where writers could work, and we could help them. I'd like to create a community that supports aspiring writers. We could have writers-in-residence to provide workshops and critiques, and it would all be free. We could even provide scholarships."

Tom looked pensive. "It could be a thing, I suppose."

I was a bit perplexed by his response. I had expected a bit more enthusiasm. "You don't think it's a good idea?"

He shrugged. "Charlie, I know you want to do something. And I know how much writing means to you. You've had your first novel published, and now you want to pay that forward. I'm just not sure this will accomplish for you what I think you'd like to accomplish."

I was more than a bit deflated, but I knew he might have a point. "What did you think of Peter's wife, Fatima?"

"A bit of a *non sequitur*," he said, sitting back in his chair beside me. "Okay, I'll bite. We're changing the subject. I thought Fatima was lovely." He smiled. "And she looks just like that TV news anchor. You know that one? Ginella something?"

I nodded. I, too, had found her lovely and quite beautiful, much like TV journalist Ginella Massa. Both had extraordinary eyes, enviable cheekbones and a flair for wearing a fashionable hijab. "Fatima has accomplished quite a lot, you know."

"Yes, I did have a brief conversation with her the night before the wedding. She's impressive, that's for sure. Wasn't she a Syrian refugee?"

"Yeah. She was in Boston doing a post-residency fellowship in obstetrics when the civil war broke out in 2011. She was able to stay in the U.S. That's where Peter met her."

"She heads up that non-profit that supports refugee women, doesn't she?"

"Yes, she does. Now there's someone doing something important. Maybe I should give her a big donation and call it a day."

Tom shrugged. "I suppose you could, my darling love, but I know you. And giving someone a crap-load of money to support their particular passion isn't going to cut it for you. Don't get me wrong. I think we certainly could make a substantial donation to her organization, but that's not going to be it for you. I'm sure of it."

I was sure of it, too.

~

Six weeks later, deep into the winter semester at school (and the long Canadian winter), I was sitting in the living room one evening, sipping a cup of tea and flipping through magazines. Tom had a dinner meeting, and I was thinking about March break. I knew Tom couldn't get away this year, but I felt a gnawing feeling that I had to. Tom walked in an hour later, poured us both a glass of wine and plopped down beside me.

"Whatcha been doing this evening?" he said.

"Not much," I said, sipping the gorgeous wine. Then I blurted, "I think I want to go to Paris for March break."

THREE

I ARRIVED AT CHARLES DE GAULLE AIRPORT on March thirteenth after an uneventful overnight flight from Montreal. At least it had been uneventful after almost missing my Montreal to Paris flight because the weather in Halifax had delayed the departure of my flight to Montreal—a fog event, to be precise. I should have given myself a longer connection time at this time of year since I really hate to rush through an airport. Anyway, I had finally arrived in Paris for five days of exploration and fine dining. Alone.

I planned to stay at the flat—*my* flat, to be precise, although I had yet to fully connect with the idea that my great-grandmother had left me her Paris apartment. After I told Tom that I planned to spend a few days in Paris over March break, he was supportive of my need to explore my family history further. He was only sorry he couldn't come with me, and I would miss him. However, I figured I'd be better off doing this alone, anyway (I didn't tell Tom that).

I didn't know a single soul in Paris except the one man I'd met the summer before during my first trip. His name was Etienne Lemieux. Etienne was the person who had contacted me about my inheritance. He was the one I had met with and who had handed me the envelope with the details—details that included the key to the apartment. So, when I decided to visit Paris once again, I contacted Etienne, hoping he might be able to help me find someone to get the apartment ready for habitation. No one had lived in it for decades.

Etienne had been charmingly helpful. He told me that it would be his pleasure to assist me in bringing the flat to life again. He also seemed to have a particular interest in antiques and old Paris apartments, so he told me to leave it to him, which I did happily.

The taxi dropped me and my small suitcase on the sidewalk outside the building on *rue de Vaurigard* on the Left Bank, a short walk from the River Seine and the Sorbonne, that storehouse of higher learning I hoped to get to know. Once again, as I had done the first—and only—time I had been here before, I gazed up at the white stone building. Since my first visit, I had done some research and discovered that the building was in what was referred to as the Haussmann style, a style peculiar to nineteenth-century Paris apartment buildings. I had learned that a certain Baron Georges-Eugène Haussmann, a minor Parisian city administrator of the late nineteenth century, had been hand-picked by Emperor Napoleon III—previously known to one and all as Napoleon Bonaparte—to undertake what we might today call an urban renewal. He accomplished nothing short of a modern transformation resulting in the wide boulevards everyone knows and loves in modern-day Paris and all these residences. I knew that not everyone loved what he had done, but I was solidly in his camp of admirers. I mean, who wouldn't love these five- and six-story buildings with their Juliet balconies and their embellished facades? As I stood there looking up at the apartment on the second floor (which I would have called the third floor, but we all know that floor numbering in France isn't the same as in North America)—the apartment that was now mine— I felt as if I were a part of history.

I used a massive key to open the enormous wooden door of the building and stepped into the lobby area. Just as I had on my first visit, I stopped for a moment to take in the scene. Directly in front of me were four steps leading up to an elevator—one of those cage-type ones I'd seen in old movies. The ceilings were at least twenty feet high, with heavily embellished crown mouldings. The walls on either side of the foyer were dark mahogany with inlaid mirrors, and the floor was white tile with black ornamentation. It was immaculate and absolutely breathtaking. I headed toward the elevator.

I scrutinized the first floor as I passed upward. The first time I'd visited the apartment, I'd been so discombobulated from discovering that I'd inherited a Paris flat that nothing else had registered. This time, I noted that the first floor had lower ceilings than either the foyer or my apartment on the second (third) floor, which was once referred to as the *piano nobile*—the floor where the wealthiest residents lived. The *piano nobile* boasted the highest ceilings in the building, illustrating a kind of pecking order of society. Anyway, my great-grandmother Frannie Phillips, as most people had known her, seems to have been among those who could afford such luxury.

I opened the cage door when the elevator stopped on the second (third) floor with a slight jerk. As I stepped out, I looked around and, for the first time, wondered about the neighbours. I wondered who might live on such an expensive floor of a Parisian apartment building since I hadn't seen a single soul on my last visit. I turned right toward the door to my flat.

When I stepped over the threshold, unlike the last time when I'd been greeted with dim light and dustcovers festooning every piece of furniture, the space was bright, clean and smelled fresh. True to his word, Etienne had indeed arranged for the place to be cleaned. Even the Chinoiserie screen in the far corner of the living room gleamed, its red and peacock blue inlaid enamel shimmering in the sunlight that now drenched the space. Now it truly did resemble the screens I'd seen in photos of Coco Chanel's Paris apartment. I made a mental note to visit Chanel's apartment to see them in person. No doubt I'd be getting a massive bill for cleaning soon, but it was hardly something I couldn't afford.

I unwound my scarf and laid it on a peacock blue velvet-upholstered sofa. I hadn't even noticed the upholstery before. The sofa flanked one side of the massive, highly embellished white stucco fireplace. Facing the sofa across a large square coffee table were two enormous, seriously comfortable-looking chairs upholstered in black velvet. Much to my surprise and delight, a fire roared in the open hearth. It was clear that Etienne or one of his employees had already been here today to turn on the heat (thank heavens since it was damp and cold outside on this March day) and light a fire. I decided I'd been very smart to tell him when I expected

15

to arrive at the apartment. As I turned to survey the other end of the room, I spied a large arrangement of flowers on a side table. There was a card.

"Bienvenue dans votre nouvelle maison. Puissiez-vous avoir beaucoup de merveilleuses expériences parisiennes ici." My improving French allowed me to conjure a quick translation. "Welcome to your new home. May you have many wonderful Paris experiences here." It was signed, Etienne. *What a thoughtful man,* I thought. *I wonder if he'll charge me for the flowers.* The moment that unkind thought entered my head, I mentally slapped myself. *Who cares? I love them. Je les aime.*

I walked over to one of the floor-to-ceiling casement windows and ran my hand down the fabric of the drapes. Ever since I had discovered my mother's hidden talent for dressmaking—and later my great-grandmother's—I had become a bit obsessed with fabrics. This was silk. I could tell by its feel as I rubbed it between my fingers. I marvelled at how fresh it seemed after all these years. I wondered when the last time Fran had been here. After all, she had died in 1989 and was by that time living in Canada. I'd have to make a note to ask Etienne if he happened to know. After all, I knew from reading Frannie's diary that his great-uncle, Jean-Christophe, had been my great-grandmother's long-time friend and sometime lover. Their story made my spine tingle.

As I turned to move away from the windows, I happened to look up at the wall between them and saw a plaque I'd not noticed on my last visit. I stood back to get a better look.

The plaque looked like it was heavy brass with a dark wood frame. It looked old to me. Engraved in black were the words, *"You don't get the life you deserve. You get the life you create."*

A shiver passed up my spine.

~

By the time I'd finished unpacking, it was still only eleven a.m. Oh, the delights of an overnight flight! I texted Etienne to thank him for the pleasant welcome I'd found in the apartment, added another log to the fireplace and decided that my best course of action was to go out for an early lunch. I knew I'd have to keep moving for as long as I could today, then get to bed early this evening to stave off jetlag. If I gave into my travel weariness and took a nap, it would take me the entire five days I had here in Paris to acclimatize.

As I stepped out into the hall and turned to lock the door behind me, I sensed that I was being watched. I turned but saw no one. There were only three other apartments on this level. I could see two of the doors while the other one was recessed at the end of the hall. I shook off the feeling and headed toward the staircase, opting to walk down instead of taking the elevator. I felt I could use the exercise. As I neared the top of the staircase, I heard a voice, almost a whisper.

"*Tu es elle, n'est-ce pas?*" You are her, aren't you?

I turned toward the recessed door and saw the top of the head of someone who couldn't have been more than five feet tall peering at me. As the face emerged, I was startled by the brilliant violet of the eyes framed by deep creases in a face that hinted at great beauty at a younger age. The woman's fine, grey hair was held back in a bun, reminiscent of what I had seen on ballerinas, with wisps trailing out at the sides. Despite her evident advanced age, she stood erect as she slowly emerged into the hallway in front of me.

"*Oui. Je vois la ressemblance.* Ah, but you are not French, are you? I am sorry. You do not understand me. I said that I see the resemblance."

I had understood what she'd said but had no idea what she meant. I must have looked very puzzled. Then the woman smiled and walked toward me. For the first time, I noticed her cane. She held out her hand to me. "You are Charlotte, *non?*" I nodded and took her outstretched hand. "I am delighted to meet you, young lady. I am Juliette Renard."

"So nice to meet you, Ms. Renard. Please call me Charlie."

She nodded. "*Oui. Bien sûr.* Of course. And I am Juliette, please." She stood back and looked me up and down. I have to admit her penetrating gaze was a bit disconcerting, but given her advanced age, I let her carry on. "I never thought I would live to meet you, you know. Frannie told me about you."

"Frannie? You knew my great-grandmother?" My heart began racing as I considered everything I wanted to ask someone—anyone—who might have known my great-grandmother.

"But of course. I knew her from a very early age—from when I was a little girl." She stood up even straighter and looked at me with those eyes. For just a moment, I thought I could glimpse the young woman she must have been. I could see fire and passion. Or was I just projecting? "Charlie, my dear. You must come to dinner tomorrow evening. We must talk."

I could not have agreed more. I did need to talk to this enigmatic woman. I suddenly realized that my primary purpose in visiting Paris and the apartment might simply be to learn more about my great-grandmother. The writer in me was intrigued. So, we arranged for me to arrive at her apartment at seven the following evening and then she bid me goodbye.

I wandered out into the street to find a café where I could drink coffee and eat Parisian croissants. And perhaps have a glass of wine—or something stronger.

FOUR

I SPENT THE FOLLOWING DAY AT THE *MUSÉE D'ORSAY*. Everyone else with little experience of Paris seemed to rush to *Le Louvre*, but it and the Mona Lisa could wait as far as I was concerned. I had to see the Degas and Van Gogh paintings and the Degas sculptures.

Before wending my way back to the apartment to get ready for dinner with Juliette, I stopped by a local market to find a bottle or two of wine. Since I had no way to determine the quality of any of the wines in the place (these were not wines exported to Canada for consumption by the colonial palate), I had to figure out a way to choose what to take. I spent some time walking around the bakery bins adjacent to the wine section until I spotted what I was looking for—the best-dressed woman to walk into the place. I then surreptitiously followed her, stopping here and there to peer at the wine bottles on the eye-level shelves. When she stopped, I carefully noted which bottle she pulled from the shelf and dropped into her shopping basket, then followed behind and took another of the same. She picked out another, and I did the same again. I figured I'd take one to Juliette's for dinner and drink the other one myself in front of that wonderful fireplace. Perhaps I could transport my mind back to when Frannie actually lived there. That made me think about the movie *Somewhere in Time* that I'd seen on television some years before and been captivated by the plot. The hero figured out a way to transport himself back in time to meet the woman whose image in an old portrait he had fallen in love with. I hoped a conversation with Juliette might also transport me back in time—at least a little. I did so want to know more about Frannie.

I presented myself at Juliette's door promptly at seven p.m. When she opened the door, her face immediately broke into a beautiful smile. Her even teeth were only slightly yellowed from what I expected was a lifetime of cigarette smoking. She leaned in for the double kiss, and I handed her the bottle of wine. She looked at it, startled. "How in the world did you know? It is my favourite. I will tell you a story about how I came to love it, but now, you must come in!"

I stepped into the foyer expecting an apartment not unlike Frannie's but perhaps even somewhat older since Juliette appeared to be at least as old as Fran was when she died thirty-three years earlier—eighty-nine—if not older. I could not have been more wrong about Juliette's style. My jaw must have dropped. She looked at me and laughed.

"I never cease to be amused by the reaction of anyone new who visits my apartment. You see an old woman, and you expect an old life." She gestured for me to come inside. "Welcome to my home."

I was mesmerized by the tableau. Although the apartment's bones were the same as in my own—high ceilings, magnificent windows, crown moulding—I felt as if I had walked into a different world. Facing me were the same two floor-to-ceiling windows that I had, but between them was a magnificent abstract painting in turquoise, white and black. Flanking a glass coffee table whose base looked like a modern bronze sculpture were two full-length curved sofas upholstered in creamy white with red and black toss cushions. The sumptuous area rug under the coffee table was a riot of patterns in cream and black. It was stunning. There was a white grand piano across the room, and beside it was a five-foot-high sparkling sculpture that looked like a gown Marilyn Monroe might have worn. I then turned toward the painting on the wall between the windows. I must then have been staring at it.

"It is the only Picasso I own," she said, sighing. "I sometimes wish my parents had liked his work better. They once knew him, you know. I had to salvage this one from them when they sold their townhouse many years ago."

A Picasso! Who was this woman? And this apartment—it was glorious. I was suddenly ashamed of myself for my preconceived ideas of how an older woman would live. I then noticed a trio of what looked like fashion illustrations on the opposite wall.

"Are you familiar with the work of Erté?" Juliette said, noticing my gaze.

"I've seen prints before." I walked over to take a closer look. "But these look like originals."

Juliette laughed. "*Bien sûr*. Of course. My parents purchased only original artwork and, of course, they knew the artist when he worked here in Paris as a designer. The art deco aesthetic is so marvellous, do you not agree?"

I did.

Juliette led me to a sofa, where I sat down gingerly, not wanting to spoil its perfection. She must have noticed my hesitation.

"Do not worry at all about the delicate colour. It is tougher than it looks. Even Ralph and Rachel are permitted to lounge here."

Ralph and Rachel? Just then, I noticed a white cat perched on the back of the sofa facing me while a white cat with black spots brushed its side against my leg.

"I see that Ralph is already making friends with you." Then she looked alarmed. "You are not allergic, are you, Charlie?"

I shook my head and smiled at Ralph, who had jumped up onto the sofa next to me and settled in.

Juliette told me to make myself comfortable while she went over to a white panelled bar I had not noticed in the far-right corner of the room. It boasted an entire wall of liquor bottles and what appeared to be crystal wine and cocktail glasses, all lit from within, against a mirrored background. She pulled a liquor bottle from the bar and placed two champagne flutes beside it. She then poured a very small amount of the dark liquor into each glass. She bent down, using her cane for support, and opened what seemed to be a wine fridge. She placed what looked like a champagne bottle on the bar.

"May I help you at all?" I said.

"*Bien sûr*. Please do. How are you at champagne corks? I used to be excellent, but my hands are not so strong these days."

I jumped up to help. Although I didn't have Evelyn's well-honed skills with corks and Tom was the usual champagne-opener in our household, I knew I could manage the job. Without too much trouble, I popped the cork off the bottle and passed it to Juliette, who poured a small amount into each glass on top of the liquor, then, after the initial bubbles had settled, topped them up. She put the glasses on a small silver tray and nodded to me. Juliette picked up a plate of canapés from the bar, saying, "Thank you, Genevieve. I do not know what I would do without that girl." I must have looked puzzled. "Genevieve is my helper, my housekeeper, my friend. We have been together for many years, and she makes the best canapés of anyone I know."

I took the tray of drinks to the coffee table, and Juliette followed, balancing the plate of canapés in one hand and leaning on her cane with the other. We both sat down. Juliette carefully placed her cane on the floor beneath her and picked up her glass. "We must drink a toast," she said. "To new friends with new stories to tell!" We clinked glasses and sipped.

"Juliette, this is wonderful. Kir?"

She nodded. "Kir royale, to be more specific." I nodded. I had forgotten that Kir was made with white wine and crème de cassis—Kir royale with the same liqueur but champagne or sparkling wine. "My favourite," she continued, "and I must say one of your great-grandmother's favourites as well. Did you know that?" I shook my head as I sipped. "Although, in truth, Frannie had many favourites! In any case, we both learned to love Kir royale from my mother."

This information was too tantalizing to let slip, so I took another sip and put my glass on the coffee table. "I think new friends do, indeed, have new stories, Juliette. I am so ready to listen!"

~

Juliette insisted that we eat dinner before beginning the stories. She said, "First, we will savour the food. A story is best appreciated on a full stomach, *non*?"

There was no arguing with her, and the aroma from the kitchen was too wonderful to ignore, so I wasn't going to disagree.

We took our places at her large dining room table, over which hung the most magnificent contemporary light fixture that reminded me of a satellite. When I admired it, Juliette said, "*Ah oui. I call it Sputnik.*" I must have looked puzzled. "Oh, but you are too young! Sputnik was a Russian satellite. In fact, it was the first satellite! In any case, is it not magnificent? I was not certain that I would love this piece, but my decorator insisted on it, and it has grown on me."

So, there we sat in the most comfortable, white upholstered dining chairs, at Juliette's table full of serving dishes that Genevieve had quietly laid—so quietly that I hadn't even been aware she was in the apartment. But really—white dining chairs? I hoped that Juliette wasn't serving red wine, but the minute she raised the cover of the first dish and exclaimed, "*Boeuf Bourguignon,*" I knew I was in trouble. Out of the corner of my eye, I could see that someone had already decanted a bottle of red wine. *Okay, I can do this*, I thought.

To say the meal was one of the best I had ever experienced in my life would be an understatement. I thought I'd died and gone to culinary heaven. I figured Genevieve was truly talented until Juliette explained that she had prepared the main parts of the meal herself with Genevieve's help as *sous-chef*. As the meal progressed, and she sipped on her wine, she became ever more talkative, and I soon discovered that Juliette Renard was a woman of many talents—and many connections, as it turned out.

~

Juliette Renard was born in Paris in 1925 to parents Kiki and Gaston Renard, whose names Frannie had mentioned in one of her many diaries. By my quick calculations, that made Juliette ninety-seven years old. As Juliette told it, her mother had been a dancer with the Paris Opéra Ballet for several years until she married her father, Gaston, a financier of some repute—a wealthy, older man to her much younger twenty-two-year-old mother. He was a widower with no children when they married, and according to Juliette, her father was devoted to both her mother and to Juliette, his beautiful daughter. I knew Juliette was beautiful as a child because she nodded to a painting on the wall behind her and snorted slightly when she told me about her parents. It was a family portrait—an oil painting—like those portraits commissioned by wealthy families of a bygone era. Although, perhaps the rich still did this even in the twenty-first century. I had no idea.

"It's an extraordinary painting," I said.

Juliette snorted again. "It does capture a moment in time. But I can tell you that my parents argued incessantly about the artist before even a single brush stroke was put to canvas."

I peered at it carefully. "I apologize for not recognizing the artist's style. Who was the portraitist?"

"Oh, some minor player in the arts scene of the 1930s. My mother—ever the artist—had wanted Matisse, but my father was aghast with this idea. He wanted us to look like we really did. Mother wanted art. I think I now wish that Mother had won that argument. I would now have a Matisse in my dining room rather than a mere moment in time. What do you think, Charlie?"

I had hoped she wouldn't ask me that question. As much as I appreciated Henri Matisse and his style, now many decades later, I found the portrait of a family as they were a bit like looking at a slice of family history. My writer's mind was beginning to race again.

I again contemplated the painting and noted the graceful posture of her mother, Kiki, and the proud smile on Gaston's face. Juliette looked like a bit of an imp. "You look like you were full of life, Juliette—and still are." I hoped I'd dodged the question of my opinion about the choice of artist for the portrait because I liked the picture just as it was, and I didn't want to argue with my hostess about how a moment in time was captured.

She waved her hand dismissively. "I was six years old when we sat for that painting," she said, "and I can tell you I had no desire to sit still. I never had. That is why my mother sent me to ballet classes." Juliette snorted slightly as she sipped her wine.

"Did you not want to take ballet?"

She shrugged in that particular Gallic way the French had (although, to be truthful, I had only really noticed it in men). "I did not want to, nor did I not want to. It was just something my parents wished me to do. As it turned out, I was very good at it, and anything I was very good at interested me—at least for a little while. But it was not my life's passion."

Juliette had been so good, in fact, that she entered the Paris Opéra Ballet herself as a member of the *corps de ballet* when she was eighteen years old. "I will show you an old photograph of me in a tutu when dinner is over. *Tu vas rire, c'est sûr!*" I was certain I wouldn't laugh, but the idea made her giggle and sound like the young woman she had been and perhaps still was. Juliette continued. "Serge Lifar, who was the director at the time, was constantly at me to work harder. He kept saying he saw talent, but that talent is not enough. He was so very right. And I had nothing more to give the ballet other than my talent. I did not have the passion. I suppose it is even sadder to have the passion and not the talent." She danced for seven years, leaving in 1950, but it was clear that even time couldn't suppress the carriage of a ballet dancer that was so apparent when Juliette moved even with her cane.

"I noted the environment in a company of dancers can grow toxic over time, and I began to think that it was, for me, simply a metaphor for the world outside. I was so very naïve, I think. I had not travelled. I did not know the world. So, much to my parents' regret, I left Paris for several years, although they insisted on financing my travels to America. Before I left, though, I sought advice from my godmother. We talked about my interest in the world and its environment—ecology, people were calling it then—and she encouraged me to follow my passion since I had so clearly found one."

"Who was your godmother?" I said, hoping that I wasn't interrupting her train of thought.

"But of course, you know, do you not?" Juliette stopped for a moment and shook her head. "Of course, you do not. How could you? Frannie Phillips was my godmother."

FIVE

I WAS STUNNED. I HAD READ MY GREAT-GRANDMOTHER'S diaries and felt I knew a bit about her life, but I had never met anyone who had known her—other than my mother, who knew her only as her own grandmother. Fran died the year I was born, so for all intents and purposes, I had never met her. I had to know more.

True to her word, Juliette sat with me on her sofa after dinner and paged through an old photo album. The faded photographs were grainy, and it was often difficult to see the people clearly, but one thing stood out. Juliette had been a great beauty and looked like a carbon copy of her mother, Kiki. And, no, I hadn't been inclined to laugh when I saw the photo of Juliette in a tutu standing *en pointe*. It had made me wonder what life as a Parisian ballerina in the 1940s must have been like. Then as she turned to the last page of the album, I recognized a face.

The moment I saw it, a jolt of electricity ran up my spine. The face had been the one I came to know when I found my great-grandmother's diaries and couture dresses. It was Frannie Phillips, and she was standing with Kiki. They were leaning against one another, laughing, each with a cocktail glass in one hand and a cigarette holder in the other. Kiki was wearing elbow-length gloves and what I would call a flapper dress. Frannie was wearing a Jean Patou original. I knew this because that very dress was hanging in my closet at home in Canada. It was one of the eight couture dresses she had kept in a locked closet for decades. I felt as if my great-grandmother were here in the room with me, blowing smoke rings over my head, sipping her cocktail and whispering in my ear.

Before I had a chance to ask questions, Genevieve quietly came into the room and nodded at Juliette.

"Oh-la-la, my child," Juliette said, picking her cane up from the floor in front of the sofa and getting up. "Genevieve tells me that it is time for me to take my medication and retire for the evening. If you would like, we can continue this the day after tomorrow. Would you like to do so?"

"I would very much like to hear the rest of the story if you'd like to tell me," I said, getting up from the sofa to help her.

"I am delighted, Charlie," Juliette said as she reached for Genevieve's arm. "I am delighted because there is something I need to mention to you. *À la prochaine.*"

~

The following day, I wandered around Paris in a daze. When I called Tom the next evening before dinner, I told him about Juliette. "I think your next book might be brewing," he said. "I can hear the excitement in your voice."

Tom knew me well. I had to admit that my imagination had begun to rev up, but I couldn't quite grasp where it might be taking me.

"Where are you off to for dinner tonight? Not dining alone, I presume?" Tom said.

"No, although I really wouldn't mind. I have lots to think about before I see Juliette again tomorrow. Anyway, Etienne and his wife have invited me to dinner. They're sending a car for me."

"Sounds fancy," Tom said, laughing. "Can't wait to hear about it. Love you, Charlie."

After we said goodnight, I was still thinking about Juliette and her fascinating story. *What in the world could she have to tell me?* I wondered. Presumably, it was about my great-grandmother (at least I hoped it was). But that would have to wait. I still had to dress for dinner.

Etienne and his wife, Ines, lived in a beautiful, pastel-hued townhouse in the Marais district of Paris, a short drive from my apartment. It was decorated in Art Deco style, evoking the era I often thought about when I thought about my great-grandmother and the style so evident in the Erté artwork on Juliette's wall that had so captivated me. The apartment's décor made even more sense when Ines explained that the apartment had originally belonged to Etienne's great-uncle, Jean-Christophe, Frannie's friend and lover, not to mention editor.

Once we had settled at the dining table, Etienne asked me about my first two days staying in my apartment. I told him it felt peculiar to be living in a space in Paris that belonged to me. It was all a bit of a dream.

"Have you met Juliette yet?"

I was surprised. "Yes, I have—just yesterday. Do you know her?"

"But of course," Etienne said. "I have known Juliette most of my life." Etienne ate his last morsel of *coq au vin*, sipped his Sancerre, wiped his mouth and continued. He smiled. "You know, Juliette was a great friend of your great-grandmother, Fran's. But, of course, she has already told you this, *n'est ce pas?*"

"She told me Fran was her godmother."

"Oh, that may be true, but of course, I do not have details. My uncle mentioned that Fran and her mother, Kiki, were very great friends when they were young, single girls in Paris."

I had thought that Juliette was the only person I'd ever met who had known my great-grandmother, but now it occurred to me that Etienne might have met her, so I asked.

"I had the great pleasure once in my young life," he said, pouring each of us another glass of wine.

"Ines," I said, "I hope you don't mind the two of us going on about my great-grandmother."

"Of course not," she said, waving her hand and smiling as she nodded to her husband to continue to pour wine into her glass. "I have spent my entire married life hearing about the personalities that populate my husband's publishing firm. I have found the discussions most fascinating. I must say that I was surprised to learn that you are an author, Charlotte. It has been my experience that most authors seem to be somewhat inscrutable. So, please carry on. I am quite happy to listen."

I turned back to Etienne. "You met Fran?"

"I did. But it was only a brief encounter. I had gone to visit with my great-uncle Jean-Christophe. He was still living here in this apartment at the time, and we often worried about him being over ninety and still living alone. I needn't have worried, though. I was only fifteen at the time, but when Fran walked into the room, I could feel the bond between them and how it seemed to cause the years to melt away. He introduced me to her, and all I could think was that I hoped to have such an elegant, vibrant woman still in my life when I am that age." He looked at Ines and smiled. "I believe that if I live that long, I just might still have her by my side." I think Ines blushed a little.

"Do you remember what year that was?"

Etienne thought for a moment. "I believe it was the late 1980s." He rubbed his chin. "Yes, I remember now. It was just after my birthday that summer. Yes, it was 1989."

"That was the year Fran died, you know," I said, thinking about how oddly disappointed I felt at never having met Fran.

"Yes. I remember when Uncle J-C told me she had died and that he planned to attend her funeral in Canada, I discouraged him. I was too young to know better than to tell someone this. I now know that I should not have done so. In any case, he did not listen to me."

"What was she like, Etienne?"

Etienne looked at me carefully. "Do you have plans to see Juliette again before you leave?" I nodded. "Well, then, ask her that question. She will have a much fuller answer for you. She knew Fran her entire life, and I do know that Juliette saw her for the final time that summer Fran was here to visit my great-uncle—the summer I met her. I remember him telling me that Fran was working on some odd new book that, as far as I can figure out now, my publishing company—her publisher for years—declined to publish. I seem to remember feeling that she was here to see my uncle and say goodbye and meet with Juliette about something. I really do not know the details, but I expect you will find them interesting. Your great-grandmother was nothing if not fascinating."

"Etienne," I said, still stuck on Fran's final piece of writing, "do you know why your publishing company declined her new book after such a long and mutually beneficial publishing relationship?"

"Not exactly, but company mythology suggests that the book was quite outside Fran's usual genre." He cleared his throat. "And you do know what her usual genre entailed."

"I do, indeed, Etienne. My great-grandmother was the master of early twentieth-century erotica." I laughed. "I can't even imagine what my grad school professor would have thought if she had known one of her students assigned to read F.E. de Plessis was the author's great-granddaughter. Come to think of it, I can't imagine what I would have thought."

"Perhaps you might have been scandalized," Etienne said, sipping the last of his wine.

"Perhaps," I said. "Etienne, does company lore have any details about the subject of Fran's last book?"

He shrugged. "I have heard it said that it was rather literary, perhaps even with a *soupçon* of social conscience." Etienne shook his head. "So, if this is true, you can see why it might have been jarring to the editors at *Éditions Lemieux*."

Literary? A social conscience? I had truthfully never seen the slightest bit of social conscience about anything in my great-grandmother's diaries and certainly not in her numerous published works. This was intriguing.

Even beyond the grave, Fran was still fascinating me.

SIX

MY PLAN FOR THIS PARIS TRIP HAD BEEN TO SPEND some time away from my regular life pursuing inspiration for what I was supposed to do with all that money. Before I left home, Tom said, "I know you're looking for that important thing for your inheritance, but promise me, Charlie, that you'll spend a bit of it just because you can and to experience what it feels like to be wealthy." And, I have to admit, Paris probably offers more than most cities when it comes to places to spend money.

I wasn't sure why Tom wanted me to have that experience, although I figured anyone who heard me question this would have reason to think I was a bit daft. After all, wasn't money next to celebrity in the grand order of things that fascinate North Americans? Then I remembered something I'd read some years back while studying for my M.F.A in grad school.

We had to read a lot of twentieth-century philosophers. I had completely forgotten most of what I'd read, but one quote stayed with me over the past seven years. It was something that French philosopher and novelist Albert Camus once wrote. He said, "*It's a kind of spiritual snobbery that makes people think they can be happy without money.*" So, as I left the apartment the next day to explore a bit more of Paris, I was thinking about what Camus had meant and what Tom had suggested. I realized that I was one of those people who could fall into that snobbery by disdaining all the money. I decided to take Tom's advice and soon found myself standing in front of the *Burberry* store on *rue du Faubourg Saint-Honoré*.

Until two years ago, I'd been one of those starving artist types, sharing a flat with several other starving artists and eking out a living as a writer with a side hustle stacking books in the university library. I would never have survived if it hadn't been for the financial support my mother chose to give me. It was much later,

32

after she died, that I realized she wasn't supporting her indigent daughter so much as she was supporting the artistic dream, something she knew a lot about, as it turned out. When I met Tom, someone I'd known only slightly back in high school, I wasn't aware that he was a wealthy young man in his own right. He was the realtor I'd hired to help me sell Mom's house, but he was also a tech wizard who'd already developed then sold a tech company for an eye wateringly high sum of money. So, when I inherited so much money, Tom and I as a couple didn't need it, but we had it. So, here I stood on the one street in Paris where I knew I could relieve myself of as much money as I wanted, and I had no idea where to begin.

I stared in *Burberry's* window and realized I wasn't a fan of their stuff. One of the mannequins in the window was wearing what looked like a shift dress with a bunch of weird things hanging down at each side. The one beside it was equally unappealing. It was a Burberry trench coat, but it had some kind of bizarre appliqué print over the front of it. I'm sure I rolled my eyes, then turned and carried on down the street.

I passed *Chanel* at number twenty-one, then *Tod's* next door. I had seen pictures of *Tod's* shoes, although I'd never worn them. I had always thought of them as far too expensive for me. I decided I might nip into the shop and try on a pair of driving shoes since they had always looked nice to me.

I pulled open the door and was immediately mesmerized by the riot of colour. *Tod's* shoes were nothing if not colourful. An icy-looking, model-thin, black-clad clerk floated toward me, murmuring, "*Puis-je vous aider, madame?*" She wanted to know if she could help me.

My French was still rusty, but I managed to indicate to her that I was just looking, so she dematerialized and left me to my own devices.

I approached one of the round tables with pairs of colourful loafers fanned out in a circle. These were appealing to me. I picked up a pair of fuchsia-coloured ones with gold buckles and surreptitiously looked for the price. *Damn it!* I thought. *Why don't shops like this have prices on things?* Then I remembered something my mother once said: "If you have to look for the price, you probably can't afford it." I realized there wouldn't be a single pair of shoes in this shop that I couldn't afford, but it still rankled.

I finally worked up the courage to ask the clerk for help (they were probably called associates or assistants, but what's in a name, anyway?). She nodded and asked me what size. I supposed I was a size thirty-nine or so in Europe. She then disappeared into the back somewhere, appearing a full five minutes later laden with boxes. It seemed she was determined I shouldn't leave the store without a pair of shoes—or two, as it turned out.

When I finally left the store, I had spent almost two thousand dollars (I had done a quick calculation when she rang it up, and I finally knew how much they cost) on just two pairs of shoes. I paid the bill and fled as quickly as I could before I passed out. When I was finally back out on the sidewalk, I began walking slowly, trying to catch my breath. This was going to be harder than I thought. Spending money like this on "things" was something I'd never been able to do. I wondered if I'd get used to it.

I slipped right past *Cartier*—although, to tell you the truth, I love *Cartier* so much (and was in love with the watch Tom gave me for a wedding gift) that I considered perusing their new handbags. Then I noticed *Hermes* across the street. I did like their scarves. Perhaps I'd come back on the opposite side and pop in. I strolled past *Lanvin*, *Prada* and *Gucci* and wondered what it had been like here in the 1920s when my great-grandmother was working as a mannequin at the salon of famed couturier Paul Poiret. I was sure Frannie wouldn't have had this much trouble spending money from what I'd read about her life in her diaries. Perhaps I could channel her a bit.

I crossed the street and was surprised—shocked, really, if you must know—to see a *Canada Goose* store taking up a large chunk of the block. I hadn't realized that Canadian fashion in the form of winter-ready parkas was a thing here. What did I know? I then passed *Valentino* and came to the next corner, where *Longchamp* seemed to have locations on both sides of the street. I suddenly realized that I hadn't embraced as much of the starving artist as I thought. I had long hauled around one of their cheapest bags—a nylon bag with a leather handle called a Pliage—but I had coveted their leathers. My breath was coming faster now at the thought that I could actually walk into the shop and buy whatever I wanted. Whatever I wanted.

I walked out of the store with a new cognac-coloured bag with top handles and a shoulder strap. It was fabricated in the most beautiful leather and was a steal at the equivalent of under nine hundred dollars (Canadian). I almost felt as if I'd found a bargain. Then it struck me: how easy it was to begin to think that a nine-hundred-dollar handbag wasn't much at all—to change your sense of value. Then I thought of something I heard country singer Garth Brooks had said once. *"You aren't wealthy until you have something money can't buy."* And I realized I had come a long distance from Albert Camus.

~

Juliette had invited me to have tea with her the afternoon before I was scheduled to fly home. I still wasn't much closer to figuring out what to do with the money, but I was beginning to see myself slightly differently.

When I arrived at her apartment, I was bearing an armload of pink peonies I'd found at a floral vendor a few blocks away and a bottle of twenty-five-year-old *Glen Farcas* scotch since she'd mentioned she enjoyed a sip of scotch once in a while. I knew little about scotch whiskey, but when I did an online search, this one came up as a very good one. It should have, given the price!

Juliette's housekeeper, Genevieve, answered the door when I knocked and took the flowers from me to find a vase. She told me

35

that Juliette was waiting for me in her den. When I knocked on the open door of Juliette's den, I was surprised to see such chaos. Juliette's apartment was otherwise immaculate. She was sitting in an oversized upholstered chair behind a white desk—at least, I thought it was white. Given the array of books, file folders, and photo albums covering it, though, it wasn't easy to tell.

"*Entrez, ma chère.* Come in, my dear." She beckoned me to sit at a chair beside her on the far side of the desk. She wanted to show me some things, and I wanted to see them.

Juliette began with a photo album her mother kept for her through the years. There were many photographs of Juliette with her parents Kiki and Gaston. The pictures told a story of a family that shared a strong bond and seemed to be having a love affair with life. There was so much vivacity in each of those grainy two-dimensional pictures—so much so that they now seemed three-dimensional. I could feel her parents' presence in the room as she talked about them.

"*Alors, ma chère.* I must not take up so much of your time viewing photographs from a long-forgotten childhood." I began to object, but Juliette continued. "I must talk to you about your great-grandmother, but in order for me to do so, I must speak just a bit more about my own background."

"Juliette, I wish you would. The story is fascinating."

"I must begin by telling you about the last time I saw your wonderful Frannie. It was right here—in this very room. Fran had arrived in Paris the week before, and I perceived she was here to say goodbye. She was, as you know, eighty-nine years old at that time, yet she could have been taken for a woman ten or even twenty years her junior. I digress."

I hoped Juliette would continue digressing since I so enjoyed hearing these things about Frannie.

"I pressed her, and she admitted that she had been diagnosed with a cancer of some sort. You probably know more about that than I do, and, in any case, it is immaterial. I did not need to know the details. All I knew was that I would likely never see my great friend and godmother again. Indeed, she had become like a mother to me since my own mother had died several years before.

"I was, at that time, sixty-four years old myself and would soon retire from my position at *Cité des Sciences et de l'industries*, the science museum of Paris. Have you visited it?"

I shook my head and frowned. This piece of information made no sense to me. "But Juliette, how did you come to work in a science museum?"

"Ah," she said, tapping her head as if she realized she'd forgotten something. "Do you remember I told you I left Paris for a time and went to America? While I was there, I attended Bryn Mawr College in Pennsylvania. It was the first women's college in America to offer graduate degrees to women, so I stayed there until I had completed my doctorate. It was in biology."

I was stunned. This was something I would never have expected, given Juliette's artistic family and friends.

"Yes, I became something of an enigma to my parents. I never married, and they eventually accepted that they would not be grandparents and that their daughter was developing something of a reputation in the sciences. I worked for many years at the National Museum of Natural History in the nineteenth *arrondissement*. It took its mission from wanting to understand how our human habits have exploited our world. Being a true Parisian, I developed an interest in how perhaps the fashion industry might be exploiting our environment. When the *Cité des sciences* opened in 1986, I was taken on as the associate director and executive curator. Of course, I was forced to retire within five years. But that was fine. I had accomplished much in my career.

"When Fran arrived that summer, she asked me about an exhibit I had curated on the science of fashion. It seemed she had developed an interest in it. This newfound interest made very little sense to me. When I asked her what had precipitated this new curiosity, she said something vague about background research for character development in a new book."

"I'm not following, Juliette. Fran was now somehow interested in science? You *do* know what kind of books she wrote throughout her life?"

Juliette laughed. "But of course. I believe I have read every one of F.E. de Plessis and Peyton Winter's books and found them endlessly useful as instructional manuals when faced with a new lover."

I think I blushed. This was the first time anyone had described my great-grandmother's erotic novels (written under her pseudonyms—F.E. de Plessis in France; Peyton Winter in America and the rest of the world) as instructional manuals.

"Charlie, my dear, this was precisely my reaction at the time. But she seemed to have been inspired to write a novel—to be her last one—that was different and to leave it as her legacy to the world."

Just then, Genevieve came through the door bearing a large silver tray laden with a teapot, teacups with saucers and an array of tiny sandwiches and cakes. She put the tray on a side table, then poured each of us a cup of tea. She then placed the plate of food on the coffee table so that both of us could reach it.

Juliette sipped her tea and then turned back to me. "Now, what was I saying?"

"You were telling me that Fran had developed a new interest in your work in science, and she was working on her last book—one she wanted to leave as her legacy."

"*Oui,* yes." Juliette leaned over to pick up a sandwich, which she placed delicately on a small canapé plate topped with a pink doily. "Fran was here in Paris for some three weeks that summer, during which we kept company at least half a dozen times. Every time we met, she would grill me on various aspects of my work and the people I'd met throughout my life and what they were like. She made furious notes as we spoke. When I asked her about it, she said she was using the material as background for the new book, which, as it happened, she was writing while she was here. She wanted at least a partial draft completed to present to her publisher before leaving Paris for the last time."

"Did Fran ever tell you what had inspired her?"

Juliette shrugged. "I asked her at the time, but all she would say is that she had a friend at home in Canada whose personal story seemed to have fired her imagination. Anyway, I was happy to help."

I was racking my brain, trying to remember something that was just outside my consciousness. It was something about an old manuscript. Suddenly, I had it. "Juliette, I think I may have read part of that book."

Juliette raised her eyebrows and cocked her head.

"Last summer, when I came to Paris to meet with Etienne about the inheritance, I found an unfinished manuscript in the bottom drawer of Fran's desk. Since it was written in English, I could read it quickly but promptly forgot about it in all the excitement. I didn't even take it home with me."

"And what did you think of it, Charlie?

"Well, to tell you the truth, it wasn't much like anything she had written before. And I was surprised, but it wasn't really very good. Even so, I did have a moment where I thought I might take on the project and finish it. I suppose it would have been a legacy of sorts for F.E. de Plessis or Peyton Winter."

Juliette laughed. "I suppose it might, at that. But that was not Fran's intention. I know the manuscript to which you refer. Fran brought it with her when she came that summer and soon after she arrived, asked me to read it. I was, perhaps, even less enthusiastic about it than you were and was in her office the evening she dropped it into the bottom drawer of her desk and slammed the drawer shut."

"So, how do you know for sure that it wasn't her legacy manuscript?"

"I know this for sure because she then pounded her fist on the top of another pile of manuscript pages on the smaller desk where she kept her typewriter. Then she smiled at me and told me that this would be a book by F.E. Phillips and that the world would finally know of her true identity as a writer."

I thought for a moment. "Juliette, did Fran finish the manuscript?"

Juliette shrugged and said nothing.

I sat back and thought for a moment. "So, where is the manuscript, Juliette?"

Juliette smiled in that inscrutable way that only someone of her advanced years can accomplish. Then she looked at her watch and said, "Oh, *mon dieu*, but it is so late." Before getting up, she said, "Charlie, are you familiar with Carl Jung?" I nodded, remembering a writers' group meeting a while back when Karl started quoting the long-dead Swiss psychoanalyst. Juliette continued. "He once said, *Your vision will become clear only when you can look into your own heart. Who looks outside, dreams; who looks inside, awakes.*" She took her cane and began to get up. "You will find it, Charlie."

SEVEN

JULIETTE AND I SAID GOODBYE, AND I AMBLED thoughtfully down the hall toward my apartment. I have to admit that I was feeling a bit frustrated, although I didn't share this with Juliette. I wondered if she knew more about the manuscript than she was letting on.

As I opened the door and stepped into my apartment, I remembered the day last year when I discovered that unfinished manuscript in the bottom drawer of Fran's desk. I remembered that after I quickly read it, I felt as if I could hear a whisper in my ear. *"Finish it."* I suppose I considered the possibility that Fran was somehow trying to reach me to get me to finish this book, but now I wasn't so sure. But was there something I had to finish? Was it another book? And if the one I'd read hadn't been Fran's final legacy book, where was the manuscript?

I still had some cleaning up and packing to do to be ready for my flight home the following day. One of the things I had to clear was the two open bottles of wine I'd recorked. The red was on the counter. The white was in the fridge. I went into the kitchen to retrieve one of them and poured myself a rather large glass of white wine (I did have to finish the bottle, after all, didn't I?). I'd save the red to have after dinner.

I reached for the last of the cheese I'd left in the fridge and the baguette I'd left wrapped on the counter and took my snack to the office. It was amazing to me how I could even think of eating after tea with the array of finger sandwiches and cookies that Juliette had served. But who could resist that last bit of Parisian baguette and French cheese? Not I, that's for sure.

Once I had settled in behind the desk, I took a sip of wine and gazed out the window to figure out where that final manuscript might be. The thought of Fran's last book was tantalizing to me as a writer. And just knowing that it was different from her lifetime body of work was even more exciting.

Juliette had been adamant that I had not yet found Fran's final manuscript—a manuscript that her long-time publisher had not been inclined to publish. And, for some reason, she hadn't been very forthcoming about whether the book was finished or where it might be. Perhaps she didn't know the answer to either question. *Well,* I thought, *I'll just have to figure out where Fran might have left it.* And now that my departure was imminent, I had to be sure it wasn't still here in Paris.

I made a few notes in the red Moleskine notebook that accompanied me everywhere. I wanted to capture my thoughts about Juliette and her remarkable life. It might come in handy someday when I was writing a new book. I put my pen down on the desk beside my laptop when I'd finished and twirled my chair around so that I could face out the window.

Fran's heavy old German typewriter sat on another desk—an elaborate antique—under the window. I remembered the first time I'd seen the typewriter. I'd run my hand over its keys, trying to channel my great-grandmother. I wondered what it must have been like to draft books on such a contraption rather than the smooth keyboard I used.

I thought it might be interesting to roll a sheet of paper into the old machine and get a feel for it. *I wonder if there's any typewriter paper left lying around this office,* I thought, turning my chair back to face my laptop.

I began opening drawers. When I opened the bottom drawer on the left, the unfinished manuscript I'd read last year was still there. I probably should have taken it home with me, but I hadn't. Anyway, if Juliette was right, this wasn't Fran's legacy novel—the one that seemed so important to her in the last year of her life. But where was *that* manuscript?

I turned to the column of drawers on the right and found some blank typewriter paper in the second drawer. I pulled out the stack and set it on the desk in front of me. As I turned to close the drawer, I noticed a key that seemed to have been hidden under the paper. I picked it up and turned it over in my hands. It was flat and resembled a smaller version of a modern safe-deposit box key. I stood up and began to look around to see if there was a box, a drawer, a cupboard—anything— that this key might open. I sat back down and turned to examine the desk where the typewriter sat. There was a narrow drawer with a decorative brass piece directly under the typewriter. I absently ran my hand over it as I looked around. My finger caught in something in the middle of the brass ornament. When I looked down, I could see that it was a slot.

My hand began to tremble as I put the key in the slot and tried to turn it. *Voila!* It opened. What I had thought was a drawer front was actually the front of a narrow niche that opened toward me when I turned the key. I leaned down to peer inside, and just as I'd hoped, I could see another manuscript. I slid the pile of pages out and turned to put it on the desk beside my laptop, and then I stared at the title page with its now fading type.

Something I'm Supposed to Do. A novel. By F.E. Phillips.

I carefully lifted the bundle of pages held together by a decaying elastic band from the drawer and placed it on the desk in front of me. Then I sat back to look at them. Like the book I'd found in the bottom drawer, Frannie had also written this one in English. I wondered if that might have been why her old French publisher had declined to publish it. However, I had a feeling that it wasn't the reason at all. The only way I'd ever know, though, would be to read it.

I took a deep breath and a sip of wine. Then I turned the cover page over to reveal the first page. Centred on the page, about halfway down, were the following words:

"The mystery of human existence lies not in just staying alive, but in finding something to live for." – Fyodor Dostoyevsky

Eight
Fran, 1989

"Charlie, my little darling, there is so much I wish I could share with you," I whispered to the tiny newborn baby I cradled gently in my arm. "You will not remember me, but remember this. Life isn't about finding yourself. It is about creating yourself. Create one for the ages, child, create one for the ages."

And somehow, I knew she would.

When I left Charlie with her mother, my granddaughter, Kat, at the maternity hospital and returned to my big, empty house, I felt alone for the first time in my long life. I had managed to keep my recent diagnosis to myself, even when Kat was concerned that I appeared to be in pain. I would hide it as long as I could, but it was inevitable that I couldn't do it forever. I would eventually have to tell my darling granddaughter I had terminal cancer. But I was eighty-nine years old, so it could never be said that I had not had a long life and a productive one by any standards. But that wasn't what troubled me. What troubled me at that moment was that there was much to do and an indeterminate amount of time left in which to accomplish much.

I had already begun making final arrangements with my solicitor. I had accumulated a great deal of money—more money than anyone who knew me could ever have imagined. James, my son and his wife, Betty, had no idea, and that is precisely as I wanted to keep it until after I died. In addition to the money, I also owned several properties—the lovely-but-too-large house I currently occupied and apartments in both New York and Paris. I planned to have the house sold as part of the estate and leave the apartments to my great-granddaughters—Charlie and her older sister Evelyn. And the money that would reside in my estate? I would arrange for them to have it when they were older. I expected that they would do great things with the money. That, however, was not the only thing on my mind.

I went upstairs to my office, slowly and carefully, taking the steps one at a time, steadying myself with the handrail. I knew I should have moved downstairs when Kat had suggested it a few years ago, but I was still stubborn and didn't wish to admit that I was as old as I most assuredly was. When I arrived at the top, I stopped to catch my breath as I always did, then went straight into my office that occupied the second story of a turret-like space. I wondered if you ever missed things after you were dead. If you did, I would undoubtedly miss the serenity I experienced when I sat here, lost in thought about life and my writing. My writing. That is what I needed to consider.

I had begun notes on a new book and had written a rough draft of a few chapters, but I didn't have nearly enough background material to begin serious writing yet. However, I was determined to finish it before I could no longer write, but I still needed to complete some background research on the story that was so inspiring me. Part of the research entailed discussions with my old friend Ellie McMaster. Dr. Ellen McMaster, to be more precise.

Ellen had lived an extraordinary, multi-layered life. The story she had been telling me lately about her granddaughter had stirred my imagination in a direction that diverged from the books I had been writing since I worked as a mannequin in couture houses of Paris in the 1920s. Her story had spurred me to wish to create a very different book from those that had assisted me in amassing my fortune. I would buckle down, listen to her, and then write for the next few months. In the meantime, I would arrange one final visit to Paris for three or four weeks. I needed to see my old lover Christophe again—for both business and pleasure. Our history goes back more than sixty years, and I could not leave this life without seeing him one more time.

I also wanted to say goodbye to my goddaughter, Juliette. Since her mother had died some twenty years earlier (her father, having been somewhat older than her mother, Kiki, had died long ago), I had become her only real family. Oh, how I remembered those extraordinary times in Paris in the '20s with Kiki and her ballet friends. Just thinking about those now long-ago days made me smile. The parties! The dresses! It was brilliant. But that was just nostalgia. Someone once wrote, "Some days I wish I could go back in life, not to change things, just to feel a few things twice." I suppose feeling the good bits again would be nice. But, even at this point, I knew I needed to look ahead.

I also need to talk to Juliette about my final work. She, too, had background material that would help me to complete the last book

I arrived in Paris at some ungodly hour in the morning after making a connection in Toronto to the overnight flight and took a taxi from Charles De Gaulle to my apartment on the left bank. Christophe had offered to pick me up, but I told him he was too old to be trekking to an airport and that I could still manage my own transportation. To my great delight, he had used his key and was waiting for me when I opened my apartment door. Despite the sizzling summer weather, Christophe had lit the fireplace just as we had often done in our youth and had laid out champagne flutes and caviar. The bottle was chilling in my silver wine bucket.

Naturally, we had both aged, yet Christophe and I still fell into one another's arms and realized that if either of us had a home in this lifetime, this was where it was. It was not an apartment or a city. It was not a country or a house. It was in each other's arms now and forever. But I digress.

The next day, I got down to business. I had a limited amount of time in Paris—or even on earth, as I well realized—and I needed some critical background material for my new novel that only Juliette could provide.

As we had arranged, I arrived at Juliette's apartment and almost immediately set upon her, grilling her for information about her work with the science museum on that science of fashion exhibit she had curated. I knew my long-standing interest in fashion, manifested in my collection of couture dresses and a lifelong interest in constructing garments myself, connected me to it in her mind. Still, I could see the question in her eyes as I pressed her for more information on the science.

"Are you writing a new book, Fran?" she said as I furiously scribbled notes. I nodded, and she continued. "But I am puzzled. It does not seem the sort of material you would need for one of your books. Where does this interest in my science come from, may I ask?"

I didn't have time for complete explanations, so I murmured something vague, and she finally gave up asking. I then returned to my apartment and pounded out the story on my typewriter every moment I was not with Christophe. I worked long into each night, and three days later, when I had what I thought was a sufficient number of pages, I bribed the attendant at the faculty copy shop at the Sorbonne to copy them. I then presented them to Christophe.

Although he no longer attended his office daily, he held considerable sway over publishing decisions. This work would be a more important book than I had ever written—a more profound story—and I was willing to have it translated so that *Éditions Lemieux* could publish it first in French before my American publisher got its hands on it. I wanted it to be my legacy rather than me being remembered in an encyclopedia entry (I shuddered at the thought) detailing my lengthy list of erotic and what some critics described as "smut" novels.

I was unprepared for Christophe's reaction.

"Frannie, *ma chère*," he said, tapping his glasses on the manuscript in his lap as we sipped wine in my living room one afternoon several days after I'd given him the pages. "This...this is...how does one say it in English?"

"I suppose that depends on how one says it in French first," I said. I was becoming impatient. I had expected him to be immediately lavish in his praise of my attempt to write something more meaningful.

"*Sérieux*," he said after thinking a moment. "It is earnest, perhaps too earnest."

"Too earnest?"

"*Oui*, but do not take this personally."

"How else can I take it?" I said, trying to will the tears forming in my old eyes not to spill out. That would be too earnest. "It is personal."

He shrugged. "Frannie, you have not changed one bit over the years. You are still headstrong."

"I find that somewhat sexist for late-twentieth-century, Jean-Christophe." He raised his eyebrows. I called him by his full name only when I was angry, and of this, he was acutely aware. I sipped my wine and realized there was no point in continuing to browbeat him about publishing the book. I would find a suitable publisher in North America if I had enough time left. He was probably right, anyway. It probably *was* too earnest. At that moment, it occurred to me that I might have become imbued with something of the Canadian culture since becoming a citizen. Perhaps it was what was referred to in the more literary circles as CanLit, a peculiar brand of contemporary literature a writer once described as "the literary equivalent of representational landscape painting, with small forays into waterfowl depiction and still lifes." I had read that in the *New York Times*, and it was clear the writer wasn't being kind. I shuddered. Perhaps Christophe was right.

In any case, I would persist with the story. I was obsessed with it for some reason that had not made itself apparent to me.

I finally said goodbye to Juliette and to Christophe. As I held each one for just a moment too long, I knew in my heart that this would be my final goodbye to each of them. Both Juliette and Christophe knew this as well and held on tight. Then I returned home to Halifax.

The minute I had unpacked, I arranged to meet Ellie for another session for background to further flesh out my novel. Of course, I would not be telling her precise story as if it were true—it would be fiction.

As I sat in her bright kitchen, sipping tea and making notes late one summer afternoon at the end of August, I was suddenly struck by the notion that I had, indeed, become an old woman. How could this have happened? How could I have forgotten something so important? At that moment, I realized I'd left the manuscript in Paris. *I must get Christophe or Juliette to retrieve it and send it to me before I run out of time*, I thought.

"Fran? Fran, are you all right?" The look on Ellie's face told me that her longstanding internal physician had kicked in, and she was concerned about my apparent mental lapse.

"Yes, yes, of course. Now, what were we talking about? Oh, yes. That young American. What is his name again?"

"Tim," she said, "Timothy Sinclair."

NINE

TIM, 1989

WHAT THE HELL AM I DOING WITH MY LIFE? This was not the first time this thought had crossed my mind, and it wouldn't be the last. I was sure of it. But today, it was different. Today, as I'd walked in the door of our apartment, thrown my keys on the hall table and tossed my briefcase onto a chair (what I wanted to do was toss it out a window, but we lived on the forty-first floor, and the windows didn't open), I knew I was ready to take action.

I hadn't planned my escape as meticulously as I usually planned my work. In fact, the only parts I had nailed down were the date—today—the route—north—and the final destination. The rest I'd have to wing.

I changed into jeans and the sweater Antonia had given me as a Christmas present last year, then poured myself a glass of scotch—my current favourite, *Glen Farcas*, expensive but worth it. I put a vinyl record on the old turntable I'd managed to scare up at a garage sale when we'd been doing what Antonia had called "antiquing" in Connecticut last year. The room was immediately filled with my favourite music: Glen Miller's orchestra and "Moonlight Serenade." Glenn wasn't the only one keeping me company on evenings like this when Antonia was out. I also had Tommy (Dorsey), Bing (Crosby) and Frank (Sinatra). If I closed my eyes, I could always conjure the feeling of being back there in the '40s, sipping a cocktail without a care in the world. Maybe I'd even be wearing a tux—I looked good in a tux. Antonia had mentioned (on more than one occasion) that I seemed to have been born in the wrong era. Maybe she was right. All I knew at that moment, there in our New York City apartment on an April evening, after spending the past ten hours taking meetings with increasingly demanding

50

and fatuous clients, was that I had to take a break. I had to get away. As I gazed out over the shimmering lights of Manhattan that were just beginning to glimmer against the sunset in the western sky, I realized that I was ready—more than ready.

I began moving stacks of shirts, sweaters and jeans from my dresser to my suitcase open on the bed. If Antonia spotted my suitcase on top of her pristine, white, 600-thread-count duvet cover, she'd have a fit. The thought made me smile. I stopped my frantic packing for a moment and walked back over to my drafting table that I had positioned to catch the best light from the floor-to-ceiling window. That way, I could slave away every weekend when there were no client meetings.

I picked up my glass, holding it for a moment to feel the heaviness of the hand-blown crystal in my hand. Then I raised it to my lips and sipped slowly, savouring the taste on the tip of my tongue then as it slid back toward my throat, warming me even as I felt a cold mantle settle over me. I knew that Antonia was the cause of that cold that was beginning to envelop me now.

I ran my hand over the unfinished drawing clamped to my drafting table. I'd started it for an ad campaign my boss seemed to think would more than make the firm's year if I could pull it off for him. The drawing showed my concept of the sinking of the Titanic with survivors in lifeboats out front. Yes, I knew it had been done before but not for this kind of ad campaign. I'd created a slogan to go along with the visuals, but I'd already inked it out because it was puerile, trifling, fatuous like the client. Maybe he'd like it, but I sure didn't. And I didn't know why.

I ran my hand over the clippings I'd amassed for research purposes. They were mainly copies of old newspaper articles. The one on the top was the front page of an old Canadian paper called the *Halifax Herald*, dated April 30, 1912, with a headline that read, "Titanic Victims Buried in Halifax." I put my glass down, pulled the unfinished drawing from its clips, gathered the clippings in a pile, and then put them all in my suitcase.

I started tapping my foot in time to the music coming from the living room and got back to my packing. Just then, I heard the apartment door opening and then slamming shut.

"Tim? Timmy? Are you in there?"

I could feel the hairs on the back of my neck stand at attention. I don't know how often I'd told Antonia I hated being called Timmy. I was okay with Tim or even Timothy, but I hated Timmy. She thought it was cutesy.

My music, which was keeping me sane this evening, stopped abruptly.

"Geez, that music makes me crazy," Antonia said as she walked through the bedroom door. "Why can't you listen to music that normal people listen to? You *have* heard of Guns 'N' Roses, Phil Collins, Cheap Trick, right? Oh, why do I even bother?" I wondered the same thing.

She sighed and threw her briefcase on a chair in the corner. Then she kicked off her black stilettos like shoes she'd bought at a thrift shop. I happened to know they were Manolo Blahniks and had cost her more money than a family of four spent on groceries for two months, and she couldn't even walk in them. Antonia wasn't one of those women who had embraced the notion of wearing sneakers to walk to work. She took a cab.

As I looked at her now, in her navy blue power suit with those shoulders that made her look like a quarterback on a football team, I realized that she was a truly striking woman. What made her even more attractive to me when we'd begun dating five years earlier was her sense of herself—that she could break through any glass ceiling, that nothing could stop her. As alluring as powerful women were to me, this constant striving for more, more, more had begun to wear thin. I couldn't put my finger on exactly when that started, but here I was, trying to make my escape.

Antonia finally seemed to notice that there was a suitcase on the bed. "What the hell is going on here?"

"Oh, hi, Antonia. You're home."

"At the risk of repeating myself, what the hell are you doing? Nathan and I thought you were at a meeting with those oil company people."

"I was. I left early."

Antonia noticed the clippings on top of the clothes in the suitcase. "What's all this?" she picked them up, and then with less than even a glance, she put them back. "Tim, what exactly is going on here?"

"You know I'm working on that campaign for the oil company. The president of the company has a thing for Titanic memorabilia, so I decided to go with a historical theme."

"Okay," she said carefully, "but what about the suitcase? Going somewhere?"

I picked up my glass and drained the last drop. "I'm taking a little research trip." I walked over to the window and put the empty glass beside the drafting table.

"Now?" Antonia was becoming slightly shrill. "In the middle of our planning? If we're ever going to get our business plan off the ground, we need to get those clients on board. We need all three of us working at top form. Now is not the time for you—or any of us—to be taking a trip."

"Look, Antonia, you and Nathan—"

The loud jangling of the phone cut me off, and I knew Antonia well enough to know that she wouldn't ignore it no matter what was happening in front of her. The phone was her lifeline to the riches that she seemed to think awaited her and that she so totally deserved.

"Yes?" she said to the caller. "Hi, Nathan. Yes, I found him."

I should have guessed that Nathan would follow up with Antonia on my whereabouts.

"No, it doesn't seem so," she said into the phone, then glared at me while she continued. "I'll be ready in an hour, though. I'll call you then." She hung up and looked at me. "You were saying?"

"I know how much this idea of us having our own ad agency means to you—"

She cut me off again. "To *us*, Tim. To *us*."

"Okay, but I need to get away to do this research. I'm sure you can see that."

"Cut the bullshit, Timothy Sinclair. We've been together long enough for me to know when I'm being conned."

I sat down on the edge of the bed and put my face in my hands. "I'm suffocating, Antonia. I just need some space to get some work done."

Antonia walked toward the window, and when she spoke, she sounded deflated, like a balloon with a hole collapsing in on itself. "Okay, Tim, so you need some space. Were you ever planning on telling me about this little junket, or was I supposed to get home today and figure it out for myself?"

"I was planning to leave you a note to explain."

"Gee," she said, her usual sarcastic edge returning, "thanks. And where exactly are you going, if I might be so bold as to ask?"

"Halifax."

"Where the hell is that?"

I explained to Antonia that Halifax is a city on the east coast of Canada. When I told her it was more or less just up the coast from New York City, she rolled her eyes. I explained that my research would focus on Halifax's connection to the Titanic disaster. She rolled her eyes again.

"Some of the Titanic victims are buried there. Also, I remember my father telling me that my grandfather was there for a short time during World War II. I thought I'd like to see it. It might be a good place to clear my head. I've got too many things on the go right now."

Antonia opened her mouth to speak, then seemed to think better of it. She came over and sat close beside me on the bed. "How long are you planning to be away?"

"Two weeks or so."

Antonia ground her teeth—I knew because I could see that slight yet telltale movement of her jaw. She seemed to be holding herself back. "Two weeks? That seems like such a long time to be away from the office." She stopped for a meaningful beat. (I'd known Antonia too long not to recognize when she was doing something for effect.) "And me." Was she pouting?

"Yeah, well," was all I could manage in response.

Then she wanted to know when I was leaving, and when I told her I'd be heading out as soon as I finished packing, I steeled myself for her wrath. Instead, all she said was, "At least let me drive you to the airport."

I finished zipping my suitcase closed. "Thanks, Antonia, but I'm driving."

Then it happened. The explosion I'd been waiting for. "Driving?" Antonia's voice was rising with every syllable. "Who drives to Canada? Are you crazy?" I shrugged. She continued. "Let me get this straight. I come home to find my colleague and future business partner, not to mention my lover and roommate, packing to go to some god-forsaken Canadian outport. He's driving there. He thinks he'll be gone for two weeks. And I'm just supposed to be okay with that?"

"I think that about covers it," I said, swinging my backpack over one shoulder, picking up the suitcase and my coat and putting my car keys in my pocket.

I said goodbye, pecked her cheek on the way by and headed for the door. Before I even had the door open, I heard Antonia angrily punching numbers into the telephone. As the door closed behind me, I heard her say, "Nathan, we have a problem."

~

I eased back into the comfort of the red leather seats I'd special ordered for my custom black Toyota Supra I'd bought last year. Then I couldn't help but smile when I remembered what Antonia had said when she saw it for the first time. "What is that, Tim? Are you having some kind of a premature mid-life crisis?" (Well, I had just turned thirty.) "Why couldn't you buy a BMW like every other up-and-coming advertising executive?" I'd wanted to tell her that I'd bought it for that very reason: I didn't want to drive what someone else thought I should drive. I wanted to drive a car I loved, and I loved this car.

That was my precise thought as I put it in gear and drove out of the underground parking garage and into the late evening streets of Manhattan. The city that never sleeps is as apt a moniker as there could ever be for New York. I loved it until I didn't. I geared down and headed out onto the parkway along the Hudson River, which would take me north through Yonkers and then onto Eastchester before I crossed the state line into Connecticut and through the rest of the New England states. I'd been to Europe and beyond, but I'd never driven through New England, and I was looking forward to it. The only place I'd been in Canada was Toronto, so this whole trip was going to open up new ideas. I didn't know the half of it.

I cranked up the volume on the first of several cassettes of 1940s music I kept in the car and revelled in not hearing anyone complain about it. Two days later, I was still humming along to the music when I put Calais, Maine, behind me and drove into Canada at a place called St. Stephen, New Brunswick. Welcome to Canada, the sign said. And just like that, my world seemed to move from black and white into full colour.

TEN

"EXCELLENT CAR, MAN."

"Thanks. Could you fill it with high test?"

"Sure thing." The young gas station attendant chewed his gum vigorously and smiled at me as he wiped his hands on a dirty rag hanging from his belt. "You headed to the city?"

I opened the car door and unfolded myself. I'd been driving for almost four hours and needed a stretch. "Halifax, yeah," I said. "The sign back there says it's fifty-six miles."

The young man glanced at the license plate on the back of the car. "It's not miles. It's kilometres. You're in Canada, eh?" Then he started to laugh as if he'd just told a joke that somehow went over my head.

"What's so funny?"

"Oh, it's just that...Oh, never mind. It's a Canadian kind of thing." Then he shrugged, removed the gas nozzle and replaced the gas cap. "Doesn't matter. Anyway, that'll be seventeen dollars, eh."

I pulled my wallet out of my back pocket and gave him the money.

"No exchange on U.S. dollars these days around here, you know?"

I smiled and nodded, then got back in the car and started the engine. Before I put my window up, he said, "Don't forget you're not in America anymore, eh!" Then he laughed.

So did I.

~

The sun was just setting when I pulled up in front of the hotel on the harbour front in downtown Halifax. A bellman dressed in a blue tartan kilt and a heavy sweater to protect him from the damp

57

April breeze opened the door for me. I got out, opened the trunk and pulled out my suitcase and backpack. He immediately took the bag from me while a valet appeared seemingly from nowhere to retrieve my keys.

"Welcome. Will you be staying with us for long, sir?" the bellman said, leading me into the lobby toward the front desk.

"A few weeks, I think," I said.

"Well, sir, if you need any recommendations for what to do and see here in the city and beyond, don't hesitate to ask. You know we have almost as many bars and restaurants per capita here as in St. John's." Then he laughed as he left me at the desk. I had no idea what he was talking about.

While I waited for the front desk clerk to find my reservation, I looked around the modern lobby. I could see people milling about, all wearing those name tags on lanyards that were the badge of the conference attendee. *Geezus*, I thought, *I hope they don't clog the bar*.

I thanked the clerk for my key and the waterfront map he'd just handed me, then headed to the elevators to find my room. I'm always on the lookout for new ideas to use in my ad campaigns, so I'm one of those people who try to read nametags if I'm close enough. Three people sporting those lanyards got on the elevator with me—two men and a woman, all north of fifty—chatting animatedly about something to do with birds. I couldn't quite catch the gist of the conversation, nor could I make out the name of the conference they were attending, but birds were of little interest to me anyway.

Once I'd unpacked my suitcase, I made my way back downstairs and took a walk along the boardwalk that snaked along beside the water. I suddenly realized I was hungry and tired, so I decided to head back to the hotel. Exploring the boardwalk could wait until tomorrow.

I found the bar just off the lobby and slid onto a barstool. The bartender nodded and put the menu in front of me. There were things like local fish and chips, burgers and something called a donair. I opted for fish and chips and a local beer made by a company called Oland's, whose name I'd heard even in New York. Less than an hour later, feeling more stuffed than I had in a long time, I headed back up to my room. (Antonia had been on a health kick over the past year after discovering the book "Fit for Life" that didn't let you combine foods like carbs and protein in the same meal. Now I could combine to my heart's delight. I felt slightly giddy at the thought.) I fell into bed without calling Antonia. *Maybe tomorrow,* I thought. *Or the next day.* I have to admit I didn't sleep that well, though, with all that unaccustomed fat.

I set out again the following day, only somewhat rested and refreshed. This time, the sun was shining, and the boardwalk was coming alive with tourists. Since it was only April, and the temperature was still cool, I concluded that the tourists were mainly conference people. There didn't seem to be any families with children. Anyway, I had a specific destination in mind. I was looking for the Maritime Museum of the Atlantic. I had checked the local map the desk clerk gave me and knew it was close.

I walked for a few minutes and then spotted the sign. I followed the arrows pointing to the front entrance, which faced the street on the other side of the building with pride of place on the waterfront. I bought my ticket and headed directly up the staircase in the middle of the ground floor exhibit space, where the signs told me the Titanic exhibit was located. I found myself taking the steps two at a time as I neared the top.

The museum was quiet this morning. With so few other people around, I had the place almost to myself. As I rounded a corner, I came face-to-face with a replica of a deck chair from the Titanic. It was set up as if to invite you to sit in it and try to conjure up the feeling of a passenger on the ill-fated ship. Behind it in a cabinet was an actual teak deck chair rescued from the wreck, a bit worse for wear.

I stood there for a moment, looked around and saw no one. I sat down in the chair and closed my eyes. I tried to feel every part of the teak wood under me. The next thing I knew, I was startled by the flash of a camera in my face—or that's what I thought it was. I sat up.

"Sorry."

I looked at the young woman standing in front of me with a camera dangling from her wrist. "What the hell?"

"We thought you were part of the display," she said.

I stared at the young woman with the camera, who was now laughing. She was probably in her early twenties, and I would have described her as attractive and outdoorsy. She seemed to have dressed from the L.L. Bean catalogue. Did they even have L.L. Bean in Canada?

"I drove a very long way yesterday. I guess I should have known better than to lie down...even for a minute."

"I don't think anyone minded," said her companion, whose presence I hadn't noticed until that moment. I wasn't sure why: she was drop-dead gorgeous with wild dark hair and penetrating dark eyes that seemed to be boring into me. "It's not very busy here today. Too nice a day for a museum."

"And you did make an attractive addition to the deck chair. My friends in Toronto will enjoy this one immensely." She patted her camera before extending her hand to me as I got up. "I'm Stephanie Jennex, by the way."

"Timothy Sinclair. Tim."

"And Timothy, this is Megan McMaster. She's shy." Stephanie began to laugh. Megan didn't look the least bit shy to me. She looked wary.

"I am not shy," Megan said to Stephanie, then turned to me. "I just like to think I have better manners than some. Please forgive my friend. Whenever she gets a chance to get out of Toronto, she gets a bit silly. I hope you don't mind the photo."

"No, I don't suppose I do. I guess I deserved it. Are you both from Toronto?"

Megan started to laugh. "Dear god, no. I'm from here. I'm just helping Steph decompress from her urban prison."

I looked at Megan closely and felt a kind of internal nudge that seemed to be pushing me toward her. "I'm looking for someone—a guide, I guess—to the Titanic sites in Halifax. You wouldn't by chance be able to help me?" What had possessed me to blurt out something like that? I hoped I didn't sound creepy.

Megan moved away from me almost imperceptibly, but I caught it. "You must be an American," she said coolly, that wary look more pronounced than earlier.

"Yes. I'm from New York."

"Oh, I love New York," Stephanie said.

Megan gave her a withering look. "You would." She looked at her watch. "Look, we have to go. We're late for a session." Then she turned and headed toward the stairs taking her down to the ground floor and out. As she was walking away, Stephanie turned to me and mouthed, "Sorry."

I stood at the railing overlooking the ground floor and watched them make their way out of the building. I wondered if the session Megan mentioned was at the conference taking place at my hotel. I hoped it might be.

~

Later that evening, I reviewed my Titanic notes and made some new sketches but found myself doodling portraits. As my hand moved, I realized the emerging sketch was a likeness of Megan. I put my pencil down and looked at my hand. I opened and closed it a few times, and then I picked up the pencil again. It felt good to be sketching something other than ad campaigns. It had been so long. I hadn't realized until that moment how much I'd missed it. I continued drawing as I reached for a tiny bottle of scotch from the mini-bar. Then I looked at the blinking message light on the telephone in the room and realized that I'd have to call Antonia sooner or later. She'd left three messages. *Might as well get this over with*, I thought.

"Hello? Tim. It's finally you," she said. "Are you on your way home yet? We've been so worried."

"Hi, Antonia. No, I'm not on my way home. I just got here. I have a lot of work to do. And who's we?"

"Nathan and I. We're here trying to figure out which clients we can take with us when our agency starts up."

"You sure that's ethical? Or even legal?"

"Don't worry about that. You worry too much about that kind of thing, Tim. It's going to hamper your career, you know. Anyway, how are you surviving in that outport?"

I knew it wouldn't do any good to try to explain to her that Halifax was a charming city and that the people were just as lovely. She would never understand. So, I just said things were going well, and I'd let her know when I had an update on my E.T.A. I could hear noises in the background suggesting that Nathan was there in the apartment, and given Antonia's slight slur, they were already well into one of my bottles of wine, if I had to guess.

"Well, Nathan and I need you here. Time is money, and you're wasting both. You're not going to need that research anyway unless we can take that client with us." I could swear I heard her take another sip of something.

"About our business plans," I said. "I'm having second thoughts."

Oh, she was angry now. The sharp and sarcastic edge she was so good at conjuring was returning to her voice. "Okay, so our creative genius is having second thoughts. Or is it that continuing premature mid-life crisis? Whatever it is, get over it, Tim, and come home. Your future is here, and it won't wait. This is so not like you."

"I think maybe it is me, Antonia. I'll call you next week." I hung up before she could say anything more.

I sat back at the desk, looking at the portrait of Megan emerging from the paper and pencil. Then I thought about Antonia and our conversation, and I could picture Antonia and Nathan sitting on the forty-first floor, trying to devise a plan to get me back on board. I was fully aware that they needed me for this business venture since I was the creative part of their nascent ad agency. Nathan was the business wizard, and Antonia's sales skills could outpace even the best (or worst) snake-oil salesman in the world. But neither of them had the creative mind and artistic skills to see the world in new and different ways. And if there was anything I'd learned after seven years in advertising, it was that clients wanted new and different—no one wanted to be seen as the same as everyone else. Yes, they needed me—perhaps more than I needed them. That was a novel thought.

ELEVEN

THE FOLLOWING MORNING, I'D PLANNED to find a taxi driver willing to take me to the Fairview Lawn Cemetery. I'd discovered that it was one of the locations of the final resting place of some of the Titanic victims, whose bodies had been retrieved from the icy waters of the North Atlantic and brought to Halifax. I thought I'd have the taxi wait for me, then drop me off at the Nova Scotia Archives, where I planned to hole up for the afternoon. My research to date told me that the archives would be where I'd find more news stories and images, and I don't know what else. I was beginning to feel a kind of obsession take over, pushing me to find out more. Since the ad campaign wouldn't need such a crazy amount of background, I wasn't sure why I was doing this—but I was doing it.

I emerged from the hotel elevator to find myself in a sea of humanity. It was late. I'd slept in and had a long, quiet room service breakfast, enjoying being truly alone. Antonia was preternaturally energetic in the mornings. All I ever wanted to do at that hour was drink my coffee in peace, and she constantly blathered on about the office. This was like being in heaven.

As I navigated through the crowd of people who seemed to be on a coffee break from the conference sessions toward the bell stand to find a taxi, I could hear faint strains of familiar music wafting down the escalator that led to the second-floor mezzanine where the ballrooms were located. It sounded like a forties swing band doing a soundcheck, if I wasn't mistaken. I took the escalator to the mezzanine and followed the sound, lured like a child following the Pied Piper. As I passed by one of the smaller ballrooms, I thought I heard someone call my name. I almost didn't turn around since I knew no one in the city.

"Tim? Hey, Tim. It *is* you. Over here."

I turned and poked my head inside the open double doors of the small ballroom. The place was packed solid with tables, each backed by a large free-standing bulletin board. Each bulletin board was plastered with pages of text, flow charts and tables. It seemed to be the poster-presentation room where conference delegates who weren't making actual presentations could present their research findings to small groups who milled around, moving from table to table at their own speed. I'd been to a conference like that when I was in college.

Stephanie—from the museum the day before—waved to me from a chair beside the second table, gesturing me over. I walked in slowly, noticing that most participants had left the room, presumably for the coffee break. As I approached Stephanie, Megan stepped out from behind the bulletin board at the adjacent table. She didn't look nearly as happy to see me as Stephanie did. Megan gave Stephanie a withering look, then turned and began tidying stacks of papers on the table. "Once again, sorry for my friend's intrusion," she said without looking up.

"Hi," I said, moving my eyes over the posters on the bulletin boards and the stacks of stapled papers on the table.

"What are you doing here?" Stephanie said, getting up and coming around the table where I was standing.

"I'm staying here in this hotel, and I heard what sounds like an orchestra tuning up. I was just following the sound."

Megan stopped tidying and looked over. "Are you a swing music fan?" she said.

"Yeah," I said, laughing. "Anything forties, really. I started collecting old vinyl records back in high school. My friends thought I was a bit of a freak."

Megan almost smiled. Had I hit upon one of her weaknesses?

"What's all this about?" I said as I scanned the materials on both Stephanie's and Megan's poster tables. "Are you guys part of this conference?" Dumb question, right? I stood back to take a closer look at the poster.

"For sure," Stephanie said proudly. "Meg and I've been working on this study for an environmental group for the past couple of years—that was until Meg branched out for her dissertation." Stephanie pointed to the poster behind Megan's table.

I moved over closer so I could read the material on the poster behind Stephanie first. The title of the study presented on Stephanie's poster was "Whales and Oil Tankers: Nature versus the Economy."

"Looks interesting," I said carefully.

"Yeah," Stephanie said, passing me a sheaf of papers stapled together. It was the text of the study. "And ever since last month's disaster in Alaska, we're more determined than ever that our stuff gets published."

I knew only too well what Stephanie was referring to. Just three weeks earlier, the Exxon Valdez oil supertanker left Alaska bound for Long Island, California, when it ran aground on a reef in an inlet of the Alaska Sea called Prince William Sound, spilling its cargo of almost eleven million gallons of oil. I had watched the news coverage, cringing at the devastation of marine life and the shoreline. It was all anyone at client meetings could talk about for days since our company represented no fewer than three major oil companies, including the one in my portfolio. I thought it might be better if I didn't mention that fact.

Megan leaned back against the table. "It's still a cause dear to my heart, although my dissertation work has taken me in a slightly different direction."

I was happy to move the conversation on from oil companies, so I turned to see Megan's poster. "Sounding the Alarm: Petrochemicals in Textile Manufacturers' Wastewater."

"Well, this sounds interesting. Textiles? Like in fashion fabrics?"

Megan looked surprised. "Yes. What do you know about fashion fabrics?"

"My mother's family was in the textile business for years. My mom worked in my grandfather's store and made all her own clothes for most of her life. And some of ours." I smiled as I remembered my mother sitting hunched over her sewing machine for hours at a time. "We had the best Hallowe'en costumes in the world."

Megan smiled. This was the first time I'd seen her really smile, and I was dazzled by the sincerity.

"Well," Stephanie said, "it seems that you and Meg have a lot in common."

Megan and I both turned toward Stephanie at the same time. I, for one, couldn't imagine what we had in common after learning about her passionate interest in the environment. Don't get me wrong. It wasn't that I had no interest in the environment. It was just that I was well aware of how I made my living. Did that make me a hypocrite? Probably, but it was, after all, my livelihood.

Stephanie continued. "You followed the sound of the orchestra, and Meg sometimes sings with a swing band."

"Stephanie," Megan said as if trying to silence her friend.

"What? It's true." Stephanie turned toward me. "In fact, that sound you heard was coming from the Allan Thomas Orchestra. They're a local group playing here tonight for a conference event." Megan was openly glaring at Stephanie at this point. "And, like I said, Megan sings with them sometimes."

I was intrigued. "Really? Are you singing with them tonight?"

"No. I'm just attending as part of the conference."

Just then, the music was louder. It seemed as if the orchestra was in full rehearsal mode.

"Why don't you two swing fans go and have a listen to the rehearsal. I'm sure Allan wouldn't mind, Meg." Stephanie then practically pushed us out the door. "I'll tidy up both our booths." Then, since everyone except the three of us had already left the room, she closed the ballroom door.

When we were standing on the other side of the closed door, Megan said, "So sorry about Steph."

"Don't be." I nodded toward the big ballroom and the music. "Could we?"

Megan shrugged and led the way toward the music.

~

"Thanks for introducing me to Allan," I said later, my search for a taxi abandoned. We had just settled into a small table at the bar off the lobby overlooking the waterfront. It had taken me all the charm I could muster to get Megan to agree to have lunch with me. I was fascinated by her style—white T-shirt, jeans, black leather jacket and all that wild hair, not to mention her dazzlingly straight, white teeth that showed when she smiled—up against her nerdy devotion to science and her love of forties music. It was a heady combination for a young man who had spent the past five years climbing the corporate ladder egged on by a woman with ambitions that outpaced even his own. Oh, and a woman who wore a power suit every day of her life.

"Allan and I have been friends for years," Megan said as the waiter placed two glasses of white wine on the table. I wanted a beer but went along with the wine to underscore our similarities. "Allan's something of a celebrity. He's not like some of those American icons," she said with a look of mild distaste, "but Canada loves him."

"About that American thing. You seem to have a problem with Americans, or is it just with me?"

Megan took a sip of wine and then placed her glass on the table. "Look, I'm sorry about the American remarks. No offence intended. It's just that years ago, my grandmother had a problem with an American sailor. I kind of got angry for her when I heard the story. It's certainly nothing personal."

I was relieved. "I'm so glad to hear that. Now it's time for me to apologize."

Megan looked puzzled. "Whatever for?"

"When I first met you at the museum, I kind of implied that you might be interested in helping me find the Titanic sites around here."

"You mean the gravesites."

"That's part of it," I said. But I was now wondering what the other part was.

Megan put her elbows on the table, leaned her chin on her hands, and stared at me. The intensity was enough to freeze a man's brain. "Why are you so interested in Titanic memorabilia and the gravesites?"

"I'm doing some research for a client."

Megan sat back. "What sort of client is interested in Titanic graves sites? What kind of work do you do?"

I took a small sip of wine. "I'm in advertising."

"Oh." It sounded cool, aloof.

"Something wrong?" I said.

Megan took another sip of wine and patted her lips with the small paper napkin. "No. It's just that...well, there are so many problems with advertising these days. I mean, all those campaigns designed to make people want to buy things they don't need and probably shouldn't have. Consumerism running rampant. You know what I mean?"

"I'm more of a creative type," I said. "I draw the pictures."

Megan at once seemed intrigued. "An artist?"

"Sort of. Anyway, I was planning to find those gravesites this afternoon. Any chance you could give me a recommendation about a taxi company?"

"I'll do you one better," she said. "I'll take you."

~

The morning sun had given way to a drizzly afternoon with a sky threatening to descend on our heads. As I opened the door of Megan's tiny car—a powder blue Ford Escort that looked to me to be five or so years old—I could smell the ocean in the distance and at once felt the damp chill of the air seep through my jacket.

"Follow me, "Megan said quietly.

As I followed Megan across the cemetery, my feet squishing into the grass that was just beginning to reveal tiny glimpses of green, I looked around at the bare tree branches. Even now, in mid-April, there were no leaves on the trees, but I could see tiny buds with the promise of warmer weather to come. I was surprised to see a few people milling around in the dampness. Then I remembered. Tomorrow was April 15—the anniversary of the sinking of the Titanic.

"It's a good thing you didn't plan to come tomorrow," Megan said as if reading my mind. "This place will be crawling with tourists. It's kind of disgusting if you ask me. Why are people so fascinated by grave markers?"

Why indeed? I thought.

Megan finally stopped and pointed to three rows of grave markers just ahead up a slight incline. "There," she said.

I looked at the undulating rows that followed the contours of the hill. There they were—one hundred and twenty-one small, granite markers. I walked on ahead, and Megan followed me slowly. I stopped in front of one marker and read it. The name on top was Freeman, and the victim was a Titanic crew member. "He remained at his post of duty seeking to save others, regardless of his own life and went down with the ship," read the epitaph. Under the actual marker on the plinth was the following, "Erected by Mr. J. Bruce Ismay." I turned to Megan.

"I didn't know that the Titanic's owner paid for headstones."

"It was the least he could do, don't you think? I mean, after all, he survived somehow."

70

I knew what Megan was talking about. Many of the first-class male passengers had escaped the disaster on half-full lifeboats intended for women and children of all classes—those were the days of women and children first. I was feeling less and less inclined to use the Titanic in the ad campaign, and I was beginning to feel like Megan's perspective was starting to trickle into my subconscious, just like the damp was seeping into my body.

I walked along the line of grave markers while Megan stood on the periphery watching me. "Does that help?" she said when I'd made my way to the end of the row.

"Help?"

"With the creative process. Does it help to see where these unfortunate people are buried?"

"You're a bit intense about this, you know."

Megan folded her arms as if to embrace herself, then turned and began to walk away. I caught up with her and strode along beside her as we made our way back to the parking lot.

"How long are you staying in Halifax?" Megan said finally.

"I'm not sure."

"Don't you have a boss who cares where you are?"

"To tell you the truth, after I talked to you and Stephanie about the work you're both doing, I had an idea. Just before you picked me up in front of the hotel, I called my boss to ask him if he minded if I worked from here for a while. I brought my new Macintosh portable computer, and I can plug the modem into the telephone jack in my hotel room, and I'm in business."

"A new Macintosh portable? Fancy," Megan said, sounding slightly impressed. "Isn't there anyone else who cares how long you stay away?"

"You mean a woman?" I said. What made me say that? Megan said nothing. I was strangely exhilarated by this turn of conversation. I'd thought she hated me. I was beginning to enjoy this. "I've had a woman in my life for the past few years. But things have changed recently."

"Is she an advertising guru, too?" Megan said as we reached the car. She smiled slightly as if she might be enjoying this just a bit herself.

"You have no idea." I reached to open her door for her. "Much more than I am."

"Timothy Sinclair," she said as she lowered herself into the driver's seat, "I have a distinct feeling that you came to Halifax for something more than Titanic memories."

TWELVE
MEGAN, 1989

"WHAT THE HELL WAS THAT ALL ABOUT?" I said to Steph as we wound our way down the stairs of the Maritime Museum of the Atlantic. I couldn't get out of there fast enough.

"What was that all about? He was cute," Steph said. "And you know very well you could use a bit of that in your life."

"Not from an American tourist," I said through gritted teeth. I ran my fingers through my unruly hair.

"Hey, wait up a bit, will you, Meg. What's the hurry?" Steph caught up to me and put her hand on my arm as we reached the door leading out of the museum. "What do you mean not from an American tourist?"

I turned, trying not to glance up toward the railing on the mezzanine where I was sure Timothy Sinclair, whose acquaintance we had just made, was looking down and said, "Years ago, my grandmother...never mind. It's a long story, Steph." Then I pushed open the door and rushed outside to grab a deep breath of fresh air.

~

As I pulled my car up in front of my grandmother's house two days later to have dinner with her as I did most Sundays, I was thinking about my reaction to Tim in the museum and the strange thoughts I'd been having since our little trip to the cemetery on Friday. I wondered what had come over me even to suggest taking him to the cemetery myself. But I was even more curious about his interest in the Titanic disaster—and there was something about him. Although I wasn't convinced he was telling me the whole truth, I was intrigued enough to have unwillingly allowed him to permeate my thoughts.

I walked up the steps and opened the front door. The minute I walked over the threshold, I felt calmer, lighter. For as long as I could remember, this house had been a safe space where I could always be myself. The house was an old Victorian with the interior lovingly cared for by Gran for years since my grandfather died and she'd retired. The wood wainscoting and hall table gleamed, and, as usual, there was a bouquet of fresh flowers adorning the table.

"Gran! Gran, are you here?"

I looked up the stairs, and Gran appeared. As always, she was the picture of the gracious, accomplished woman that she was and that I had always hoped to emulate—I didn't think it was working for me, though.

My grandmother, Dr. Ellen McMaster—Ellie to her friends—swept down the stairs in a pair of perfectly cut black pants and a cashmere sweater. I looked down at my bulky fisherman-knit sweater and jeans and almost laughed at the vast difference in our styles despite my yearning to emulate her.

"Meg, darling. You're loud as always. And I love it."

Gran embraced me in a tight hug, and we walked arm in arm into the living room. "Dinner's not quite ready yet. Let's sit and have a glass of sherry." She looked at my face. "Or would you rather have a beer?"

I smiled. "You know me well, Gran. You pour your sherry, and I'll get a beer." As I retrieved a beer from the kitchen, I wondered what had made me order a glass of wine when Tim and I had a drink together after he met Allan. Surely, I wasn't trying to impress someone from the big city.

When I returned to the living room, Gran was pouring her sherry from a crystal decanter on the coffee table. Gran frowned at me as I began to take a sip from the bottle. I stopped with the beer halfway to my mouth and went to the liquor cabinet in the corner to get a Pilsner glass. She smiled, and we sat down.

"You're in a good mood, Meg." She peered at me. "You've met someone."

"Gran—

"Am I wrong?"

I sipped my beer and smiled. Then, as I thought about the situation, my smile faded quickly. "He's an American."

"Is that a problem?" Gran said.

"Well, I thought you might not approve."

Gran placed her sherry glass on the coffee table and turned to look at me. "And why in the world would I not approve?"

"Because of your experience," I said carefully. I really did think Gran might have a problem with this situation.

Gran rolled her eyes and sat back on the sofa. "You mean because an American sailor jilted me over forty years ago?" She laughed. "Megan, that was a long time ago. And I daresay some of the terrific things that have happened to me since that time were a direct result of that encounter—even if it didn't work out the way a love-struck eighteen-year-old might have wanted it to."

"Like what?"

"If I hadn't been pregnant, I wouldn't have left to go to Montreal. If I hadn't been in Montreal, it is highly likely that I would never have gone to university. If I hadn't gone to McGill, I would never have gone to medical school there or perhaps anywhere else. It was the 1940s, my darling, and women didn't do that." She got up from the sofa and went over to the mantle where there was a photo that had been there ever since I could remember. I knew it was a photograph of Gran with a group of medical students on the day they had all graduated from medical school at McGill University in Montreal. She picked it up and looked at it before replacing it and continuing. "And you, young lady, probably wouldn't be here. I couldn't bear that. So, what's the problem?"

I felt a bit deflated and perhaps just a bit silly. "Nothing, I guess."

Gran sat back down beside me and sipped her sherry. "So, why is your American boy here in the city?"

"He's hardly my American boy—or man—Gran. Anyway, he says he's here researching the Titanic disaster for some ads he's working on."

"Hmm. And ad man as they say. It sounds to me like you don't quite believe him."

"Well," I said, not knowing where this conversation was going, "it just feels like he's here for some other reason."

"Is there any chemistry?"

"Chemistry?" I didn't feel all that comfortable going there with my grandmother.

"How does he make you feel?" she said softly.

I picked up a cushion and hugged it to me. I couldn't stop myself from smiling, yet I had no idea where this feeling was coming from. Didn't I dislike him on sight, and hadn't I known him for less than a New York minute anyway?

"That good?" Gran laughed and got up. "I'm going to check on the roast and open some wine. You put on some of that Allan Thomas music I love so much, and you can tell me all the juicy details." She turned. "By the way, if your young man wants to do some real research, you can tell him a friend of mine survived the Titanic sinking."

"What? Who? How is that possible, Gran?"

"It's Fran Phillips, my dear. Remember when she showed you her collection of vintage couture dresses?"

I certainly did remember. How could any little girl forget trying on a St. Laurent gown (yes, she let me try it on)? "Wow, Gran. I didn't know that about Mrs. Phillips." I was genuinely impressed by this piece of news.

"She was only twelve, and she's eighty-nine now. I may not have mentioned this, but she's not so well, so if your American friend wants to talk to her, he better let me know, and I'll see what I can do."

"Do you think she'd want to talk to him?"

"Knowing Fran Phillips as I do, I'd say she'd be more than delighted."

~

The sun was shining, and the wind was blowing hard as we picked our way across the massive granite boulders toward the lighthouse. I'd been surprised (and oddly happy) when Tim called after I returned from Gran's house on Sunday evening, asking me if I would like to spend a few hours with him at Peggy's Cove, a quaint fishing village just outside the city. He wanted to see what all the tourist brochures were boasting about. I hesitated for just a moment before I agreed. So, on Monday afternoon, I ditched my library work, and Tim picked me up in a car I thought I'd never set foot in. No one I knew drove a sports car, and this Supra was something else. He took the curves—and there were lots of them on the way—at a speed I would have found excessive if it hadn't been so exhilarating. We were both still laughing as we approached the lighthouse. I didn't even pull away when Tim reached for my hand as we neared the edge of the boulders and looked down at the waves crashing against them, sending sprays of white foam high into the air.

"So, you said you wanted to see Peggy's Cove lighthouse. How would you like to see it from a different perspective?" Tim looked puzzled. I pointed toward the little harbour protected from the wave action where fishing boats were moored beside wharves laden with empty lobster traps piled high. "See the sign? Murphy's Whale-Watching?" Tim nodded. "You don't get seasick, do you?"

"Hey, I grew up outside Boston. I think I spent every summer weekend from the age of four until I left home on my father's sailboat."

I took Tim's hand and led him down the hill toward the sign where Patrick Murphy, the proprietor and my old friend, was waiting. I'd called him in advance, and he was ready to take us out.

"Ready to go?" Patrick said, handing each of us a life vest and a heavy jacket.

We climbed aboard his boat, and he expertly motored toward the narrow opening leading out of the tiny harbour and into the open ocean.

"You don't get a lot of this in New York City," Tim said as he stood in the stern, looking at the ever-widening distance between the boat and the shore.

"Do you miss being on the water?" I said, winding my scarf more tightly around my neck as the wind came up.

"I don't think I realized quite how much," Tim said. He sounded wistful.

I picked up a pair of binoculars that were sitting on the bench. "There!" I said, gesturing toward a point in the water. I handed Tim the second pair Patrick had left for us to look for whales.

"I see it!" Tim sounded excited.

Patrick slowly turned the boat toward the sighting and cut his engine. He was good at this, but he knew that he didn't need to provide any commentary with me on board.

"It's called an Atlantic Right Whale," I said, training my binoculars on it. "The shape of the spout of spray is specific to each species. Isn't it magnificent?" I always felt the same way when I spotted these sea creatures. They took my breath away. "Could you believe that oil tankers have been leaking oil out there, threatening their habitat?"

"No," Tim said softly as he peered through his binoculars. "I can't."

I had a sudden urge to kiss Tim, so while Patrick wasn't looking, I threw my arms around his neck and gave in to the urge. I immediately pulled away. "Oh my god, Tim. I'm so sorry. I don't know why I did that." Then he kissed me back.

THIRTEEN

I WASN'T SURE *HOW* IT HAPPENED, but it was one of those things that just happened—and felt right. When I awoke the following day, I had the feeling that something was different. Light was streaming in through my bedroom window overlooking the water as it always did when I woke up this late, but nothing seemed the same. I turned toward the window and saw Tim's silhouette against the glass as he gazed out toward the cove. Then I remembered.

"Nice, isn't it?" I said, grabbing a bathrobe.

"I don't think nice quite captures it, Meg." At some point the evening before, Tim had started calling me Meg. It sounded right, but more to the point, it *felt* right.

"Is it very different from the view you usually have when you wake up in the morning?" I said, sitting on the side of the bed.

"I might as well live on a different planet," Tim said, turning toward me.

"How does it make you feel?"

"Grounded," he said, turning back toward the view.

"So…," I began slowly, "why don't you stay?"

Tim turned to me, smiling. "I'd love to spend the day here with you, Meg. Don't you have work to do?"

I got up and walked over toward him. "No, Tim. I mean, *stay*." What in the world had come over me? Did my usual good sense not have any control over my tongue this morning?

"Stay," he said as if he might be turning the word over in his head.

I took a deep breath and charged forward. "I get the feeling you're searching for something, Tim, and I don't think it's Titanic souvenirs or research materials. Last evening, you told me that you're tired of drawing what other people want you to draw. Well…maybe it's time you stopped doing that. Maybe it's time for you to start following your passion for once." Tim encircled me with his arms. "And I don't mean me." He laughed.

While we were drinking beer (we finally both admitted we loved a good beer) and looking at the moon over the ocean the evening before, Tim had told me about his passion for sketching and watercolour painting. He was using his graphic design skills in his advertising job, but he was no longer doing any of his own art. He didn't have time.

Tim took my hand, and we walked out into the living room, where I could smell coffee. Tim had clearly been up for a while.

"Meg," he began, "I told you about those business plans." Yes, he had also told me about some business plans. "And about my two business partners. And remember, I'm such a city person. I mean...this is paradise, but I somehow don't think it's actually real. I almost think I don't deserve it."

I moved away from him. "I think I'll get some coffee." I made my way into my tiny kitchen, where there was a full pot of coffee. I needed to think, to catch the moment. I poured each of us a mug and went back into the living room, where Tim was putting on his sweater. I handed him a mug.

I decided to ignore the direction our conversation seemed to be going. "Tim, I have a friend with a furnished cottage on the water ten minutes from here for rent. I know he'd do a short-term lease, which would be much better—and cheaper—than a hotel while you're here. Plus, you could get more of a sense of the place." I put my mug of coffee down on a side table and plugged a cassette into my big tape player on a credenza beneath three shelves of cassette tapes. The Allan Thomas Orchestra filled the room with "You'd Be So Nice to Come Home To." I immediately thought, *Oops, maybe that isn't quite the right song for this moment*. But I let it play anyway.

Tim smiled. "Cole Porter, 1943. Right?" I started to speak, but he stopped me. "Wait. Wait. From the movie *Something to Shout About*. I think it was nominated for an Academy Award that year, but I can't remember if it won."

I was impressed. "It didn't," I said. "Yes, Cole Porter by way of the Allan Thomas Orchestra. Impressive, aren't they?"

"Yes, you are," he said.

And I had him.

~

Tim decided to spend the day, so I planned a little road trip. We'd get into his car and head around the bay to Queensland Beach. Then we'd carry on to Chester, a chi-chi little village where rich Americans and a few Canadians still owned huge summer homes. Then we'd carry on to a port town called Lunenburg, where we'd have lunch at one of the seafood restaurants housed in the colourful clapboard buildings overlooking the waterfront. It would take us about an hour and a half to get there. I hadn't been to Lunenburg for a couple of years, so I was looking forward to it—and to showing off my province to an American tourist!

I was getting my purse ready when I heard the phone ring in the living room.

"Could you get that, Tim?" I said. I knew it wouldn't be anyone I would mind him talking to.

As I came into the living room, I heard Tim say, "And I must be speaking with Dr. MacMaster. Megan's told me a lot about you." Then he laughed. "I'm looking forward to meeting you, too."

Gran! She could be so charming. I lunged for the phone.

"Here she is now, Dr. MacMaster—Ellie...Yes, nice to talk to you, too...Thanks, I look forward to it." Then Tim handed me the receiver. With a grin plastered on his face. Yup. She had charmed him. And I had little doubt that the charming had been mutual.

FOURTEEN
TIM, 1989

AS MUCH AS I TRIED, I COULDN'T REMEMBER a time in my life when I'd felt so alive. And it wasn't just because I'd spent the night with a new and exciting woman, either. The day Meg and I travelled the tourist route around St. Margaret's and Mahone Bay was the most fun I'd had in my adult life. Antonia and I spent holidays during the past five winters on islands like St. Lucia, Antigua and Barbados in the Caribbean. We had travelled together to Paris and recently London. We stayed at cosmopolitan hotels and ate at highly recommended restaurants. And yet, I had never felt as free, as interested, as content. What was happening to me?

When it was time to leave, I drove back into the city in a happiness fog. Meg had to work, and so did I. I spent the next day in the archives with a side trip to an art store for supplies and was now sitting in my hotel room, alone, trying to create a watercolour of the cemetery we'd visited. I could have convinced myself that I was creating the image for the ad campaign, but I knew I was only kidding myself. It just felt good to be painting what I wanted to paint. That hadn't happened in years. I was trying to get the contour of the land right when my concentration was interrupted by the ringing phone. I smiled, thinking it might be Meg.

"Hello!"

"Well, don't you sound cheerful." It wasn't Meg.

"Antonia, hi," I said, enthusiasm draining from every fibre of my being. "I was going to give you a call tomorrow. I'm thinking of extending my stay a bit longer."

"What?" Her friendly(ish) demeanour had evaporated. "Tim, have you completely lost your mind up there? Things are crazy here." She stopped for a beat. "And I miss you. We really need to talk."

I could tell just from hearing her voice that this last pronouncement was delivered with just the faintest of pouts. I wasn't sure I bought that sentiment. "I have a lot more to do here than I had originally thought." Way more, it seemed, but I didn't think it was a good time to discuss this. "I need more time. I've talked to Ken, and he's okay with me working from here for a while." Both Antonia and I reported to Ken, one of the senior partners.

"Screw Ken," she said, that edge I knew so well returning to her voice. "You and I have been lining his pockets for long enough. It's our turn. You and I and Nathan are a team, and if we're going to go out on our own, we need to be a tight working group. You need to be here. *I* need you to be here."

"Please, Antonia—" Antonia slammed down the phone, cutting me off.

I calmly picked up a brush, dipped it back into the sap green, mixed it on a palette with a bit of burnt umber, and went back to work on the scene's foreground. I hummed a bit. I knew Antonia so well that when the telephone rang again, I let it ring three times before picking it up.

"Antonia?"

"Where will you be?" she said, far more calmly than before.

"I'll let you know," I said, trying to sound noncommittal.

"You know I love you, don't you, Tim?"

I think I rolled my eyes.

~

True to her word, Meg hooked me up with her friend with the cottage for rent. I wasn't convinced about this idea, but I couldn't bear to let her down. I was maneuvering the car along the road that snaked along the bay while rehearsing what I'd say to Meg. I was thinking about how to let her know that a cottage on the bay might work for her, but it really wasn't who I was when I suddenly realized I'd reached my destination. I abruptly turned the wheel, pulling into a gravel driveway alongside a beige mini-van. I turned off the ignition and got out of the car. The moment I slammed the door shut behind me, a middle-aged, bearded man wearing a plaid jacket and jeans opened the front door and walked out onto the porch.

"George Smithers," the man said, reaching out to shake my hand as I walked up the three steps onto the wide porch that spanned the length of the small, single-story house. "You must be Megan's friend Timothy."

"I am, sir," I said, shaking his hand. The grip was stronger than I expected, and he held it for just long enough for me to get the message.

Narrowing his eyes, George said, "I hope you're treating that girl well, Timothy. She's like a daughter to me."

"I'll remember that, George."

Then George turned and walked into the house, beckoning me inside. I was prepared to be polite and conduct a respectful conversation with George, letting him know I wasn't sure and would get back to him. I wasn't prepared for the sight before me as I looked out the back of the house facing the water.

From the road, the house looked tiny, almost swallowed up by the trees surrounding it. Once inside, though, it was clear that the trees flanked only three sides. The fourth side—well, let's just say that nothing flanked it. The house was on a promontory that dropped off down to the water. The view across the bay to a mysterious-looking dark island was breathtaking.

"Wow," was all I could manage.

"Yeah. Most everyone has that reaction. That there's Shut-In Island," George said, noticing the direction of my gaze. "Uninhabited."

I could immediately see an image of Shut-In Island emerging from watercolour paints in my mind's eye. I could see and feel an easel and a coffee pot on the small, chipped table in the window. I looked around at the meagre furnishings and the massive beach stone fireplace and pictured a roaring fire. I looked up at the pitched-roof plank ceiling soaring twenty-five feet above me, and before I knew what was coming out of my mouth, I said, "I'll take it."

"Don't you want to know the rent? Or the lease arrangements?"

"I don't think they matter," I said.

The following day, I checked out of the hotel and drove out to my cottage. *My* cottage. Wow! After checking out the view from the back deck that I hadn't noticed on my first visit, I set up my computer, plugging it into the telephone line. The telephone service was the only thing I'd been concerned about when George asked me if I had any questions. However, after I told Meg I'd rented the house, she began listing off all the things I'd have to pay attention to: the well, the septic system (what the heck?), the electricity that evidently had a habit of going off in high wind (she said there was a generator that I had no idea how to use—but I could learn). The telephone service was key, though, since it was the reason Ken, my boss, had agreed to let me work from a distance for a while.

My firm had recently subscribed to something called CompuServe, a new-fangled internet service that let us send electronic mail to one another. This electronic communication was a new thing for our company, and some of the older account executives were actively resisting any change. They were the same ones who had fought voice mailboxes a few years earlier. On the other hand, I was more than happy to keep connected to my office this way.

Once I had everything set up, I dialled into my account and found a message from Ken himself.

"Tim: Hope you're enjoying your sojourn in the wilds of Canada. The Eastern Oil folks liked your initial Titanic pitch. One of their managers is

thinking of taking a trip up there to see how you got so inspired. I think he was joking. Anyway, I want to send you some notes, so I'll need a mailing address asap. By the way, Eleanor thinks we should spend our summer holidays in Nova Scotia. We've never been to Canada, and she says our dollars will go further up there. Would you recommend it? You know how wives can be. Or you will someday! I do know Antonia. Haha. Cheers, Ken."

I was just sitting down to send him a reply when I heard a faint knock on my front door. I was still preoccupied with my thoughts about what to say to Ken as I opened the door to find Meg standing on the porch with a bottle of wine and a bag of groceries.

"Welcome to the neighbourhood!"

Since she lived about a ten-minute drive away, I thought that neighbourhoods up here were much bigger than I was used to.

"I'm beginning to feel like I'm in Oz," I said, taking the wine and groceries out of her hands so she could come inside.

"Not a chance," she said, unwrapping her scarf and looking around. "If this were Oz, there would be a wicked witch around the corner." Then she stepped back and looked around. She glanced over to my computer and then to the easel I'd set up in the window just as I'd imagined. "Not bad, Timothy Sinclair. Not bad."

FIFTEEN

WHEN I LEFT NEW YORK, I'D PLANNED ON SPENDING two weeks or so doing some research (ostensibly) and clearing my head (mostly the latter). I was unprepared for the feeling that came over me as I stood on the waterfront that first week while still at the hotel. I had simply stood there, staring. I was staring at the little ferry that carried people from one side of the harbour to the other. I stared at a navy ship as it glided majestically out of the harbour, bound for foreign lands. I stared at the small groups of people meandering along the boardwalk. And I smelled the ocean. It was probably that smell that brought back all those summers on the sailboat—memories that had been deeply buried for years as I clawed my way through the urban landscape on my way to—where exactly? That was now the question.

So, now here I was a month later, still here and staring out at what I'd begun to think of as *my* window at the water below, shimmering in the noonday sun. I scratched my two-day growth of beard as I sipped a coffee and marvelled at how I could never get away with this semi-scruffy look at my Manhattan office. I was almost surprised at how much I liked the feeling of freedom I had here. My mid-day reverie was interrupted by the phone. I was expecting a call from Ken at the office in New York but was hoping it might be from Meg.

"Hi there," Meg said. "What's going on?"

Just hearing her voice made me smile—stupidly, I'm sure. "Just enjoying the sunshine at the moment. Taking a bit of a lunch break. What's up?"

"A couple of things. First, Steph just called from Toronto. I'm so excited for her. She has a new job!"

Her excitement was infectious. I could feel myself getting excited, and I didn't have a clue what this job was about. But if it was important to Megan MacMaster, it was increasingly important to me. "Tell me about it," I said, tucking the receiver under my chin to pour another cup of coffee.

"She's just been appointed issues manager for that environmental company we both worked part-time for when we were in grad school up in Toronto."

"Issues manager?"

"Yeah. Her job is to follow what's happening in the media and related industries and help her company figure out which issues could become problems. Remember that article I showed you a few days ago? The one about offshore gas pipelines?"

We'd been having dinner at Meg's cottage when I'd noticed a pile of clippings on her coffee table where she often worked. It had been about new offshore gas pipelines in the North Atlantic and their potential to affect the environment. I told her I remembered.

"Well, it seems there may be important concerns about how the pipelines might affect the whale population."

I was becoming increasingly aware of Meg's passion for the environment, in general, and whales, in particular. To tell you the truth, I had never given either of them much thought—until now.

Meg continued. "And after that Exxon disaster on the west coast, it's more important than ever to be sure the oil and gas companies do what's right. And I'm not so sure they will. That's why watchdogs like Steph's organization are so important."

I ran my hand across the pile of illustrations and paintings on the table beside my easel and rested my hand on top. The rendering for my next iteration of the ad campaign for the oil company was peaking out. I still hadn't mentioned any of this to Meg.

"The second thing," Meg said, "is that the Allan Thomas Orchestra is playing at *The Old Jube* in town next weekend—a week from Saturday. You interested?"

"*The Old Jube*?"

Meg laughed. "Sorry. I completely forgot that there's no way you could know what that is. It's a new dance hall of sorts. But it has a history. Well, you know that Halifax played quite a role in the second world war? You know that convoys of ships gathered here in the harbour before sailing to Europe, right?"

"Yeah, I do. I think my grandfather was here briefly."

"What? Really? Wow, so this will *really* interest you. There was a place down by the Arm—it's a kind of inlet that comes up on the other side of the peninsula—that used to be called *The Jubilee Boat Club*. It was a rowing club, but it also had a dance hall where soldiers and sailors used to go when they were on leave. A couple of years ago, some local entrepreneurs got together to rebuild it. Allan's orchestra usually plays there when they're in town."

"Count me in," I said. "And what about the singer? Are you by any chance singing?" I remembered Stephanie had mentioned that Meg sometimes sang with the orchestra, but I had yet to see any evidence.

Meg started to laugh. "Not that I had planned!"

~

Our plans to go to the dance hall were still more than a week away, but I was looking forward to it. I planned to pick Meg up, have dinner at a restaurant in the city called *Zapata's*—evidently, they even had a Mexican restaurant here—then go on to the dance at *The Old Jube*. My problem, however, was that I ran into a bit of a snag the day before when my car wouldn't start. I decided to call George, my landlord, since he seemed to know everyone on the bay and beyond. There must be someone who could come and get it started. Sure enough, George sent over his friend, Axel, the mechanic. I'm not kidding—his name really was Axel.

Axel arrived in a souped-up pick-up truck. He launched himself out of the cab the moment he spotted my black Supra.

"Wow, man. That the car I'm supposed to fix?" He started walking around, running a hand over the shiny surface and whistling.

"It is indeed," I said, although I was beginning to wonder if he'd ever worked on one of these before. I didn't have to wonder for long.

"Radical! I've been wanting to get under the hood of one of these babies ever since I saw them in that auto mag I read every month."

I was starting to worry. "So, you've never worked on a Supra before?"

"Nah, but don't worry. A car is a car, and I'm the best car man on the bay."

I wasn't so sure I agreed that a car was a car, but what was I supposed to do?

"Mind if I get behind the wheel, then take a look under the hood?"

I nodded and watched as he confirmed that the engine wouldn't turn over. He got out and opened the hood. Then he leaned his head into the engine for a few minutes before standing up. "Yup. Needs to go to the shop," Axel said, wiping his hands on the dirty rag he was holding.

"How long will it take to fix it?"

Axel looked up at the sky as if he could see the time in the puffy clouds drifting by overhead. "Well, let me see. I can send a tow truck this afternoon. Then I'll need to take a closer look. Then we'll have to get parts." He tapped a finger on his lips. "Ten days, I think."

"What am I supposed to do out here without a car for ten days?"

"What? Not a problem, man. My cousin rents cars. I'll give you a lift."

So, Axel's cousin rented me a car. Well, it wasn't really a car. It was a van. A mini-van. All the times Antonia and I had ridiculed the mid-west moms and their min-vans came flooding back to me. Now, I was one of them—minus the kids in the back. Life does have a way of getting even with you.

~

The more I drove the van, the more I liked it. I mean, seriously? I liked it? Yeah, I liked it. I drove it to the grocery store at the end of Peggy's Cove Road to get supplies. I drove it to the liquor store. I drove it to pick up a pizza at the local diner a ten-minute drive from my cottage, the only game in town for takeout. (And I even started to love that they put so much gooey cheese on it that it dropped off in masses when you picked up a piece. The fact that Antonia would have been apoplectic seemed to make it even more enticing to me.) I drove it into the city to visit the archives and the museums and have lunch at a waterfront restaurant. When Meg and I got together, though, she drove her little Ford Escort. She laughed so hard the first time she saw the van I thought she might split apart.

I was thinking about this as I fumbled with my keys in the dark to open the front door, my arms loaded with grocery bags. But I didn't need the key, after all. I hadn't remembered leaving the door unlocked, but I guess I was starting to act like the locals. Who would drive down the dark driveway and break in anyway?

I opened the door, dropped the bags and stumbled over some unknown object as I reached for a light switch. "What the hell?" I was sure there had been no object there when I left. I flipped the two switches on the wall simultaneously. One flooded the interior entrance with light from the small hanging fixture overhead, while the other lit up the porch outside.

As I looked down at the offending object—an eerily familiar-looking small leather satchel—the voice came from the living room. "Finally. You're here."

I clutched my chest as if I might have a cardiac arrest in the next second. It was Antonia. "Geezus, Antonia," I said as she appeared in the doorway, a silhouette against the moonlight shimmering on the water beyond. "What the hell...?"

"What the hell am I doing here? Nice to see you, too," she said drily. "Well, you know the old saying...If the mountain won't come to Mohammed...Well, you know the rest." She walked back into the living room and turned on a lamp before taking up position in one of the single chairs beside the fireplace.

"Geezus, Antonia." I was suddenly reminded of what Meg had said when I told her I felt like I was in Oz. She had said there would be a wicked witch. *God*, I thought, *what's making me think that way?*

"You already said that. The proper follow-up might be hello," she said, looking around the room, her eyes resting on the easel and drafting tables.

"Sorry," I said. "Hello. You just took me by surprise."

"Good," she said. "That was precisely what I intended. There's nothing quite like a good surprise."

I thought this was an odd statement coming from a woman who had, on more than one occasion in the past, clearly told me she didn't like surprises. Oh well. We all change.

"Well, it's clear to me that you can't be planning on spending any more time here." I think her nose twitched just slightly as her head swivelled to take in my entire living room. "I'll just wait for you to throw your things in a suitcase, and we'll go to a hotel. I took a suite in a very nice one in town. I was surprised that they have such nice hotels here. Anyway, I'll just wait."

I was puzzled. "Why would I want to go to a hotel?"

"I mean, Tim," she said, sweeping her arm around, "just look at this place. It's so not you."

I looked down and noticed that I was still clutching my car keys. I threw them on a table and sank into the sofa facing out onto the water. "And just what would be me, Antonia?"

"Oh, Tim, let's not get into that now. I haven't seen you in a month, and we have a lot to talk about."

"How did you get here, anyway?" I said, cutting her off. "I didn't see a car outside. And how did you even find me?"

"Believe me, it wasn't easy," Antonia said, examining her nails as if the process of getting here might have damaged them. "It almost seemed like you didn't want to be found. But, as you know, I have my ways. And Ken is so easily manipulated. You did give him your mailing address. Then I managed to find a cabbie in town who seemed to know this area and was willing to take me out here for a decent price. I must say I had no idea it was this far outside town." She stood up and walked over to the small window overlooking the driveway. "You know, I've even missed that nasty Supra of yours." She stopped for a moment as she gazed out into the driveway lit only by the light from the porch. "Where is it?"

"In the garage—getting fixed."

"How did you get home?" She looked out the window again, and the penny seemed to drop as they say. "You haven't been driving that disgusting minivan parked out there?" She was beginning to sound just a tad hysterical. "It wasn't there when the cab dropped me off."

Strangely, I was beginning to enjoy this—just a bit. "Why not?" I said.

"God, Tim. Only carpool parents and hicks drive vans, for god's sake. Remember what we used to say about them?"

I shrugged, remembering a sticker I once saw on the back of a mini-van that said, *Condoms prevent minivans*. I did my best to suppress a smile.

Antonia plunged on. "I cannot believe that your standards have begun to deteriorate in such a short time. Things are more desperate than we thought. You've got to come home." There was the royal "we" once again—Antonia and Nathan, no doubt.

"I can't," I said, getting up and walking over to the drafting table. "I'm not finished here yet."

"From what I've seen of this hole so far, Canada is a refuge for the dull and the commonplace."

I could feel anger rising in my throat, and I remembered all the times over the past two years when Antonia's unwarranted snobbery and condescension had begun to wear on me. "Where do you get off—"

I was interrupted by a loud knock on the door.

"Tim?" I heard the door open. "Tim, am I early?"

Antonia sat down, folded her hands on her lap and took on that expression I'd seen so many times before. She had that sucking-on-a-lemon look on her face. "It seems we have company, Timothy. I guess our talk will have to wait."

Before I could say a word, Meg came into the living room in her chinos, white T-shirt and espadrille sandals in stark contrast to Antonia's travel outfit: a black Escada jacket with power shoulders, black T-shirt, black slacks and boots. Maybe there was a wicked witch after all. I almost smiled. Almost.

The moment Meg saw me standing in the window, she made directly for me, throwing her arms around my neck. "You'll never guess what I..." She stopped as she spied Antonia out of the corner of her eye. She pulled away. "Oh, I'm so sorry, Tim. I didn't know you were expecting anyone else."

"I wasn't," I said quietly. Then I turned to Antonia. "Meg, this is Antonia St. John. Antonia, meet Megan McMaster."

I was staring at Antonia—I had no idea what was coming next. She didn't get up, so Meg walked over to where she was sitting and extended her hand in greeting. As Meg approached her, I could see Antonia doing that thing she always did whenever she met other women for the first time. Antonia was looking Meg up and down from the top of her wild and wonderful hair to the tips of her scuffed espadrilles she told me she'd picked up on a backpacking trip in Spain a few years earlier. I had often mentioned to Antonia that she ought to try at least not to be so obvious about her scrutiny of women she was meeting for the first time. She didn't see any reason to be more subtle.

"Charmed," Antonia finally said as Meg reached her.

"You must be one of Tim's New York colleagues," Meg said, friendly as usual.

"You could say that. *You* must be one of Timothy's Canadian—"

"Antonia!" I had to cut her off. I couldn't risk her naming what she thought Meg might be.

"I was just going to say one of Timothy's new friends." Antonia gestured toward the sofa near the chair where she was sitting. "Please, Megan, sit." Meg sat down. "Timothy, why don't you get us a glass of wine. Megan and I can just get to know one another." Timothy, was it now? Such formality didn't bode well. It didn't bode well at all.

As I stepped into the kitchen, I looked back to see Antonia turn to Meg. "What is it you do in this part of the world, Megan?" I knew I had to be fast to get back in there.

"I'm just finishing up my Ph.D. in environmental science."

"I didn't know you had such brilliant friends, Timothy," Antonia said. "Soon, you'll have to call her Dr. McMaster."

I selected a bottle as quickly as I could and grabbed glasses, hoping I could get them to the living room before breaking one and before Antonia had time to do any damage. I managed to get all items onto the coffee table just as Antonia said, "Environmental science. So, you're an activist?" Meg shrugged and smiled as I pulled the cork loudly from the bottle. Antonia continued. "And has Timothy been helping you with your work?"

Meg shook her head, looking puzzled. "No, of course not."

"Pity," Antonia said, taking the glass I offered her. Then she shrugged off her jacket and placed it gently on the arm of her chair. "I was just telling Timothy that we're all looking forward to his return to New York, wasn't I, Timothy?"

God, how many times is she going to say Timothy? I thought.

Meg turned to me. "Are you leaving already, Tim?" She looked puzzled.

I was beginning to feel any control I might have had in this situation slipping away moment by moment. "No. I mean..."

"You mean yes?" Meg said, frowning.

Antonia took a long drink of her wine, quickly draining her glass. "A nice wine, Timothy. I remember it well. I'm a bit surprised you can even find it here." She put her glass on the table and stood up. "Good heavens. Where are my manners? It seems I'm interrupting your evening here. I do apologize. I'll just get my things and call a cab." She picked up the jacket she'd just removed and began putting it back on. I wondered what she was playing at. Then she continued, and I could hear a slight edge of sarcasm begin to harden the edges of what she said next. "I'm sure you two have a million things to talk about. I'm sure Megan must find the work you're doing with your latest client fascinating."

"We don't really discuss Tim's work," Meg said.

I could feel a tightness across my chest as if I were being squeezed in a vice.

"You don't?" Antonia said. "Well, that's a shame. Timothy, do you mean to tell me you haven't told young Megan all the details of those terrific Titanic-based ads you're creating?"

"Antonia, that's enough!" My anger was just at the surface, and Antonia knew exactly which buttons to press to make it boil over.

"Oh, I don't think so. I don't think it's nearly enough," Antonia said through clenched teeth as she turned to Meg. "You really should have a look at the new work he's doing for Eastern Oil. I'm sure an environmental scientist such as you would be fascinated. I do believe that they might have been indicted last year for oil spills—not as substantial as that recent Exxon disaster, mind you, but deadly, nonetheless." She turned to me, and I could see the smug look on her face. "Weren't they responsible for all those dead whales that washed up on the beaches in Maine?"

Meg's face was a mask of disbelief. She watched wordlessly as Antonia walked to the foyer and picked up her satchel. I heard the sound of gravel crunching on the driveway.

"Well, what do you know?" Antonia said. "I don't need to call a cab after all. My cabbie has returned."

I knew she knew this without even looking. She had pre-arranged it. It was so Antonia—always wanting to be in control, even of her exit—perhaps especially of her exit.

Antonia turned once more before leaving. "Tim," (we were back to Tim now), "we need you. Your home is waiting for you. And don't take too long. I'll be at the Harbour Plaza Hotel for two days." Then she turned and was gone.

Meg and I stood there, saying nothing and avoiding eye contact. The sound of crunching gravel on the driveway told us the taxi was departing. Then there was total silence. All I could think about was how it made more noise than a broomstick in flight—and that Antonia had ruined everything. Or maybe I'd done that myself.

Meg walked over to the drafting table and picked up a drawing. "Was she telling the truth? Are these for Eastern Oil?" She looked up at me, and I could see tears glistening in her eyes. I nodded. "Why didn't you tell me?" Her voice was low and even.

"How could I?"

"How could you not? I trusted you."

"What have I done?" I said lamely. "I haven't lied to you." Her eyes flashed at me. I could feel her fury pierce me just as surely as if she had shot an arrow into my heart. "How I feel about you may be the most honest and genuine thing I've ever experienced in my adult life."

"How you feel about me?" Tears were now spilling down her face. A single tear splashed on my watercolour rendering of the Titanic gravesites. "You know how important my work is to me. You've known about my passion for the environment from the beginning." She looked down at the page still in her hand and then threw it back on the table. "You've sold yourself out, Tim. You're no artist. You're a prostitute." Then she turned and fled.

Sixteen

I WAS ANGRY. I WAS ANGRY AT ANTONIA for barging into my life and blowing everything up in front of my eyes. But what did I expect? How could I blame her? She had valid reasons for doing it. She and I had been together for five years, and the pull I'd always felt toward her had never waned despite everything. But over the past two years, I had begun to see Antonia for who she truly was or was becoming. And I said nothing, even going along with her hare-brained scheme to steal clients away from our current employer to form our own company. It turned my stomach. Then, what did I do? I took off like a coward instead of staying and facing the situation—a situation I wanted (perhaps needed) to extricate myself from. I at least owed it to her to man up here. The truth is that I was mostly angry with myself for being that coward—and so much more.

Despite my protestations, Meg was right. I hadn't been honest with her. I had chosen not to tell her about my current client because I knew exactly how she would react. And now, with all that had happened in less than a month, I was beginning to realize that she was probably right—or at least on the side of decency. Meg's comment about me having prostituted myself to the oil industry hit me hard because it was so close to the truth that it hurt a part of me buried so deep inside that I knew she had hit on the truth of who I was. Even more than selling out my passion for art and my talent, I had long harboured the feeling that I was lying to myself every day of my life since I'd moved to Manhattan. And I'd allowed myself to be sucked into a life that wasn't who I truly was. But I sure gave a great performance. Maybe I'd get some kind of award for being the great imposter. All the self-flagellation in the world wouldn't get Meg back in my life, though. Of that, I was sure. I had to do something.

After Meg left, I sat and stewed for half an hour or so, resisting the urge to have a drink. I picked up my car keys, threw on a heavy pull-over sweater I'd bought at a local gift shop and headed to the van. Forty minutes later, I got out of my car in front of the Harbour Plaza Hotel and handed my keys to the valet, who cast a dubious glance at the van. I shrugged and headed into the lobby.

I walked through the lobby, past the open entrance to the bar where groups of jacket-and-tie-clad people laughed and drank, toward the back with my head swivelling back and forth until I spied what I was looking for. As I was about to pick up the house phone to find Antonia and get some things sorted out, I heard her call me.

"It's okay, Tim. I'm here. I knew you'd come." I turned to see Antonia leaning on the wall in the doorway leading to the bar. "I saw you as you walked by. Nathan and I are having a drink. Come join us."

I was momentarily confused. "Nathan? He's with you?"

"You didn't seriously think Nathan would leave it entirely to me to bring back our business partner, did you? You know Nathan better than that. He has the crazy idea that our rather intimate history might just cloud my otherwise impeccable judgment."

Yeah, I did know that about Nathan. It was one of the things about Nathan that was beginning to get on my nerves. Ever since the three of us had decided to start our own advertising firm (or rather, I let myself be dragged along with Antonia and Nathan), Nathan had been an increasingly large thorn in my side. Nathan was a business whiz with a Harvard M.B.A. and a serious case of narcissism. He knew, though, that an advertising firm would need principals whose talents complement one another and complete the set of skills we'd need. I was the creative talent with the innovative ideas and design skills. Neither of them had that.

Antonia took me by the arm and led me back to the bar, where we were swallowed up in the dimly lit space among the suits. Nathan was sitting at a booth in the far corner, one arm draped across the back of the leather banquette, the other holding a martini to his lips—extra dry, two olives. How many times had I heard him berate waiters when they didn't quite get his martinis dry enough?

Nathan, as usual, was impeccable with his expensive New York haircut, his Brooks Brothers button-down shirt with his monogram on the cuffs, and the inevitable cashmere sweater slung around his shoulders like the preppie he'd always been and the Yuppie he was becoming. Suddenly I felt a bit underdressed. As we approached, Nathan looked up.

"Well, old man, I have to admit I didn't really think she'd pull it off this time. Do have a seat. You look like you could use a drink."

Geezus, I hated it when he called me old man, and he knew it. He only did it to push my buttons—not unlike Antonia did. I took the seat opposite Nathan while Antonia slid into the booth beside him. Nathan gestured to the passing waiter to bring two more drinks the same as his. I didn't want the same drink, but I let it go.

"I didn't expect to see you here, Nathan," I said. "Antonia hardly needs a caretaker."

Nathan shrugged. "Quite right. Look, Tim, we've been talking about our agency ever since we started working for Ken. Our time has come, and we need all our talents." He made a grand hand gesture to include all three of us. "Regardless of what you might think, you are important to us—both of us."

Antonia leaned across the table toward me. "Listen to him, Tim. Nathan and I started worrying about you a couple of months ago when you started questioning every little thing about our lives—nitpicking, really. First, you started questioning the type of clients we'll be representing. Then it was the networking parties, even though you know how important those are and will be in the future. Then you questioned taking clients—*our* clients, mind you—from Ken." She leaned back against the banquette. "I suppose I shouldn't have been surprised to find you at home packing after that fiasco with the gallery opening the night before. You didn't have to be so rude about that young man's work."

I looked down at the table, fiddled with the napkin, then said quietly, "The work looked like some kid had puked on the walls." Then I looked up and started laughing as I remembered the event the evening before I left. "And there was all of the New York elite, falling all over themselves to shake his hand. What a crock! I suppose they might not have been quite so enthusiastic if daddy hadn't been a hotel tycoon they all wanted a piece of." I was really laughing now.

Antonia shook her head. "There. See what I mean?"

The waiter appeared and placed a drink in front of each of us.

"You know, guys, I really don't know why I came here this evening," I said, knocking back the martini and gesturing to the waiter for another.

"I think you're ready to come home," Antonia said.

"Don't put words in my mouth." The martini was starting to settle in my empty stomach. When Meg walked out, dinner walked out with her, and I hadn't eaten since noon. It was now almost eight-thirty. I reached over and picked up Antonia's glass, then downed hers, too. "There is something I want to say to you, though, Antonia."

She looked over at me, her eyes narrowing in preparation for what I supposed she expected was coming.

I continued. "I wanted to tell you that you're a damn bitch. That little scene you put on earlier was out of line."

Antonia smirked. "You've always known I can be a bitch, Timothy Sinclair. I always thought it was one of the things you liked about me. I see what needs to be done, and I do it."

"Come on, you two—"

"Just shut up, Nathan."

Antonia opened her mouth to speak, but the waiter arrived at that moment and set my fresh drink down in front of me.

"No, Nathan. Now I see things a lot more clearly than I have for the past six months," I said.

I saw Nathan glance at Antonia, who wouldn't catch his eye. Then Nathan gestured toward the three empty glasses in front of me. "Too many more of those, and you won't be seeing anything clearly."

"Shut up!" My voice was rising, and I could feel eyes from other tables begin to settle on us.

"Tim, keep your voice down. You're making a scene." Antonia had never been averse to creating her own kind of scene, but these scenes never included a public airing of her dirty laundry.

"Why should I care? Everyone around here is...," I looked around the bar at the tables full of people, "...how did you put it, Antonia? Oh yes. I remember. It was dull and commonplace. Surely that means that whatever they think can't possibly count."

Nathan began to rise from his seat, nudging Antonia, who was blocking his way. "I think we've taken this as far as it can go," he said.

I stood up, and something overtook me. I didn't seem to be able to control myself as I got out of my seat and grabbed Nathan by the collar, pushing him back down in his seat. "No, Nathan, I don't think we have. Sit down, you pompous ass." People were starting to gape. I could feel it, but I was on a roll. "Here's the way I see it. You two need me for your little business venture. Neither of you is above stealing clients you have no right to steal, and..." I stopped for the briefest of seconds to gather my momentum, "I know that you, Antonia, you've been cheating on me with Nathan for months." Antonia started to protest, but I cut her off. "Be quiet and listen. I chose to ignore your little dalliance until I could figure out what to do about it. I may not have handled it well, but I handled it."

"You're hardly one to be taking the moral high road. You, the wounded lover? As if. I saw you looking at that Megan person. And I saw how she looked at you. A little young for you, isn't she?"

"Shut up, Antonia. I'm not finished. The two of you have figured out that you can't make your business plans work without a creative, and I'm the best in the business at this stage in my career.

You know as well as I do that clients won't agree to go with you if I'm not on board. So, you need me."

Antonia sat back and examined her perfect fingernails. "Well," she began languidly, "from the reaction I got out of your little friend Megan, I'd say you don't have any reason to stay here any longer. I'd say we have a pretty good basis for a working relationship."

I pushed myself up from the table, furious. I stood above Antonia and Nathan, who were still shoulder to shoulder in the booth. "Go to hell, Antonia." I turned to Nathan. "Thanks for the drinks, Nathan. Enjoy your conquest."

I stormed out with all eyes in the bar boring into my back.

~

I have no idea how I made it home without either an accident or the R.C.M..P—Royal Canadian Mounted Police, the local equivalent of highway patrol—pulling me over and charging me with a D.U.I. I must have stumbled into the cottage and fallen asleep because I was lying on the sofa, fully dressed, with an empty bottle of scotch on the floor beside me when I woke up. I don't think I'd ever had a hangover as bad. I could barely open my eyes, but when I did, I checked my watch and found that it was still an hour to sunrise, but I felt so ill that I had to get up. I dragged myself into the shower, dressed, had a coffee and decided I needed some fresh air.

Hoping I wasn't still drunk, I got into the van and headed out toward Peggy's Cove, thinking I could breathe in some air and watch the fishing boats head out. I'd read somewhere that it was lobster season, and I'd noticed all the lobster pots on the wharves when Meg and I had been there just a few weeks earlier.

I parked the van and walked along the road through the fishing village. The sun was just rising, and I could see Patrick, Meg's friend who'd taken us out whale watching, getting his boat ready for the day. Meg had told me he also had a lobster license. He looked up from the ropes he was arranging just as I made my way down over the hill toward the water and waved. I waved back and headed toward him. I had an idea.

"Hello, Patrick," I said, nearing the boat. "Any chance I might be able to go out with you today?"

"Well, hi yourself. Tim, isn't it?" He leaned over from where he was standing in the boat and shook my hand. "Now, why would you want to do that? Plenty of pleasure boats around for tourists. We're a working lobster boat this morning."

"I'd like to know more about what you do, and to tell you the truth, I thought the salt sea air might help me clear my head. And I'd prefer to be out on the water with someone who makes his living from the sea rather than with a bunch of tourists."

Patrick seemed skeptical. "The whale-watching with Meg was pretty tame. You got much experience on the water?"

"Summers sailing with my father."

Patrick snorted derisively. He looked toward the fish house on the wharf where a young boy, maybe twelve or so, was picking up a large box of equipment. "Seamus!" Patrick called out to him. "Bring another life jacket for our tourist here."

Seventeen

Patrick expertly maneuvered the boat away from his wharf, past other wharves and lobster boats in the tiny cove. Then he headed out through the opening between the boulders lining the passage that led to the open ocean. As we left the safe harbour, I stared to my left at the famous lighthouse that has pride of place on the large granite outcropping that is Peggy's Cove—the lighthouse that has graced many a postcard. I wondered how many tourists had ever seen it from this vantage point other than on those postcards. I suspected only those who took whale-watching tours. I considered myself lucky.

It was a cool morning, bordering on cold. I looked off into the distance toward the horizon and saw clouds gathering—not unusual for this time of year in this part of the world. I knew this. I stood beside Patrick in the wheelhouse, listening to him as he explained how we'd make our way first into St. Margaret's Bay, the bay where my little rented cottage took up its tiny piece of coastal real estate. From my living room window, I'd noticed red and blue buoys that Meg had explained signified the location of lobster traps. When I asked him about the ones I'd seen, Patrick told me they weren't his but that he had some close by. We'd go there first.

Seamus poured us each a cup of steaming coffee from a thermos, then took up position on a padded bench seat near us to bury his head in a book. Patrick explained that they had several locations where they'd dropped lobster traps, which would constitute our route this morning. When we arrived at our first stop, I stood back and watched Patrick and Seamus do their work.

As he worked, Patrick seemed happy to explain that they would first identify their own lobster pots that they'd set out the day before, pull them to the surface and check to see if the lobsters in the traps were up to size. Patrick explained that they had to measure

105

what he called carapace length—basically from behind the lobster's eye to the end of the carapace or the body.

He showed me how he used a curved plastic tool whose tips were exactly 82.5 millimetres, the minimum length permitted. "It takes a lobster seven or eight years to reach that size," Patrick explained. They returned the undersized lobsters to their home in the sea. After checking current traps, they'd return them to the water and set a few more. It was back-breaking work, as far as I could tell. I helped Seamus pull a few traps and was surprised that such a slight kid had the strength he did.

After the first stop, Seamus pulled out a large plastic box that contained several types of sandwiches. He told me his mother had made them and then offered me tuna salad, ham and cheese or lobster salad. Of course, I took the lobster. Seamus screwed up his nose and shrugged. "Whatever."

"Don't you like lobster salad?" I said, shocked that anyone would pass up lobster for tuna salad.

"God, no," Seamus said, taking a big bite out of his tuna sandwich. "You get kind of sick of it after a while, you know."

Patrick laughed.

"Wind's coming up," Patrick said as we pulled the final trap. He turned from the wheel toward where I was sitting in the back of the boat. "You don't get seasick, do you?"

I laughed. "No. Not at all. Everyone around here must think all Americans get seasick."

"Well, Tim, I've seen a lot of it. I got damn seasick myself when I started fishing with my father." Patrick lifted his mug and sipped his coffee. "Now, tell me, son, why are you *really* out here with us this morning? I don't think you needed a lesson in lobster fishing, did you? Something to do with our Megan?"

I shrugged. "You could say that."

"Now listen, Tim. Megan McMaster and her grandmother are two of the most important people in my life next to my wife and that kid over there." He nodded toward Seamus, who was again engrossed in a thick hardcover book. "Meg is the closest thing I've got to a daughter. Known her since she was a kid. I was there for her after her parents were killed in that car crash."

"Car crash?" I said. "She never told me about that." My mind was reeling. Why hadn't she told me something so significant? "Is that why she's so close to her grandmother?"

"Ellen McMaster has been mother, father, sister and grandmother to that kid since she was ten years old. And all while running a medical practice and making a name for herself as an artist."

"An artist? What kind of artist?"

"Let's just say Ellie McMaster's fibre art sculptures are nothing short of breath-taking, and I'm not the only one who thinks so. As I recall, she had a show in New York not more than two or three months ago. Meg showed me a couple of newspaper clippings from New York art critics. They called her a genius."

The wheels in my brain started turning slowly, then faster and faster. "Patrick, you don't happen to remember the name of the gallery in New York where the show took place, do you?"

Patrick laughed. "No, sir! Art galleries aren't exactly the kind of places I follow. Why?"

"Nothing." I stopped for a moment. "Well, are her sculptures kind of like, say, a disembodied shimmering, strapless Marilyn Monroe-type gown sort of lit from within?"

Patrick laughed again. "Kind 'a, sort 'a, eh? Yes, I suppose you could say that, but that's not how the art critics described them. But I think I've seen one you're describing. So, have you seen it?"

"I think I might have," I said, remembering that fateful evening I spent at that terrible art show Antonia forced me to attend. I had lingered at the gallery window next door, admiring that glittering sculpture and trying to picture it in my New York apartment—our New York apartment. Before I had a chance to point it out to Antonia, she dragged me onward into the breach.

I shook my head as if that might give me some clarity. "I thought Meg and I were getting close. But she never told me any of this."

"She wouldn't. She doesn't trust you enough yet." Patrick looked away from where he was now steering the boat into another cove and peered at me. "Any reason why she shouldn't trust you?"

"Maybe." I must have looked so crushed Patrick didn't say a word.

We had arrived at our next cove, so Patrick stopped the boat, and he and Seamus began hauling in traps again. He asked me to keep it steady, and I was happy to help.

When they'd finished at that site, Patrick returned to the wheel.

"How old were you when you started fishing?" I said.

"Really fishing?" Patrick nodded toward Seamus. "About his age. I used to go out when I was very young, but Dad would only let me go on calm days back then."

"Did you always want to fish?"

Patrick peered at me closely for a moment. "Tell me something, Tim. Do you think people who come from families who fish ever think about doing anything else? Like, going to university or something?"

I'd never really thought about it, but I could see how Patrick might interpret my question as possibly prejudiced—and I suppose it was, in a way. I guess I did harbour some preconceived notions. Patrick turned back toward the bow and steered us up and over a couple of increasingly large swells. "As it happens, I didn't think I wanted to follow in my dad's footsteps. I got a master's degree in marine biology, you know." That startled me, although it probably shouldn't have. "Yeah. Six years in university, then five years working for the government department of fisheries and oceans. But, you know, Tim, I was never really happy."

"Are you happy now?"

"We've all got something we're supposed to do, Tim. This," he said, slapping the wheel, "is what I'm supposed to do."

"What about your son? Will he do this work with you?"

Patrick looked toward the stern where Seamus was tidying up the pots on the deck and checking on the lobsters they'd already pulled. He smiled. "Seamus?" Patrick started laughing. "Don't let him hear you say that. No, Seamus is a musician, believe it or not."

I looked at Seamus, who, at that moment, looked every bit the part of someone whose future might very well lie at sea. He was wearing knee-high rubber boots, jeans, a plaid shirt under a bulky jacket that doubled as a life preserver, all topped off by a peaked cap that looked like it had seen better days.

Patrick continued. "Yes, my son, the violinist. Bach, Beethoven, Vivaldi. That kind of stuff. I'm surprised he hasn't put Nigel Kennedy playing *The Four Seasons* on the cassette player yet. Maybe he thinks you won't like it."

"I love it."

Patrick called out to Seamus to put on some Vivaldi, and the familiar strains of the spring symphony began to mingle with the crashing of the waves against the side of the boat that was now rocking from side to side.

"Seamus is just coming out with me when he's off school while my first mate's recovering from gall bladder surgery. Then he'll go off to Acadia University later in the summer to a music camp. Yeah, Tim, he's a concert violinist in the making!"

I was suddenly embarrassed for drawing prejudiced conclusions. I'd have to do better.

Seamus was standing in the stern, looking at the white caps and the swells. "Weather's getting bad, Dad."

"We better batten down the hatches," Patrick said, laughing. "Let's get going back to port."

Just as we set the course back to Peggy's Cove, the rain began pelting down, and the wind from the northeast whipped across the swells, causing the spray from the white caps to blow horizontally. I couldn't remember ever seeing a sky that menacing in all my summers on the water. It was as if it wanted to swallow us whole. I stood at the door to the wheelhouse, staring out at the white caps trying to remember the last time I'd felt this kind of swell on the ocean. Seamus's voice interrupted my reverie.

"Dad! Dad, help!"

Patrick and I both turned in the direction of the panicked voice. Seamus had been knocked over by a wave crashing over the back of the boat and was gripping the side as the rain pummeled him. Patrick cut the engine and sprang into action, reaching Seamus just as he lost his grip. "Help me, Dad!"

Patrick threw a life preserver to the now-floundering Seamus, bobbing in the massive waves like a toy. "He's not wearing his jacket!" Patrick yelled. Why Seamus had removed his flotation jacket was a mystery until I saw it dragging behind the boat, where it must have been caught on something and torn off him as he fell. I remembered noticing that he hadn't had it zipped up.

Without even thinking, I kicked off my boots and grabbed hold of a rope on the back deck. As I plunged into the water, I wasn't prepared for the shock of the icy ocean, which pushed all the air out of my lungs for a split second. Seamus struggled to stay afloat as I tried to reach him. I was almost there when Seamus disappeared under a massive wave. I couldn't let this happen.

I remembered all the life-saving classes my parents had insisted I take back when I was a teenager who wanted to sail by himself. I balked at the time, but their instructions came flooding back to me, and I managed to lunge toward Seamus just as he bobbed up to the surface. I could see from his face that he had swallowed a lot of water. I grabbed hold of his shirt with one hand and made sure I still had a hold of the rope in the other.

"You damn fool!" Patrick was yelling as he pulled me toward the boat.

When we reached the side of the boat, Patrick pulled Seamus's limp body up onto the deck and then reached down for me, where I was clinging to the side. "No!" I shouted. "Get him breathing first!"

"Seamus," Patrick yelled, tears streaming down his face and mixing with the rain. "God, don't let him die!"

While Patrick was turning Seamus on his side, I managed to pull myself into the boat. Every muscle in my body was shaking, and I could feel my teeth chattering. I slid over to Seamus, who was still unconscious and felt for a pulse. "C.P.R., Patrick! Now!"

And so we began. Finally, after what seemed like a lifetime but was perhaps thirty seconds, Seamus coughed up a lung-full of water—or so it seemed. I managed to get Patrick, who by this time was almost inconsolable, to pull himself together, and we pulled Seamus into the wheelhouse to wrap him in a reflective blanket and head home.

~

"Mr. Sinclair, you have no idea how grateful we are to you. I don't know why the Lord sent you to Peggy's Cove today or to Patrick and Seamus. All I know is that our pride and joy would be gone if you hadn't been there." Patrick's wife, Bridget, wiped a tear from her face as she stood in their warm kitchen two hours later, making coffee and soup.

"Please, it's Tim, and I only did what anyone would have done in the same circumstances."

"Oh, but you're wrong, Tim. You see, I worry every day that Patrick goes out to sea. It's just part of our lives. But it's Patrick's life choice. Seamus is different. And you were there to save him."

"I was just glad I was there to help." And I really meant it. I sipped the hot coffee and looked up to see Patrick coming into the kitchen wearing a heavy, fisherman-knit sweater and dry jeans.

Patrick came directly over to me and shook my hand. "Now I know why you came to us today. You're quite the hero."

We chatted about Seamus, who would be as good as new and that Patrick had decided Seamus had spent his last working day on the water. Patrick then poured himself a cup of coffee and sat down

111

at the table opposite me. "You ever saved anyone's life before?" I shook my head. "Well, if there's ever anything you need..." His eyes began to fill with unshed tears.

"Thanks, Patrick. It's like you told me about fishing. It was just something I was supposed to do."

~

I was home alone a few hours later, sitting on the sofa looking out over the water. The storm outside was subsiding, but the one inside me was raging. I had to talk to Meg. I had to see her again. I picked up the phone and dialled her number. No answer. I let it ring a dozen times, but she wasn't there. I threw the phone down and made a decision. *No matter what happens next week,* I thought, *I will be there at that dance next Saturday. And I'll find her.*

~

I picked up my Supra the following Saturday, and Axel was as good as his word: it worked perfectly. When I pulled up in the van, Axel was still running a rag over the hood, shining it to perfection. As I left the van behind, I had a momentary feeling of nostalgia. I think I was beginning to like that bulky old vehicle—but not enough to give up my Supra—as Axel waved goodbye, shouting, "If you ever want to sell it, you know where to find me!"

I then spent the rest of the morning just driving the coastal road, enjoying the sense of freedom and peace—or at least as much peace as I could manage, given that I was planning to find Meg this evening at the dance.

When I pulled into the parking lot at *The Old Jube* at nine p.m, it was already almost full, so I drove around for a few minutes hunting for a space. I drove past a familiar powder-blue Ford Escort and pulled into the last parking space in the line. I got out of the car and walked down past the little Ford, sure it was Meg's. My heart began

112

beating faster. I had to talk to her, and I hoped she would hear me out. As I approached the well-lit entrance, I could hear voices and music wafting from the open windows. I peered beyond the building and could see the moon glinting off the tiny ripples in the water of the Northwest Arm. I took a deep breath and opened the door, where a blonde woman who looked about seventy smiled and said, "Welcome to the *Jubilee Boat Club*, sir."

Eighteen
William, 1942

"HEY, SINCLAIR! BILL! OVER HERE!"

I removed my cap and tucked it under my arm before flicking a bit of lint off the one and a half stripes surrounding the cuff of my uniform jacket—the ones that proclaimed me as William C. Sinclair, proud U.S. naval lieutenant, but my friends called me Bill. I looked toward the familiar voice beckoning me toward a space along the wall near the bandstand. As I made my careful way through the throng of dancing couples, groups of women in brightly coloured dresses smoked cigarettes while they waited their turn to dance. I navigated past groups of uniformed men sporting American naval uniforms like mine, a group of Canadian soldiers and a bunch of British sailors. And there were groups of all three nationalities jumbled with women in swishing dresses and high heels. I was smiling, but I could feel a dash of nostalgia—I only hoped it didn't show. Most of these men would be shipping out in the convoy of ships that, at that very moment, waited in the Bedford Basin. Over the next several days, they would make their way out of the Halifax harbour and off into the North Atlantic toward Europe and the war. I knew this because I was one of them. I kept walking.

As I neared the edge of the dance floor where my friends waited, smoking and drinking, I tried to shake off the feeling of wistfulness at the thought that some of them might never go home. It was hard not to smile around this lot, though. Their zest for life was contagious, and I could use a bit of that zest just now. I was finally close enough for them to hear me over the music and laughter.

"Hi, guys. This is quite a place, isn't it?" I smiled at the two young women taking up wall space next to us. One of them smiled

114

and raised her glass to me. If I wasn't a married man—I couldn't finish the thought.

"We were beginning to think you weren't coming, Bill," Jack, naval Lieutenant (junior grade), said. "Take a seat."

I shook hands with Jack and Leroy, Lieutenant (junior grade like Jack), another one of what our captain liked to call The Three Musketeers. I turned to look toward the canteen on the far wall, where there was a sign telling me that they sold "Pop 25 cents." So, the canteen was dry. I turned back to my table mates. "What are you all drinking?" I said.

Jack pulled a flask from a paper bag he had in his pocket, shook it at me and said, "Get yourself a pop, and we'll talk."

I got up from the table and stood for a few moments in the short line for the canteen. I took this as an opportunity to familiarize myself with my surroundings—something about my training as a naval officer, I guess. The windows lining the wall on the opposite side of the large room overlooked the water, but I could see couples walking outside on what must have been a porch the length of the building. The band in the far corner was called "The Skinny Thomas Band." I knew this because of the placard set on an easel just to the right of the stage. As I reached the front of the line at the canteen counter, the band began belting out the strains of "Straighten up and Fly Right," a favourite of mine from Nat King Cole—man, I loved that man's music. It seemed to be a favourite of many since the floor immediately filled with dancers, all smiles and flailing arms and legs. It was hard not to share their enthusiasm.

I returned to the guys with my glass of pop, to which Jack added a stream of the brown liquid in his bagged bottle. "Just a bit," I said, holding my hand over the top to prevent him from overdoing it, which he tended to do a lot.

"You need to get your buzz on, man," Jack said, capping the bottle. He then raised his glass in a toast and said, "Well, I guess if you have to be anywhere before you ship out to fight the Krauts, Halifax is as good as any to have a drink and a laugh."

"I'd rather be in Chicago," Leroy said, wiping his nose with the back of his hand before gulping his drink.

"Of course, you would," Jack said, laughing. "With that new bride at home, I'd want to be there, too. Even with all these dames available!"

Leroy had married his high school sweetheart a few weeks before reporting for overseas duty, and I wondered how he could stand to be away at this point. I had married Gwen so young and had now been married for eight years. Those early weeks after our wedding were precious memories, but the bloom was off the rose (and had been for some years), a situation that I found profoundly sad because I had no idea how or when it had happened. I had thought that when my son, Douglas, was born seven years earlier, a year after our wedding, it might have brought us closer together, but it hadn't happened. Now I hoped this distance would bring us the closeness we'd once felt—as long as I made it home.

My reflections were interrupted by the bandleader himself—Skinny Thomas—who had taken the microphone.

"Ladies and gentlemen...and you sailors, too!" The crowd roared with laughter. "Welcome, welcome, everyone, to the *Jubilee Boat Club,* and welcome to Halifax. What a great crowd we have here this evening. We're right proud of what you fellows are about to do. I know most of you are shipping out in the next few days. So, let's make your last few days in civilization the very best they can be. To that end, we have a very special treat for you all this evening." The applause was deafening. Skinny continued. "Here in Halifax, we take our entertainment very seriously, you know. Some of you have already seen the Halifax Concert Parties Guild perform onboard your ships in the harbour. Tonight, we have with us one of the best voices to grace their stage. And one of the best pairs of legs!"

I was almost deafened by the wolf whistles all around.

Skinny smiled and waved his hand to silence the crowd. "Ladies and gentlemen, please welcome to the stage our very own Ellie McMaster!"

116

I joined in the clapping and watched as a young woman—she couldn't have been much more than eighteen years old—took the two steps up to the stage. She was wearing a red satin dress that swished and swirled around her legs and clung in all the right places. It had a fitted bodice, and that flowing skirt stopped just at her knees. Her legs ended in a pair of matching red pumps, and she wore elbow-length white gloves. Her lipstick was the exact shade of her dress, and when she smiled, she flashed a set of perfect white teeth.

I had to agree with Skinny about the legs. They were killer. But that luminous smile—I couldn't take my eyes off her. Ellie McMaster was one of the most stunning women I'd ever set eyes on.

Mesmerized, I watched as Ellie caressed the microphone while the band leader melted into the background. The lights in the hall went down, and one spotlight lit Ellie, her dark hair shining under the light. She looked out over the crowd that had fallen silent and nodded to the band.

I immediately recognized the intro bars of another favourite song, and when Ellie McMaster opened her mouth to sing "I Hear a Rhapsody," I thought I was hearing Dinah Shore in the flesh. I could feel the hairs on the back of my neck stand straight up. I could hardly breathe as I stared at her in the spotlight.

All around me, couples began taking to the dance floor. The young woman who had raised her glass to me earlier looked imploringly, but I couldn't budge. I was spellbound.

Jack leaned over. "She's something, isn't she?"

"Something," I breathed.

When Jack and Leroy turned to ask the girls next to us to dance, they seemed more than happy to oblige. As the final notes of the melody faded, the dancers all stayed where they were on the dance floor while Ellie McMaster stood embracing the microphone again, looking out over the wildly applauding crowd. I thought she caught my eye for a moment, but the glance was gone in a flash. Then the piano began. I recognized the intro notes and remembered Gwen once remarking that I seemed to have an encyclopedic knowledge of music these days and wondering why I didn't have the same interest in fixing things around the house. But as Ellie's voice again filled the hall, all thoughts of Gwen and home seemed to evaporate. "Romance is a game," she began to sing. And then the song itself—"Fools Rush In." And for the first time in my life, I felt like a fool. I stood there, stone still through to the end of the song and through the next one. As the last strains of the music faded away and Ellie excused herself from the stage, Jack and Leroy made their way through the crowd back to where I was still standing. Just before they reached me, I began to walk toward the stage. As I passed Jack, he said, "Where are you headed?"

"To get a bit of air," I said, not stopping. I could see Ellie just about to disappear out a door beside the stage. I figured it led out to that wrap-around verandah.

Jack looked over toward where I was heading. "Better hurry, Sinclair, before all the air gets taken." He slapped me on the arm, and I moved even faster.

I noticed a vase of roses on a table beside the door. As I walked by, I slipped one out. I couldn't see where Ellie was gone, but I knew I'd find her. I had to find her.

~

I felt like a man possessed. This behaviour was not like me, not like me at all. I was a straight-as-an-arrow family man who never even looked at another woman regardless of the fraying of my relationship with Gwen. I didn't know what I was doing, and I didn't know why, but my sense of desperation was bubbling to the surface as I stepped out onto the verandah and couldn't see her. I stood looking out over the water, still clutching the rose and trying to calm my breathing. What was wrong with me? I was a twenty-seven-year-old naval officer with a wife and son back in Boston. And here I was, drooling like a schoolboy, hoping to catch a glimpse of a girl. It was pathetic. Or it would have been if it hadn't been so genuine.

I must have stood there for a full five minutes before noticing that most of the other people out getting air had gone back inside as the band started up again.

"There's something about the sea air, isn't there?"

I turned, confused about the voice coming from farther down the deck.

"Of course, you look like you've taken in your share of sea air. That's a naval uniform, if I'm not mistaken."

I turned, and there she was. Standing with the moonlight framing her dark hair, Ellie McMaster stood at the corner of the verandah, her gloves now off, her arms crossed across in front of her, smiling a kind of enigmatic smile. I couldn't tell if she was making fun of me or not. I must have looked like a pitiful, love-struck schmuck, standing there alone, holding onto a rose.

"I saw you in there," she said, keeping the distance between us.

"How could you see anyone with that light on your face?"

"You'd be surprised. It's not that big a place." Then she walked toward me, holding out her right hand with her white gloves tucked in her left, and I could see that her bright-red nail polish matched her dress just as perfectly as her lipstick. "I'm Ellen," she said. "But you can call me Ellie."

I stuck out my hand and took hers in mine.

"Are you going to tell me your name?" she said when I appeared unable to speak—or think, for that matter.

"William, but you can call me Bill," I said finally. "From Boston." I'm not sure why I added that.

~

The next couple of hours were like a dream. Ellie had two more sets, and between each set, we sat together on a bench on the verandah outside while she told me about her ambitions. Her father was a local doctor, and she hoped to go to university and follow in his footsteps, as difficult as that might be for a young woman. I was surprised that she didn't seem to want to pursue a singing career. When I asked her about it, she laughed.

"Of course, we all have such dreams," she said. "I've gotten a lot of accolades for my singing—family, friends, school choir directors. But I'm a realist. I know the odds against me as a singer, and I don't plan to spend my life singing at the *Jubilee Boat Club,* if you know what I mean."

I did, and I didn't. I thought that singing here, entertaining people, making them happy must be the nicest feeling in the world. I had joined the navy when I was twenty-one, just out of Boston College and had never seemed to be able to make anyone happy—even myself. But the odds against her seemed to me to be just as daunting in her desire to be a doctor.

"How many women have graduated from the medical school here?" I said when she told me about her plans.

She shrugged. "I'm not sure, but I do know that the first woman to graduate from Dalhousie Medical School here in Halifax was someone named Annie Hamilton, and she graduated in 1894. So, there's a history, for sure."

"Did she practice here?"

Ellie shook her head. "No. As far as I know, she was some kind of a medical missionary in China. But there have been other women here since. And, after all, it is 1942. It's high time there were more women in medicine, don't you think?" In fact, I did think it would be a good idea. I nodded. She turned to face me. "Anyway, what about you? Tell me about *your* life."

I told her about living in Boston and attending Boston College for a liberal arts degree. I told her about my father being a naval officer all my life and his love of the sea, and how we sailed every summer. I told her about joining the navy while never really thinking I'd be a war-time naval officer. But it was what I signed up for, and I was, if not happy, at least willing to serve my country. However, there were things I did not tell her.

I saw her eyes flutter to my left hand several times where there was no wedding ring. I had developed an allergy to my ring shortly after Gwen and I were married. I never searched for another or even tried to wear it again. I didn't know what was going on here, and something inside me wouldn't let me tell Ellie the whole truth about me. I looked at her as she glanced at my hand again, and I was sure she knew my secret.

After her last set, the orchestra continued to play, so we danced. We danced as if no one was watching—as if no one else was even in the room.

"Hey, you two."

I heard Jack's voice near my ear but couldn't quite place why he might even be here.

"If you two decide to come up for air, we're all going downtown. There's a great selection of pubs." Then Jack and his partner danced away.

Before the last strains of the last dance faded out, Ellie said, "When are you leaving?"

"In four days."

"Four days," she said softly.

"Four days can be a lifetime if we let it."

Ellie pulled back and looked at me. "William—if it's all the same to you, I'd prefer to call you William. What can I say? I like the name. Anyway, my parents are leaving tomorrow to spend next week at my grandparents' summer house in Herring Cove outside the city. I can't go because I have to sing tomorrow evening at York Redoubt, and I have school on Monday so I can't go with them. If you have the time—"

"If I have the time? You bet I do. What time are they leaving tomorrow?"

"They usually leave before nine."

"I'll be there by 9:30. I'll borrow a car—somehow."

She smiled and hugged me. "I'll pack a picnic."

~

I had never met anyone like Ellen McMaster. She was smart, funny, and so beautiful. She had a mind of her own. Until that moment the next day, when we were sitting on an old plaid blanket somewhere called Lawrencetown Beach watching the waves, I hadn't even known I liked that about women.

I had managed to borrow a car from the friend of a family member of a Canadian officer I'd met at a function ashore when we first arrived in Halifax. The Canadian navy had hosted the officers from the American ships, and I'd been chatting with a local officer. When I called him later that night, he was gracious about being woken up so late and put me in touch with this friend, who reluctantly agreed to lend me his car since I was shipping out in a few days. I picked Ellie up in the late model roadster with a rag top. Together we folded the top down and headed out. Ellie had pointed me in the direction of the beach.

The more we talked and the more I got to know her, the more I realized that I was falling in love. *Is this even possible?* I thought as I watched her talking and laughing as she sat across from me, sipping a glass of wine I'd managed to scare up from one of my buddies late last night. I knew that it was *more* than *impossible*. Not only could I not be in love, but I also couldn't even be here, and yet I was here—and *I was in love*. I knew I was playing with fire, but I could feel myself looking forward into a future where I left Gwen and spent the rest of my life with this extraordinary woman. The next few days went by in a blur, then the day arrived.

~

"I'm so scared for you," Ellie said as we stood together for the last time on the pier before I boarded the tender that would take me to my ship in the basin and away from her. She held both of my hands and looked straight into my eyes. "I'll never see you again, will I?"

I held her as close as I could, oblivious to all the other couples embracing as if to shield themselves from what they knew was happening. Like us, they were saying goodbye. "Damn this war," I said. "But if it hadn't been for the war, I would never have been here this week, and we would never have met. I'll be back for you, Ellie."

Her eyes were wet now. "No, William, I don't suppose you will."

Nineteen
Charlie, Present Day

"So, that's it? That's supposed to be the whole story?" Miriam was perplexed. I'd just finished my reading for the evening. Since I'd met her many years before, I'd never seen Miriam take such an interest in anything I'd written—not even since I'd managed to have my first novel *Kat's Kosmic Blues* published, and we'd reconvened our writers' group. Miriam was usually so cool, sitting there like the queen in her flowing caftans, the very picture of the Bohemian artist—an image she loved to cultivate.

I nodded. I was hosting our little group of five writers in our spacious den with its wood wainscoting and walls of bookshelves. For years, I'd never been able to host our group since I had lived in such small spaces—that is until I met Tom and was now lucky enough to be sharing his Victorian mansion on the chicest street in the city.

Wendy, the children's book writer, said, "But it's not finished. The story isn't finished." The furrows between her eyebrows deepened with every word.

Joseph, who wrote dubious poetry and now worked from time to time as an actor, said, "You have to tell us how it ends."

I looked at Karl, our truck-driver-turned-romance-writer. He sat back, his muscular arms resting on the chair's wide, padded, leather arms. "Wow, Charlie. It's quite a story—almost." He sat up and leaned into the group. "It's even almost a romance. But only almost. It isn't completely anything. And it isn't anything like what you usually write. Where did the story come from?"

When I decided to read the story in installments at meetings over a few weeks, what I didn't tell them was that the story was written by my great-grandmother.

"We need to know what happened to these characters. What happened to Megan? To Tim?" Miriam said.

"First, I have a confession to make," I began. "I didn't write the book I've been reading to you in sections over the past few meetings. My great-grandmother, Frannie Phillips, who died the year I was born, did."

I looked around at my fellow writers. Miriam looked at me, her wine glass stopping just short of her lips. Joseph cocked his head and stopped chewing the piece of cheese he'd just popped into his mouth. Wendy's eyes widened even more than usual.

I looked at Karl. He looked at me. "Spill, Hudson." He only called me by my last name when he was really serious.

"Okay," I said, taking a deep breath. I had never told anyone (yet) that my great-grandmother had been a writer. In my defence, I had only recently learned this myself. I had also not told anyone yet about my inheritance from her estate. I took my time here trying to figure out precisely what I would—or should—say. "Okay," I said again. "My great-grandmother, Fran Phillips, was not only a writer. She was a famous writer—a very famous one."

"Still waiting, Hudson." Karl had now crossed his arms and was looking at me suspiciously.

"Ever heard of F.E. de Plessis?"

I could see by the confused looks on Joseph's and Wendy's faces that they hadn't. Miriam pursed her lips and rolled her eyes up and to her left as if she were trying to access a memory. The edges of Karl's mouth began to twitch as if he might be trying to suppress a smile.

"He was French," Miriam said, still gazing upward. "I remember something about erotica. Yes," she said, coming back to the present moment, "that's it. He was a French writer of Victorian smut." She took a large drink of wine as if to congratulate herself for being the only one present who knew the identity of this obscure writer.

"But that's not the whole story, either. Is it Ms. Charlotte Hudson?" Karl said.

"You're familiar with F.E. de Plessis, aren't you, Karl?" I said. When I'd been cleaning out my mother's house the year after she died, Karl had come to my rescue a couple of times to help with the heavy lifting, so to speak. We'd had a lot of time to chat about various things. That was when I learned about his interrupted Ph.D. studies and his love of romance writing. I did not doubt that he'd read F.E. de Plessis in grad school.

"I am, Charlie. I'm just a bit surprised you are, although I suppose you had to read this work while doing your M.F.A. I'm intrigued, though, by why you might be asking us this odd question. Unless..." He trailed off.

"Unless what?" Joseph was still stuffing cheese into his mouth between sips of wine.

Karl looked at me. "Unless there's something about F.E. de Plessis that you know, and we don't. Although I have to tell you that I've read that there were rumours about *him*."

"What rumours?" Wendy had come back to life.

"Yes," I said, "there were rumours as you say, Karl, and most of them were right."

"I knew it," Karl said, smiling broadly. "I knew that no man could have written that stuff. I've always thought that de Plessis was a woman. What a scandal that would have been if anyone had known in those days. So, what's the rest of the story?"

So, I sat down, took a deep breath and told them. I told them that F.E. de Plessis was, indeed, a woman, and that woman was my great-grandmother. We discussed her French and later American erotic novels, written under her North American *nom de plume* Peyton Winter and the ones that had been turned into films. All of them were stunned, but none of this story really helped explain why Frannie had been writing this sort-of romance set in, of all places, Halifax, Nova Scotia, Canada, where we were all now sitting and eating and drinking in an old Victorian house. I was thinking about

126

that little voice in my head that said, *"Finish it."* And although I had no way of knowing if this was what I was supposed to finish, it was the best place I knew to begin. It seemed that my audience wanted me to finish it, too.

~

After carefully re-reading the unfinished manuscript, I discussed it with Tom. I wanted his opinion on whether I should pursue finishing a book begun years earlier in another time and place by someone else.

"Can you see a story for these characters?" He said.

"I'm not sure. I like the idea of finishing something my great-grandmother started, but I would want it to be true to her vision. I don't think I know how to do that."

"Shouldn't any book you write be true to *your* vision?" Tom asked.

"I suppose so, " I said, "but this was her book. I think I would have to do it as a tribute to her. This novel was supposed to be her legacy work."

Tom shrugged. Then he asked me if he could read it himself.

A week later, we sat again in our beautiful living room after dinner, sipping wine.

"I finally finished reading it," Tom said. I must have looked puzzled. "Frannie's manuscript."

I hadn't noticed it before, but Tom had placed the increasingly tattered manuscript on the coffee table. Tom picked it up and removed the elastic band I'd put on it after breaking the decaying one Frannie had applied all those years ago and then lifted the title page

"Have you seen this?" Tom handed the single page to me.

"Of course. It's the title page without a title." In the place where a title should be, Frannie had typed, "Title placeholder." Then a few spaces down the page, it said "a novel by F.E. Phillips."

"Turn it over."

I did as he asked and immediately saw what he wanted me to see. It was a hand-written note that I hadn't noticed before. Why had I not seen it? Anyway, I had missed it when I'd turned the page. Count on Tom to examine the manuscript closely.

I recognized Frannie's handwriting from the diaries I'd read. It said, *"Note: Check on permission to use names: Tim, Megan, Ellie."*

"What do you suppose it means?" I said.

"Why would a writer need permission to use specific names? Tom said.

I shrugged and thought for a minute. "No reason I can think of. A writer chooses a character name to suit that character." There was a thought just outside my consciousness that I couldn't quite grasp. "Unless...unless the characters themselves were..." I stopped.

"Real people," Tom said, completing my thought.

I looked at Tom, who was staring down at the note. "And would it matter if they were alive or dead?" he said.

"Probably."

"And you're saying this manuscript is nothing like what Frannie had ever written before?" Tom said.

I nodded again. But there was something in the back of my mind that I couldn't quite access. What was it Juliette had told me? Then I remembered. "Tom, when I was in Paris, and Juliette told me Fran was writing this book the year she died, she made a passing remark about something Fran had said. Juliette told me that Fran mentioned a friend in Canada whose story inspired the writing. Inspiration doesn't mean actually using the living characters, though. You don't suppose one of these people in the book was that friend?"

"Sounds plausible," Tom said.

But why? I wondered. Why would she be writing a novel based on the life of real people? It didn't make any sense. It wasn't what Fran did.

"Let's do some digging," Tom said, pulling his laptop onto the sofa beside him. "Maybe we can find out if any of these people really existed." I knew that if anyone could find them, tech-whiz Tom could. "Oh, before I forget," he said, clicking into his favourite search engine, "Elizabeth called. She said something about wanting to talk to you about getting involved in one of her projects."

"What kind of project?"

"She didn't say, but it probably has to do with her sewing stuff."

He was probably right. My mom's old friend Elizabeth had been my junior high school sewing teacher. More recently, she had reignited in me an interest in sewing, but I didn't have much time for that these days. I did miss it, though. I'd get back to her soon.

"Maybe you could work on those snacks we were planning while I get started," Tom said.

"Started at what?"

"Research, my darling Charlie. Research! And I think I'll take a wild stab and start with Ellie McMaster. If she was a doctor here in Halifax, there might be something about her on the web."

And that was how I discovered that there was a real person named Dr. Ellen McMaster from Halifax and that she really had graduated from medical school at McGill University in Montreal in the late 1940s. Unfortunately for our research, we found this information in an online obituary. She had died two years earlier. But we also found something else. There was a gallery downtown near the waterfront called *The Sinclair Gallery*. Its founder was an artist called Timothy Sinclair.

TWENTY

ACCORDING TO WHAT TOM AND I COULD FIND on the web, *The Sinclair Gallery* was something of an institution in the city. We found hit after hit in our search results that told us this gallery was a long-time purveyor of contemporary art in the city, although I'd never darkened their doorway. I loved art, but until recently, I hadn't been in a financial position even to consider buying something of value, and if the rumours were correct, *The Sinclair Gallery* carried only the best. So, I figured the best approach would be a casual visit to the gallery to see if Mr. Sinclair was still around. I had done some calculations. This Timothy character in Fran's book was somewhere in his early thirties in 1989, which would mean that he would be in his early 60s today. It was conceivable that, if he were the real person, he would still be alive and working. Again— a long shot.

Later that night, as I lay in bed, unable to sleep, scenes, characters and artwork jumbled around in my monkey mind. As I stared up at the dark ceiling, I made a decision to visit the gallery, although I wasn't really sure how to approach this in-person part of my research—or even if I should.

I decided that the gallery would probably be less busy on a weekday, so I planned to visit on a Tuesday morning between classes. I had no way of knowing if this Timothy Sinclair was the same one Fran had written about in the manuscript, but I had to meet him anyway if he was still alive. It was a long shot, for sure, but I had to start somewhere. I had a deep feeling that I needed to finish the story, or at least figure out how the real one ended—if it was real at all.

I finally drifted off into a fitful sleep, my mind only slightly more settled.

~

The gallery was downtown near the waterfront. As I turned the corner and slowly walked toward the red canopy with the gold lettering proclaiming that the establishment was *The Sinclair Gallery*, I felt my pulse quicken. I wasn't sure why I was so nervous. Then I considered the possibility of meeting another person who might have known my great-grandmother. In addition to Juliette, this would be the second—if this Timothy were the one in Fran's notes. No wonder I was nervous.

When I reached the red canopy, I stopped for a moment to consider the art pieces displayed in the windows on either side of the massive oak door with its brass fittings. To the right of the window was a large painting that looked like a photograph—but I knew better. I recognized the artist at once. The piece was by Canadian Paul Kelley, an internationally recognized artist who called Nova Scotia home.

The piece was about two feet by a foot and a half. I got as close to it as I could and saw it was called "Purple Umbrella." From what I'd read about his work, I figured that a Paul Kelley of this size would probably sell for well over five-thousand dollars. Naturally, though, there was no price on the window display. I wondered what Tom would think about it. We'd talked about buying some original artwork for our house, and a Paul Kelley would be a superb acquisition. But I was procrastinating. I knew this. Then the piece to the left of the door caught my eye.

This one was a piece of sculpture. It stood about five feet high and looked like a dressmaker's mannequin wearing an elaborate floor-length dress. The dress was obviously stiffened by some process and looked like it was blowing in the wind. The piece had the effect of being a headless fashion model. The dress had been fabricated from chiffon or some other sheer fabric, and it was lit from within, casting a glow all around it. I could picture this one in the corner of our living room. This might just prove to be a very expensive research trip. I took a breath and opened the door.

I stepped into the gallery space to the ringing of a small buzzer that the door opening had set off. Immediately, a young woman, perhaps a few years younger than I was—which would have made her around thirty—materialized from somewhere behind a screen that I hadn't noticed. It looked like she was stepping out of the wall. She was so perfect that I thought she could have been one of the artworks.

"Good morning. My name is Ava. How may I assist you?"

Ava was about five-foot-two—a good four inches shorter than I was—with shoulder-length, jet-black hair cut in a severe bob that would have looked creepy on anyone else. On her, it looked magnificent. She was dressed from head to toe in black, from her black turtleneck that looked too warm for such a nice day to the thigh-high leather boots. I supposed that working in a gallery demanded such a wardrobe. It was a bit intimidating.

"I'm just browsing. I'm interested in both pieces in the window."

"Oh, the Paul Kelley. He's one of my favourites."

"Yes, that one. I'm also interested in the sculpture piece. Is the artist local?"

Ava's face fell. "She was. I'm afraid she died a couple of years ago. She was my mentor."

"I'm so sorry," I said, genuinely feeling for her. "Are you an artist, too?"

She brightened up again. "I am. I'm following in my father's footsteps—a bit of my own art along with some gallery work."

"Your father is an artist, too?" Ava nodded enthusiastically. "Would any of his work be here?"

"Yes, of course. Would you like to see some of it?"

I said yes, and Ava led me to a door hidden in another screen at the back like the one from which she had emerged. The door led into a private gallery space. The lights were low except for the spotlights illuminating the numerous paintings giving each of them a three-dimensional quality. As I walked around, I noticed that some were

132

oils on canvas while others were watercolours. In fact, most were watercolours.

My eyes wandered from one to the other until they fell on a watercolour of a beautiful young woman who resembled Ava, but it clearly wasn't her. I was mesmerized.

Ava walked up behind me. "That's a portrait of my mother. Dad did it when they first met."

I peered at the signature on the bottom right-hand corner of the painting. Startled, I looked at Ava. "Timothy Sinclair is your father? And these are all your father's work?"

Ava nodded. I began walking slowly. I was stopped short by another portrait—another watercolour of a woman. But this one was different. This one looked like a formal portrait of a woman from back in the 1920s—no, earlier. She was wearing a high-necked blouse with a cameo in the centre front of the neckline. Her hair was tied back in a chignon, and she was sitting with her arms resting on a book, a far-away look in her eye. It wasn't just how the artist captured the subject that hypnotized me. It was something more—something more overpowering. As I gazed at her eyes and she looked back at me, I felt like a ghost had passed through me. I felt the hairs on the back of my neck stand at attention. I'd seen this picture before—yet I'd never seen it before.

"She's wonderful, isn't she?"

I turned to see the source of the deep voice. Standing beside Ava was a tall man with a full head of silver hair, a face lined and yet still handsome.

"Are you the artist?" I said.

He nodded and extended his hand for me to shake. "Guilty as charged. I'm Timothy Sinclair. Welcome to my studio."

"Charlotte Hudson," I said, shaking his hand. "But please call me Charlie." I turned back to the portrait. "Mr. Sinclair, who is the woman in this portrait? I have the strangest feeling I've seen this picture before."

"I doubt it. And please call me Tim." He stood beside it, looking first at the painting and then at me. "You've probably noticed that it looks like the portrait of a woman from the early twentieth century. If I remember correctly, it was about 1915. But you couldn't have seen this portrait before because I only finished it six months ago."

I shook my head. "I know this sounds odd, but I do think I've seen it." I stared for a moment. "Did someone sit for you, and you created it to resemble an old portrait?"

He shook his head. "No, although I wish I'd known this woman when she was that age. I painted it from a sketch I made many years ago when I met the woman in the portrait. At that time, she was already in her late eighties."

I could feel a light go on in the back of my mind. "Mr. Sinclair—Tim—was this woman's name Fran Phillips?"

It was his turn to look as if he'd seen a ghost.

~

Half an hour later, Tim, Ava and I were sitting in his private office just off his gallery. The minute I mentioned Frannie's name, the colour had drained from Tim's face, and he suggested we sit for a few minutes in his office. On the way there, I'd passed several watercolour renderings of the Titanic and a single watercolour of a deck chair. Now, Ava had made coffee, and I felt it was time to come clean about why I had come to the gallery this day. I told Tim I had been looking for him and why. I listed the other names—Megan McMaster, Ellen McMaster, William Sinclair—the names I'd read in Frannie's manuscript. He sat back against the cushion on the back of his office chair.

"I've been searching for some way to figure out the end of the story," I said when I'd finished explaining how I'd gotten here.

"The end of the story," Tim said with a faraway look in his eye.

"I have a feeling you may be able to help me."

Ava said nothing, but she held herself in such a way that made me think she had something she wanted to add. If she did, she kept it to herself.

"So, you say that Fran Phillips was your great-grandmother," Tim said. I nodded. "And you think you've seen that portrait before—although I assure you, I painted it within the past year." I nodded again. "Well, maybe I do owe you a story since I painted that portrait from a quick sketch I made of a photograph—a photograph Fran showed me the one and only time I met her."

I gasped. "I have that photo now," I said.

Tim reached down, opened a drawer in his desk and pulled out a large black leather portfolio, the kind I'd seen graphic artists carrying. He placed it in the middle of his desk and gestured for me to come around so we could both see it from the same direction.

As I stood beside him, he opened the portfolio and began to page through the contents. One after the other, there were pencil sketches and watercolour renderings of what looked like an advertising campaign. I was puzzled. "You're a graphic artist?"

"Was," he said. "Past tense. I was a graphic artist—the creative director for a New York advertising company, to be exact." He pulled out what looked like a completed advertisement for Eastern Oil. It looked like a Titanic motif. I began to shake, remembering Fran's novel—the one she hadn't finished.

"Didn't that company go bankrupt in the early 2000s?" I remembered something about an oil spill they couldn't clean up, but I didn't remember seeing this advertisement. I asked Tim about it.

"I never submitted the final version of the ad campaign, so it was never used."

"How in the world did you ever end up in Halifax?" I asked. I wondered if I might already know at least part of the story. Or at least Frannie's version.

"That, my dear Charlie, is where the story begins—and ends. How much time do you have?"

TWENTY-ONE
TIM, 1989

I STOOD AT THE BACK OF *THE OLD JUBE*, LISTENING to the music and staying as far back in the shadows as I could. I needed to find Meg. I knew she probably didn't want to see me—and she had ample reason to distrust me at this point—but there was no way I was leaving town without seeing her again. I wasn't even sure at that stage if I was leaving. Finally, there she was.

Appearing from the shadows to the left of the stage, Meg walked up the three steps and took the microphone from Allan Thomas, who had just introduced her. I could feel my heart skipping a beat, and I had trouble catching my breath. Meg was wearing a wide-necked red dress that swirled around her ankles and caught the light, giving her an ethereal glow. Her usually wild hair was smoothed down and fell over her shoulders, shining under the lights. She started singing. And I had to agree—it did seem as if we had stood and talked this way before.

I was glued to the floor against the wall, watching the dancers. It was like an old, black-and-white World War II movie, but this time, I was there, and it was in full colour. The music transported me to another time—but not another place. When Meg finished her set, I was still standing there and couldn't move for a moment or two. By the time I'd come to my senses, it was too late. She'd already disappeared through the door leading out onto the verandah. I made my way through the crowd as quickly as I could, arriving in the parking lot to find her car had vanished—with her in it. I had to find her.

~

For the next few days, Meg continued to ignore my calls. I even drove by her cottage twice, but her car wasn't there either time. I'd have to figure out where else she might be. It took a bit of sleuthing—and tracking down Stephanie in Toronto. I remembered the name of the organization where Steph had her new job, so I was able to get a phone number. When I finally got hold of her, she was more than happy to tell me that whenever Meg needed moral support, she visited her grandmother, Dr. Ellen McMaster. That was how I found myself standing on the porch of a huge Victorian house on the chicest (and most expensive) street in town, waiting for someone to answer the doorbell.

After a moment, the door opened to reveal a well-dressed older woman with shining silver hair pulled back off her face and the bluest eyes I'd ever seen next to Meg's. This lovely woman, who bore an uncanny resemblance to Meg, had to be her grandmother.

"Dr. McMaster?" I said. "I'm Timothy Sinclair—Meg's friend. I'm sorry to intrude. I wonder if I could talk to you for a moment?"

For a moment, the woman said nothing. I noticed a strange look cross her face as if she might be trying to figure something out.

"Sinclair?" she said, peering at me. Then she continued softly. "Meg didn't mention your full name. Please, come in," she said, standing aside to let me in. "Oh, yes, I am Dr. McMaster, but you can call me Ellie."

"I'm sorry if I startled you, Dr. McMaster…Ellie."

"I'm the one who should apologize. I'm afraid you simply took me by surprise." She led me into the living room. "Please, take a seat, and I'll get us some coffee. Or perhaps you'd rather join me in a drink of something a bit stronger. We Nova Scotians are great rum drinkers." Ellie looked down at her watch, which looked suspiciously like a Cartier. "Forgive me. It's a bit early for a drink, isn't it?" She moved in the direction of what I supposed was the kitchen. "Although frankly, I could use one," she said slightly under her breath. She stopped at the door and looked back at me for a moment. "I expect you'll want one, too."

While Ellie was in the kitchen, I looked around at the impeccably appointed room. It wasn't done in a Victorian style, as the house's outside might have implied. It was a contemporary design with art deco touches in the beautiful sconces and the burl wood furniture.

The couch looked comfortable, so I took a seat and sank into the cushions. When Ellie returned, she carried a large tray of coffee and muffins. She laid it on the coffee table, then went over to the bar on the sideboard and brought over two crystal old-fashioned glasses and a bottle of rum, placing them beside the coffee.

"We might need this," Ellie said, pointing to the rum bottle before pouring the coffee. "I suppose you want to talk about Megan. She's my pride and joy, you know. I expect she's already told you that her parents died in a car crash when she was ten. We've been constant companions ever since."

I didn't tell Ellie that I had to learn this from Patrick. I thought she might think Meg hadn't told me because she didn't trust me. I supposed we'd get to that. "What about her grandfather?"

Ellie got up and went over to the grand piano in the corner. She picked up a framed photo and then brought it back to where we were now sitting side-by-side on the couch. She passed it to me and sat down again. "This picture was taken on our graduation day. My husband was a classmate of mine in medical school in Montreal. I was the only woman in the class, you know. In fact, I thought I might never be able to pursue my dream to become a doctor." She laughed at the remembrance. "He was the only man in the class who would even speak to me. How could I not fall in love with him?" Ellie took the photo from me, put it on the coffee table, then sat back, her hands in her lap. "You know we practiced together until he died fifteen years ago—I just retired this past year. But you didn't come to listen to an old woman reminisce, did you?"

"Not exactly, but…"

"So, tell me about you and Megan."

"Ellie," I began but didn't know how I could say this to Meg's grandmother except just to say it. "I think I'm in love with your granddaughter, but I think I've messed it all up." I was miserable.

"Megan told me about it, and frankly, Timothy, I think she has a point." Ellie sipped her coffee. "She told me about your work and how you omitted important details."

"I know, I know," I said, standing up. "I'm not even sure why I'm here."

"I think I do," Ellie said. "Sit down, Timothy. It's important that we talk about this."

I did as I was told and sat down.

Ellie placed the cup she'd been holding back on the coffee table and leaned toward me. "Timothy, why did you come to Halifax in the first place?"

"To do some research for a client."

"Yes, that's what Megan said when she told me about you initially. In fact," Ellie leaned over to reach for a small piece of folded paper on the side table, "this is for you. When she told me you were here researching the Titanic, I told her you should meet a friend of mine. I'm true to my word. Here's her name and number. She lives a few doors down from here." She passed me the paper.

"I'm not so sure I'm going to need it now."

"Hmm. Maybe, but visit my friend anyway, won't you? I told her about you, and I think she'd like to talk to you in any case." I nodded before she continued. "But back to the matter at hand. You know, Timothy, dear, I've been around a long time, and I don't believe you. Try again. Why did you come to Halifax?"

"Research for the ad campaign." I looked at Ellie, and it seemed she wasn't buying this. "Well, that may not be the whole reason. My grandfather was here during the war." Ellie was stone-faced—as still as a sculpture. I took a deep breath. "Okay. The truth is I just needed to get away from my life in New York. It was starting to choke me." I shook my head either in disbelief or to clear the cobwebs. I wasn't sure which. "I don't know. Don't you think I'm too young for a mid-life crisis?"

"I don't know, Timothy. How old are you?"

"Thirty-one."

"Hmm. That does seem a bit young," Ellie said thoughtfully. "What is it about your life in New York that's suffocating you? Your work? The people?" She stopped for just a beat. "Yourself?"

"Myself?"

"Timothy, everyone goes through periods when they have to figure out what they're supposed to be doing in their lives. You've hit your time."

I was suddenly scared. I was afraid because I knew she was right. "I always thought that when I started making real money, I'd know that I'd hit on the thing I would do for the rest of my life. I hit that too early, though, I guess." I started to run my hand through my hair, something I only did when I was frightened. I hadn't done it in years.

"*Money often costs too much.*"

"Excuse me?"

"Emerson once wrote, *Money often costs too much.*"

I stared down at my hands clasped in my lap, thinking about just how much making money had cost me. "I always thought I'd be an artist."

"Isn't that what you're doing for that advertising agency?"

"Not really." I looked up at her. "I mean, I always thought I'd be an artist who painted pictures he wanted to paint whenever he wanted to paint them." I got up from the couch, stuffed my hands in my pockets, and walked toward the vast window overlooking the front garden. "I never thought I'd end up taking orders from clients and painting layouts to deadline."

"So, I take it you're not feeling fulfilled in your life. You know, Timothy, when you get old, you begin to realize that sometimes how you make a living isn't always how you make a life. But you also

140

learn that things can be sequential. Sometimes you must go through one chapter of your life before the next one becomes clear."

I walked back over to the couch and sat down beside this wise woman. "I think I might know some of that, but it's more. It's almost like I feel I've cheated myself. So, I came here to get away, and now I'm more confused than ever."

Ellie patted my hand and stood up. "At the risk of adding to your confusion, I want to show you something." Ellie moved with the elegance of a dancer (I wondered briefly if she'd ever been one) as she approached a chest sitting under the window on the side. She removed the toss cushions and lifted the top. She knelt down and began searching for something. Finally, she lifted out an old picture frame. For a moment, she looked longingly at the yellowing photograph. Then she stood up, held it close against her, and returned to the couch. Before she sat down, she poured two ounces of rum into one of the glasses, then glanced at her watch but didn't take a drink. Then she sat beside me, placing the photograph flat on her lap.

"Timothy, what was your grandfather's first name?"

"You mean Grandfather Sinclair?" I said. Ellie nodded. "It was William—Bill."

I could hear her draw a breath as if something had frightened her. She then spoke quietly. "Is he still alive?"

I shook my head sadly. "No. As a matter of fact, I never really knew him. He died a few days before I was born." I was becoming increasingly puzzled by this enigmatic woman.

Ellie passed me the photo. I looked down at the image. It looked like a picture from the 1940s, judging from how the two young people in the picture were dressed and the young woman's hairstyle. Then I did a double-take and found myself squinting hard. They were standing hand-in-hand on a beach, smiling widely into the camera. I shook my head. I didn't know what I was seeing, but I knew I couldn't be seeing what I thought I was seeing. It was a photograph of Megan—and me.

141

Ellie watched me for a moment or two, lifted her glass to take a sip of rum then spoke quietly again. "Did you know you are the spitting image of your grandfather?"

TWENTY-TWO

MY GRANDFATHER? THIS WAS A PHOTO OF MY GRANDFATHER? I looked down at the grainy photograph and ran my fingers over the images as if I might be able to bring them to life with my touch. How could this be possible, and why did it look like Meg was in the picture with him? Suddenly I knew. I looked at Ellie, whose eyes were glistening with unshed tears. And suddenly, I was looking into the face of Meg—at age sixty-five. It wasn't Meg in the photo with my grandfather. It was Ellie. She had known my grandfather, William Sinclair.

Then I thought about what Meg had said about Americans and her grandmother's experience. Could she have been referring to my own grandfather?

"Ellie, I..." I wasn't sure what to say.

Ellie put her hand on my arm and squeezed gently. "Now you can see why I thought I was seeing a ghost when I answered the door earlier." She took a deep breath. "Noontime be damned," she said. "I expect you'll be wanting that drink now."

Oh, how right she was. "Do you happen to have any scotch?"

She looked at me and smiled. "I suppose I ought to have expected that."

"My grandfather?"

She nodded. "His drink of choice—when given a choice." Ellie went to the liquor cabinet and returned with a bottle of scotch.

"It looks exactly like Meg," I said, unable to breathe for a second.

"Yes," Ellie said, "I did, didn't I?"

"God, this is an incredible coincidence. I can sure understand how you must have felt when you answered the door and saw me standing on your porch. I've seen a few old pictures of my grandfather before, but this is the first time I realized how much I look like him." I took a sip of the excellent scotch, wondering briefly what kind it was, but it seemed an inappropriate time to ask. I turned from the photo that was still on my lap toward Ellie. "But what's the rest of the story?"

"The rest of the story," she said, taking her time. "The rest of the story is that Bill and I spent four of the most wonderful days of my entire life together before he shipped out." She took another sip of her rum as if to fortify her. "What neither of us knew on that day as I stood with him on the pier was that I was pregnant."

I began to choke. Ellie patted me on the back and continued. "Times were different then, you know, Timothy. It was a family disaster of sorts. My parents decided that what was best for me—and for them if truth be told—was to ship me off to a more liberal aunt and uncle who lived in Montreal at the time. They told me it was best for me to go away and return with a clean slate as if nothing had happened. But something did happen. It turned out to be the pivot point of my life." Ellie stopped and stared blankly into space for a moment before continuing. "I remember arriving by train. My aunt and uncle were good to me, but I still felt so very alone. Anyway, I had the baby and then went back to school. I couldn't face returning to Halifax at that point, so I decided to stay in Montreal, living with my aunt and uncle for a few years. I did well at university and eventually got into medical school. It was ten years later before I returned to Halifax."

"What happened to your baby?"

Ellie smiled. "My baby. She was a beautiful baby girl. My parents had insisted I give her up for adoption, but my aunt helped me. I named her Anne after my grandmother. I raised her, and when I married, my husband loved her as if she had been his very own. She was the light of our lives."

"Was?"

Ellie raised her eyebrows. "You know this. Anne and her husband died in a terrible car crash."

144

I swallowed, trying to keep the lump forming in my throat from rising further. "Anne was Meg's mother, wasn't she?" The enormity of what Ellie was telling me was only beginning to seep into the edges of my consciousness.

Ellie nodded, and the tears that had been threatening began to spill from her eyes. Silence hung heavily between us as we sat there, each with our own thoughts. I could hear a clock ticking somewhere in the depths of the house and noticed that birds outside the front window seemed to be chirping louder than ever. A breeze from the open window blew the airy drape so that I could see it shimmering just outside my field of vision.

"So, Timothy Sinclair," Ellie said, breaking the silence, "I believe you came to Halifax for a very important reason. I don't believe in coincidences. I know in my heart that it was no coincidence that you and Megan met." She stopped for a moment. "You may find this difficult to accept, but I believe Bill had some unfinished business, and you're here to finish it."

My head was spinning. This was not what I had expected when I arrived on Ellie's doorstep. It was not what I expected, nor was it what I wanted. But what did I want? I still didn't know.

"Timothy, you and Megan do, indeed, have a connection. But you now need to work out exactly what it is and where that takes you."

I shook my head as if to clear the confusion. "So, I guess that makes Meg and me kind of related."

"Yes, kind of, as you say. I'm not your grandmother, Timothy, but I'm going to play that role for a moment. I feel something of a proprietary interest in you, I suppose. You need to figure yourself out, get over yourself, and figure out your relationship with Megan."

"How can I do that? She won't speak to me. I don't even know where to find her."

"I do. And when the time is right, leave Megan to me."

I glanced down at the photo I had placed on the table while Ellie spoke. My grandfather seemed to be staring through me, daring me to make a move.

~

When I left Ellie's house, I got into my car and sped away. I had to drive. I had to think. I headed back toward the bay and my cottage, taking the long way around.

For the next few days, I could think of nothing else but the story Ellie had told me—and Meg. Always Meg. The following day, I piled my easel, sketching pencils and watercolour palettes into the minuscule trunk of my impractical sports car (when had I begun thinking about it as impractical?).

I stopped the car just outside Peggy's Cove, pulling off onto the narrow gravel shoulder. I got out of the car, took my art supplies out of the trunk, and walked across the boulder-strewn landscape toward the water's edge. I had read somewhere that these small and enormous granite boulders had been picked up and dropped by receding glaciers in the last ice age, chiselling and scraping the landscape as they retreated.

When I reached the shore, I stood on a granite slab several metres above where the waves hit, causing a small spray today. I stood there looking out to sea and thinking about how this had all been covered with one of those glaciers something like fifty thousand or more years ago. It was unfathomable. Time passes, and here we are. Then I thought about how even forty-seven years was such a long time. Incomprehensible in its own way—at least to me. That was how long ago my grandfather had been in Halifax. There had been a war, and everything was different. Now, I felt different from what I had only hours ago—before Ellie told me her story.

I then spent the day sitting on my small stool, my easel set up in front of me on a granite boulder on the edge of the cove. From where I sat, I could see a small slice of gravel-covered beach where small waves lapped against the stones. All day, I stared at an old, ruined Cape Islander boat that had washed up on the shore and now lay there, lonely and forlorn on its side on the beach. I could feel its loneliness in the depths of my soul. Now and again, seagulls swooped and wailed overhead, then glided down to perch on the old wreck, staring at me. I began sketching the boat and soon found myself so immersed in what I was doing that I even managed to forget the extraordinary situation I found myself in. *What a mess. I should never have come here*, I thought when I did remember.

With my sketch nearly completed, I stood up to stretch my back. Now that I was no longer focused on my painting, my mind started roiling again—thoughts of Meg, Ellie, my grandfather. I couldn't clear them. I had just decided to leave my half-finished painting and take a walk to clear my head when I thought I could hear the faint sound of music coming from somewhere over the next rise. I figured I was having auditory hallucinations. *Great,* I thought. *Now all I need is to start losing my grip on reality—if I ever knew what reality was.* But the music seemed real.

I paid attention and tuned into the sound of a violin playing Vivaldi. I thought I recognized the music as the autumn part of *The Four Seasons* concerti. It was coming from somewhere over the next boulder. I stood for a moment listening to the music as it drifted over the airwaves, mixing and jumbling with the sounds of the water as it splashed and gurgled against the rocky shoreline. I started walking in the direction of the music.

As I reached the pinnacle of the next rise, I looked down to see a young musician doing what I'd been doing—practicing his art encircled by nature in all its majesty. He was standing on a rock, facing out to sea, his violin under his chin. I stood and listened. The young man was lost in the sounds of autumn, created so many years ago by an Italian composer. When he reached the end of the movement, he seemed to sense that he was no longer alone. He put down his violin and bow and turned toward me. It was Seamus, Patrick's son.

"Bravo," I said, closing the distance between us.

"Mr. Sinclair," he said, recognizing his audience. "What're you doing out here all alone?"

"I could say the same to you, but I think I can see what you're doing," I said.

"Oh, I come here sometimes to hear the nature sounds jumbled up with my music. How about you?"

"I was taking a walk to clear my head." I didn't want to get into a discussion about my so-called art.

Seamus nodded. "Know what you mean. Sometimes things just get rolling around in there." He peered at me closely. "You don't seem like the kind of guy who gets bothered about much, though."

"You'd be surprised what bothers me," I said.

"My violin teacher at the conservatory tells me I overthink. Sometimes I wish I had a light switch that I could just flip when I want to stop thinking about stuff."

I laughed. "Me too."

"My teacher gave me a saying in a frame, and I have it on my bedroom wall now. It says, *Put your thoughts to sleep. Do not let them cast a shadow over the moon of your heart. Let go of thinking.*"

"Wow. That's pretty heavy stuff for a kid your age." Seamus shrugged. "Did your teacher come up with that one?"

"Uh-uh. It's by some guy called Rumi. Ever heard of him?"

"Thirteenth-century? Persia?"

Seamus laughed. "You know, Mr. Sinclair, you're pretty smart. Maybe you *are* an overthinker like I am."

Maybe I *was* overthinking. "Can I give you a lift, kid?"

TWENTY-THREE
MEGAN, 1989

As I GRABBED THE STRAP ON THE END OF MY SUITCASE and tugged, it promptly fell over. It was the millionth time I'd wished someone would invent a rolling suitcase that didn't tip over. How hard could it be? At least I didn't have to carry it like I had to before Gran bought this one for me a few years ago. These were the thoughts whirling around in my head as I made my way to the ticket counter for Air Canada to check in for my flight to Toronto.

After the encounter at Tim's with that vile Antonia—not to mention the revelations about his work—I couldn't wait to put some space between us. And to think I had thought I was falling in love with that man. How could I have been so naïve? I'll never know how I managed to get through my Saturday night gig at *The Old Jube*. I was just happy to sing my songs, look out into the crowd and not see him. That was the moment I began to feel a kind of gnawing emptiness in the pit of my stomach. I rattled around Halifax for as long as I could, avoiding Tim's calls until I just had to put some more space between us. When I called Steph and told her I needed to get out of town, she immediately told me to get on a plane, fly to Toronto and stay with her for a few weeks. So, I booked a ticket, told my dissertation supervisor at the university that I was going to Toronto to do some research and called Gran to tell her where I'd be.

As expected, Gran was immediately concerned about me. "Are you sure you're all right, darling?"

"Oh, Gran, I'm not really. How could I have been so stupid?"

"Megan, darling, I know that Timothy may not have turned out to be what you had hoped, but I think you still need to face the

149

situation. You need to hear him out. I take it you still have not spoken to him."

Hear him out? What in the world was she saying? Why was she saying this? I thought she understood that he stepped over every moral line I had drawn in my life—or most of them, anyway.

"Gran, I can't. You know I can't."

"Megan, ever since your parents died, I've watched you push everyone away. Stephanie and I seem to be the only ones you haven't pushed away. I've watched you throw yourself into your work with such a vengeance that I sometimes think you'll never have time for anything else in your life."

"But you were my role model. You were a doctor. You devoted yourself to your patients through all the years you were in practice. And you had your music and art. I have music, too. It's all I need."

"Megan, I had your grandfather in my life for most of those years. That relationship was so important to me. And I had you. Perhaps you need to figure out how to open up your heart. You're a beautiful, incredibly intelligent young woman, and I hope you'll be able to find love in your life."

"But not children," I said, a tear starting to drip down my cheek.

"No, not children, perhaps," Gran said quietly. "But miracles can happen."

"I don't believe in miracles, Gran. I believe in science. And science told me I wouldn't be able to have children." I wiped my face, cringing at the horror of finding myself with a sexually transmitted disease that had rendered me sterile as far as the doctors could figure out. It had happened back when I was a master's student. I tried never to think about it if I could help it. "Anyway," I said, "we shouldn't even be talking about this."

"No, of course not, dear. But I'm not sure running away will help you in this situation. I can tell you're hurting, and you need to find some closure."

150

"I'm not running away, and I have all the closure I need on the Timothy Sinclair front, Gran. Look, I have to get some packing done. I'll be back in a couple of weeks. Talk to you then. Love you, Gran."

"Love you, too, beautiful girl." Then the line went dead.

I was thinking back to this conversation as I sat in the departure lounge surrounded by a throng of people yet utterly alone. I was surprised—no, shocked—at Gran for suggesting I somehow find a way to bridge the gap between Tim and myself. It was never going to happen. Just then, the voice on the loudspeaker made the boarding announcement. I closed my paperback novel and shoved it into my big purse. I had finally gotten around to reading *Bonfire of the Vanities*, a bestseller from last year. *"Your self...is other people, all the people you're tied to, and it's only a thread,"* Tom Wolfe had written, and I had highlighted it because it made me shiver. I didn't want to think that my self was other people. Perhaps, if he was right, not being tied to anyone was the key. At least I wouldn't be in the same province as Tim for a while.

~

As expected, Steph wasn't at the airport to meet me. Unlike in Halifax, few Torontonians met visitors at the airport. It was so big and busy with traffic that snarled around for miles. I was just as happy to find a taxi and spend a king's ransom to get to Steph's new flat in the city. I was looking forward to seeing it.

When the taxi pulled up in front of a huge, red stone mansion in the area of the city known as The Annex, I felt a bit like I was home. When Steph and I had been doing our master's degrees together here at the University of Toronto, we had lived only three streets over on the twelfth floor of a sixties-style apartment building that teemed with students. She was still in the same neighbourhood but seemed to have come up in the world.

As I stood there on the sidewalk, the taxi pulling away behind me, I looked up at the house that had once been owned by a wealthy

Toronto family back in the day—industrialists, if memory served. When Steph told me about moving to this building, she said it now contained six flats, and she'd been lucky enough to find one of them vacant when she was apartment hunting. I knew she was on the third floor, and she had warned me that there was no elevator. So, I dragged my enormous suitcase up the steps to the porch, rang the bell and waited for her to come down.

The minute she spied me, she opened the door and threw her arms around me. "Sorry about not being at the airport, but you know how it is around here. And sorry about all the stairs. Oh, and sorry, I look a mess."

I laughed. "For heaven's sake, stop apologizing." I stood back and looked at her. "And I've seen you look worse!"

She laughed and slapped my arm. "Let's go up, shall we?" she said, taking my purse from me. I was on my own with the awkward suitcase.

By the time we reached the top of the elaborate, wooden staircase—clearly original to the house—Steph opened the door to her flat and pulled me inside.

"God, Meg, I'm so happy to see you again so soon. Now, I'll open some wine, and we can sit down. You can tell me all about this fiasco you made with the dreamy Tim."

~

"I still can't understand you, Meg. I mean, I do, and I don't. Not everyone has the passion for environmental issues we have, but that doesn't mean we have to cut anyone who doesn't share our zeal out of our lives entirely. After all, maybe we could make a difference if we focused on one person at a time. Maybe you could turn him."

It was three hours, two bottles of wine and one large pepperoni pizza later, as Steph and I sat in her living room, sprawled out on the couch. I was too tired—and honestly, too drunk—to have this conversation with her—again. We'd already been over the Tim situation several times. Steph was convinced I was letting a good man get away just because I have principles. I didn't understand her at all.

"Steph, it's not just because of his sell-out work for oil companies. In fact, I guess you're right. Maybe I could get him to change his mind if I had any inclination to do that. It's the lying."

"Oh, you mean about that Antonia woman," Steph said, looking at the empty wine bottle.

Just the thought of that vile woman made me squirm. I guess I must have lived a sheltered life because people like her hadn't ever really been a part of it. Maybe that's just how they were in New York City. But I couldn't admit that to Steph. I could hardly admit it to myself.

"It's not Antonia." Just saying her name caused the hair on the back of my neck to rise. "It's because he didn't tell me about his work at the outset." And because he didn't tell me about Antonia. And because I couldn't understand how anyone could have a relationship with a woman like Antonia.

"So, let's say Tim had told you one of his main clients was an oil company the first time you'd met him." She drained the last drop from her wine glass. "What would have happened?"

"I would never have gone out with him, and none of this would have happened."

"Oh, Meg, can you honestly say that you'd be better off if you hadn't fallen in love?"

I began to interrupt her to tell her in the strongest terms that I wasn't in love, but she cut me off, raising her hand in front of her face. And I wasn't sure who I was trying to convince anyway—Steph or me.

"Meg, I've watched you push people away ever since we met that first day in research methods class." Steph and my grandmother seemed to share the same view. "Do you remember that guy who was so infatuated with you that he used to leave you love notes?"

I cringed at the remembrance. He had been a Ph.D. candidate and my thesis supervisor's research assistant when I was doing my master's degree, and he was the reason I couldn't have children. I couldn't even remember his name—and I didn't want to remember it.

Steph pressed on. "Then there was that guy from that environmental lobby group. He was seriously hot. I was so jealous. Then there was Donald."

I cringed again. Donald had been a young psychology professor I'd met at a Christmas party at York University. I had kind of liked him but had pushed him away, telling Steph that I couldn't date him because he was a professor and I was a student. Of course, she pointed out that he was a professor at a different university altogether, but I wasn't to be swayed.

"Okay, okay, Steph," I said, surrendering. "You're right. I have pushed lots of people away, but that doesn't change how I feel about Tim."

She wrinkled up her face and said, "How *do* you feel about Mr. Timothy Sinclair, Miss McMaster?"

I didn't answer her because I didn't know the answer. By the time I had finished contemplating this question, I looked over, and Steph was snoring. I got up shakily, grabbed the arm of the couch and took a throw from the chair next to us. I put it over Steph, whispered good night and passed out on her bed.

~

It was late August, and the international students were beginning to filter back onto campus at the University of Toronto. I visited two former professors and a couple of former classmates who were now young assistant professors themselves. I spent some time in the library, ostensibly doing research, but in truth, I spent most of my time gazing off into space. What was the matter with me?

I was walking along St. George Street on my way back to Steph's one afternoon in the middle of my second week in Toronto when I had the feeling someone was staring at me from across the street. I tried not to catch his eye, but as the light turned green and we both began walking to the centre of the crosswalk, I saw him stop and say, "Megan, it *is* you!" By this time, I had reached the sidewalk on the other side. I turned to see the man who had been staring. He had stopped in the middle of the street, and as the light changed, cars began blowing their horns at him. He moved quickly in my direction as I stood there, glued to the sidewalk. It was Donald.

"Megan, what are you doing in Toronto? I heard you moved back to Halifax. How wonderful to see you." Then he encircled me in an awkward hug, the kind you give someone when you think you should, but you're not sure they want it.

"Donald," I started, "ah, nice to see you. Are you still at York?"

"No. I'm here at U of T now. I'm in the psych department. Have you moved back to the city?"

We stood there uncomfortably, staring at one another as pedestrians passed us on both sides.

I told him I was still in Halifax and had almost finished my Ph.D. He asked about my research, and I told him briefly about it.

"Let's have a drink together," he said. "For old times' sake. And I'd love to hear more about your research. It sounds fascinating."

I opened my mouth to tell him I wouldn't have time before I returned to Halifax but instead heard myself say, "That would be nice. How about later today?"

And that was how I ended up at the pub having a beer with Donald, the psychology professor.

~

As I sat in the wooden booth, staring out into the fog of cigarette smoke, it was as if the past five years of being back home in Halifax in the safe, sheltered, protected womb of the Maritimes had never happened. This place was the pub where young graduate students used to hang out and commiserate about the capriciousness of professors' marking and the life-sucking ennui of required courses, all the while lubricated by pitchers of draft beer and bottles of *Blue Nun* wine. Just the thought of that sorry excuse for a wine now made me feel like I wanted to run to the washroom and puke. It wouldn't be the first time. As I waited for Donald to return to our table with beer and potato chips, I wondered what happened to that girl who thought she could change the world. I hadn't finished my doctorate yet, and I was already feeling jaded about what I could really accomplish. Of course, the other thing on my mind was the question of what I was doing here with Donald in the first place.

Donald returned. As I watched him navigate past wooden tables and chairs filled to capacity with laughing, talking, smoking students, I examined everything about him. His sandy hair was still cut in a kind of buttoned-up mullet, if there could be such a thing. It wasn't quite as puffy on the top or long in the back as most of the younger men around. He was wearing an oversized printed, short-sleeved button-up shirt tucked into a pair of chinos. He had removed his jean jacket and slung it into the booth beside him, a nod to the fact that it was steaming hot in the pub that evening. When asked, the bouncer at the door had mumbled something about the air conditioning being broken. As I looked at him, it occurred to me that Donald was desperately trying to project the image of a cool young professor. I wondered how that was going for him.

I was wearing a lightweight cotton jumpsuit with white sneakers. As I looked around at the younger students wearing their slouchy jeans, even on this hot August night, I felt years older—and lightyears different. I felt like I was from another planet. How had I begun to slide into middle age in my mid-twenties? I sighed as Donald placed the beer in front of me and slid into the seat opposite.

"Penny for your thoughts?" he said, lifting the enormous glass mug to his lips.

"I was just thinking how much has changed over the past five years and yet how much is still the same."

"Tell me about it. Students aren't what they used to be."

Our conversation was interrupted by the music that someone had turned up to full volume. Billy Joel began singing "We Didn't Start the Fire" at the top of his lungs, and everyone joined in the chorus. *No*, I thought, *I don't suppose you think you started this fire, but rest assured you'll start one for the next generation.* I think Gran had said that to me once.

"Tell me more about this research of yours," Donald said. "How did you become interested in pollution in the textile industry?"

"My grandmother has a friend—her name's Fran—who's now in her late eighties but spent her early adulthood in Paris as a fashion model. I used to love to talk to her about clothes, and she showed me her closet full of couture dresses. One day, I was looking at how they were made and compared one of them to the shirt I was wearing. It struck me that the difference in the quality was astounding, so I started thinking about Fran's dresses that were handmade in a couturier's workshop and mine that was mass-produced in some factory in China." I took a sip of beer and picked up a potato chip from the bag that Donald had torn open and put in the middle of the table. "Then I thought about how I had so many cheap tops and pants. I talked to my grandmother about it. She had been making her own clothes for years."

"Was your grandmother a dressmaker?"

I laughed. "No. She was—is—a doctor. She just always made her own clothes. I suppose that's why she always looked so much better than the other kids' parents." Donald gave me a funny look. "I think I told you my parents were dead. Gran raised me." He nodded, remembering. "Anyway, Gran always had this attitude that I should consider quality over quantity. So, I started wondering how clothing manufacturers could afford to produce so many cheap clothes month after month. I started to do a bit of reading and found that they could only do this by using production methods that were harmful to the environment."

"Like what?"

"Well, take cotton, for example. You'd think it was the best thing of all to use for making clothes. After all, it's a natural fibre that can be replanted and doesn't seem to cause any environmental problems." Donald was nodding. "The problem is that it takes excessive amounts of cropland to produce and excessive amounts of water to get it to the point where it can be used to make fabrics. Then it's dyed, and the dyes produce harmful chemical run-off. Then it's made into cheap clothing that we all buy and discard whenever we feel like it. And that's only the beginning." I had to stop myself. Whenever I got talking about my passion for my research, I could easily get carried away. "Anyway, what are you working on these days? Publishing anything?"

Donald started talking about his department and his psych research, and my mind started wandering. What was I doing here? I wasn't sure I was any closer to figuring things out or giving Tim another chance, but I knew it was time to go home.

TWENTY-FOUR

I MET WITH MY DISSERTATION SUPERVISOR the day after I returned to Halifax. Dr. Fumiko St. James was one of the reasons I'd come back to Dalhousie University to do my doctorate after finishing my master's degree at the University of Toronto—well, Dr. St. James and the fact that I wanted to return home. As I sat in Fumiko's office that morning, looking at the three walls of books that surrounded me, I was picturing myself here, in this office—or one like it—on a university campus advising a student like me. Fumiko was a role model for me—a smart woman who had managed to claw her way at least partway up the academic ladder in a field that was dominated by men. Environmental science wasn't the most welcoming field for people like us. Fumiko also had an interesting personal story that she shared with a magazine writer some years ago, which is when I'd learned about her.

Fumiko's parents had been living in Canada for ten or so years when World War II started. When Japan entered the war in 1944, when she was just six years old, her parents were offered repatriation to Japan. Of course, as Canadian citizens by that time, they had refused and were forced to move east from Vancouver—away from the coast—where they'd been living to prove their loyalty to Canada. They settled in Toronto and raised a young woman who was fiercely proud to be a Canadian. She had been singled out for her talents at an early age. Her parents wanted her to be a concert pianist, but as much as she loved music, she loved science more. So, she ended up here as a professor, married to a Canadian man named Eric St. James. Her love of science and music was enough to draw me to her. When she had agreed to supervise my research, I was elated. And here I sat, some years later, nearing the end of my educational journey.

"Megan, your work has been coming along nicely until recently," Fumiko said as she looked over the material I had sent her a few weeks earlier, just before I'd fled to Toronto. "Did you find what you were looking for in Toronto?" She peered at me closely. As usual, I felt like she could see right into my head.

"I did some background stuff…" I trailed off, not knowing what to tell her since the trip had been a bust as far as research-related work was concerned.

"Your head hasn't really been in the game for the past month or two," she said. "I thought you'd have a finished draft of your dissertation on my desk by now. This isn't like you."

"No, I guess not," I said.

"When can I expect the draft? You know it will need polishing before you can submit it to the rest of your committee. And if you want to graduate this coming year, you need to get on with it."

I knew exactly what she meant. She had told me repeatedly over the past few years that women in our field—as in most fields at the university these days—needed to be better, faster, smarter and more thorough than their male counterparts. I knew all this.

"I suggest you deal with whatever it is that is keeping you from complete concentration on your work, Megan. You're the only woman in this year's potential list of doctoral graduates from our department, and I want to see you at convocation next year. Are we clear?"

I nodded. Fumiko was so right. I did need to deal with what was bothering me. I'd have to visit a friend.

~

I left the campus and headed toward home, but while I was sitting in Fumiko's office, I figured out that I needed to talk to the one person who might help me make sense of this situation I found myself in. So, instead of driving straight home, I took the long way around Peggy's Cove Road and pulled my car off onto Patrick's driveway.

I could see Patrick down on his wharf, and it looked like he had just finished a whale-watching tour. I could see the excited tourists making their way from his wharf up the hill toward the lighthouse, where they'd probably all want to buy souvenirs in the gift shop or have a lobster roll at the *Sou'wester Restaurant*. They'd have the fish and chips if they were smart, though. That was my favourite. I could tell by their excited jabbering that the tour today must have been a good one. They must have spotted a whale.

Patrick looked up from his ropes and waved. He wound them neatly and placed them on the wharf as I walked down.

"Just about to get my thermos here, Meg. I'll pour us a coffee."

We sat on the bench outside his fishing shack on the wharf, and I watched him get his thermos and two chipped ceramic mugs. He poured the dark liquid into the mugs and passed me one. It had been hot and steamy in the city, but it felt almost cool as I sat there on the dock with the fog just offshore. I could feel the breeze on my face, and it felt good.

I took the mug from him and lifted my face toward the sun and the breeze, listening to the seagulls squealing and squawking overhead. I breathed deeply and took the salt air into my lungs. Gran had always been a believer in the healing effects of the salt sea air. I hoped she was right.

We sat in companionable silence for a few minutes. Knowing someone for so many years permits that kind of silence. It never hangs—it's just there. Finally, I looked down into my coffee, my hands grasping it tightly and said, "Patrick, did you ever meet someone who was so wrong for you but who you couldn't get out of your head?"

Patrick looked out over the water, lapping gently against his wharf and said nothing.

"Oh, never mind." I got up and walked over to the edge of the wharf, then turned to look at him.

"Okay, kid, what are you really doing here having coffee with me on a sunny summer afternoon when you could be doing a million other things? Maybe finishing that dissertation for one."

"I just needed some air and thought an old friend might need some company."

Patrick snorted at me. He knew me so well. "I'd say it's you that needs company, kid. Does this have anything to do with that young man I saw you with earlier in the summer? That young man, Tim, I took out whale-watching with you?"

"Maybe." Why couldn't I just come out with it? Perhaps it was because I didn't know precisely what "it" was.

"Megan McMaster, don't you be coy with me. I've known you since you were a kid. I took you on your first fisheries tour when you were still an undergrad in university. I was probably the inspiration for that whale research you did with Stephanie when you were doing your master's. Don't give me any crap."

Patrick was at least partially right about the inspiration. I *had* been inspired that day in third-year biology when we'd taken a field trip to see if we could spot the whales. But Patrick had become so much more. He had been a kind of guru to me.

"Okay," I said, sitting back down beside him. "It does have something to do with him."

Patrick grinned triumphantly. "Well, I've got a news flash for you, kid." A news flash? That was puzzling. "Seamus and I—well, we took your Tim out lobster fishing a while back."

"Lobster fishing? You and Seamus took Tim Sinclair lobster fishing? Are you daft?"

Patrick laughed. "Maybe, but that doesn't change the fact that it was your Tim Sinclair we took out. Helluva guy, too, I might add." He sipped his coffee.

"A helluva a guy? What's that supposed to mean?" What Patrick was saying wasn't making any sense.

"I mean, he's a guy who's just trying to figure out what his life's supposed to be all about. I can identify with that, you know. And I think you can, too."

I was still trying to get my head around the fact that Tim had been here without me, and he had clearly made an impression on Patrick—and a good one—when he continued. "Saved Seamus's life, too, while he was at it."

Patrick spoke these last words softly—so softly, in fact, that I could hardly hear him. I thought I had misheard. I asked him to repeat what he'd said, and he did—louder this time. I didn't quite know how to respond to something that sounded so farfetched. "What do you mean, Patrick?"

"I mean, he wanted to go fishing with us, and I took a chance on him. He seemed to need it somehow. The weather got bad, and Seamus..." Patrick's voice trailed off for a moment. "...well, Seamus got himself heaved overboard—and his flotation jacket got ripped off in the process." He wiped an eye. "If Tim hadn't been there...well, let's just say the world woulda lost a great musician. And me a great son."

For a minute, I thought that Patrick had lost it. But I had never seen him so emotional before in all the years I'd known him. I shook my head, trying to get this idea sorted out in my mind.

"God, Patrick. It just seems a little out of character for Tim to play the hero."

"I'm not sure you really know much about his character, kid. And believe me, he wasn't playing at anything out there." Patrick got up and took our mugs into the shack. When he emerged, I was still reeling from his revelation. "Remember, kid, *the love you withhold is the pain you carry*." I looked at him. "I didn't say that. Emerson did."

TWENTY-FIVE
TIM, 1989

"*PUT YOUR THOUGHTS TO SLEEP. Do not let them cast a shadow over the moon of your heart. Let go of thinking.*" Rumi might have said it, but he probably hadn't met anyone like Meg McMaster, and it was unlikely he faced a complete mid-life crisis at the age of thirty-one. Then again, maybe he had experienced those things back in thirteenth-century Persia. How did I know?

After my visit with Ellie, I found myself at more of a crossroads than I could ever have imagined. I spent the next couple of weeks madly sketching and painting every day. One morning two weeks after our visit, the phone rang while I was sitting at my easel in the window, finishing the last watercolour strokes on a large piece. Like every other occasion when my phone rang recently, my heart jumped to my throat, hoping it would be Meg—yet knowing it wouldn't be. I wasn't going to get my hopes up. That was wise.

I wiped my hands on a rag on the table beside me and answered the phone. I noted with a moment of disdain that the table where the phone sat was covered with dirty coffee cups and two or three dirty plates. I was turning into a slob. I made a note to do something about that as I reached for the receiver.

"Tim, my boy." Definitely not Meg. "Nice to find you alive in the far reaches of the world."

"Hi, Ken. I'm not exactly at the end of the earth. I'm just up north of you a bit."

Ken laughed. I could hear a slight edge to his laugh and knew what was coming.

"The thing is, Tim, we need you here. I'm going to need those finished storyboards for Eastern Oil. You *do* have them finished, don't you?"

164

"More or less, but I'm not ready for them to be released yet."

"Okay, Tim. You can bring them with you when you come home. When can I expect you?"

"The thing is, Ken, I'm not coming home—I mean, not yet."

"I can't give you any more time, Tim. You can't work from a distance forever. You need to be here for client meetings."

"Well, I guess we could call it a sabbatical if you like, but," I hesitated a moment before continuing, "I really don't see my future in advertising anymore."

"What the—"

"Ken, it isn't the firm. It's me." Geezus, that sounded like a break-up line if ever I'd heard one. "I'll be in touch."

The moment I hung up, I felt a bit lighter—only a bit, though. There was more I needed to do, and that would start with cleaning up this mess.

~

After washing the dishes, dusting and vacuuming, I decided to tackle the stack of dirty clothes in my bedroom. I discarded my clothes every couple of days simply by putting them in the pile. I guess I somehow figured they might clean themselves. But it wasn't happening, so I got at it. I started by checking all the pockets of my pants. I'd had one too many receipts go through the washing machine in my adult life. That's when I found the note Ellie had thrust into my hand when I visited her a few weeks earlier.

Ellie had said something about her friend who wanted to talk to me and had some knowledge about the Titanic that I was ostensibly researching. There didn't seem to be much point in interviewing this Fran Phillips, as the note indicated was her name since I was reasonably sure I was going to ditch the ad campaign. But Ellie had seemed insistent that I should follow up, and it occurred to me that it might be nice to keep me in Ellie's good books, as they say. So, I called Mrs. Phillips and set up an appointment for two days later.

~

As it turned out, Mrs. Phillips lived in a house that I would have called a mansion, even by my Boston-roots perspective, two doors down the street from Ellie McMaster. I parked my car on the street out front and stood there gazing at this magnificent specimen of Victorian architecture with its turret at one end and its wrap-around porch. I wondered what was in that turret. It wasn't long before I found out.

I rang the bell, and it was answered promptly by someone I assumed was a housekeeper (it could have been a daughter for all I knew) who told me her name was Gladys. "Mrs. Phillips will be straight down," she said, leading me into an impeccably appointed sitting room. My eye was immediately drawn to three prints (at least I figure they were prints) by Erté. With my hands behind my back, I walked over to take a closer look. I did love his style. I was slightly taken aback when I looked at them. Instead of each having a series number as I'd seen on previous Ertés, they seemed to be signed in ink by the artist rather than pencil like the prints.

"I do love those pieces."

I turned toward the source of the voice and was greeted by the most elegant-looking older woman I think I had ever seen. She carried herself regally—much like Ellie—but was several inches taller, giving her a majestic look. She was wearing a well-cut summer dress and espadrille sandals. Ellie had told me this woman was in her late eighties, but I would never have believed it seeing that twinkle in her eye.

"I met him several times, you know. My friend Kiki and I had such fun prying some of his work from him many years ago in Paris," she said, coming toward me, her hand outstretched. "I'm

Fran Phillips. You must be Timothy Sinclair. Ellen has told me about you."

I found myself tongue-tied in the face of this magnificent woman in her magnificent house with her magnificent artwork who seemed to have just told me that she had known the great Erté. When I finally found my voice, I squeaked out that I was, in fact, Tim Sinclair and that I was happy to meet her.

"Please call me Fran," she said. Then, turning toward the artwork on the wall where I'd been staring, she said, "Do you like Erté's work? These are originals, as you may have noticed. As I recall, he was a difficult man to wrestle his original work from." She laughed. Just then, Gladys reappeared to ask if we'd like tea. Fran told her we'd take it in her office. Then she led me up the stairs into that turret. It was, indeed, her office.

As Fran gestured me inside, I felt as if I might be walking into the inner sanctum of some kind of incredible writing rocket ship. The turret had windows on three sides, so the bookshelves were confined to the space below the windows and part of the one wall. The rest of the wall was plastered with what appeared to be framed book covers. Many of them were in French, but I even recognized several. The writer's name was F.E. de Plessis.

"Was F.E. de Plessis a relative?" Either that or Fran Phillips was an enormous fan.

Fran smiled as she took her seat behind the grand, highly polished mahogany desk on which there was a bulky computer on one side and what looked like an ancient typewriter on the other. There was a large felt blotter between them. "You could say that," she said. "What do you know about the work?" Then she gestured toward the oversized leather chair opposite the desk.

The chair made a rude noise as I sank into it. "I believe the author was known for his French erotica. I also seem to remember there may have been a few movies made from his books."

"*His* books, you say? Could F.E. de Plessis not have been a woman?"

167

I wasn't as familiar with this author as I now figured I should be. I thought it was best to come clean before getting deeper into this discussion. "I haven't actually read any of this author's books. I was more of a graphic artist kind of student back in my university days."

"That explains your interest in Erté's work. In any case," Fran said as Gladys quietly entered and set the tea tray on the blotter between the computer and the typewriter, "I am F.E. De Plessis. I wrote all those books."

I was dumbfounded. And I felt a bit embarrassed at not having read any of the books in question. I looked at this octogenarian sitting across from me and tried to picture her as a writer of well-known erotica. I was having trouble getting that picture in my head.

"I wasn't always an old woman, you know, Timothy. I've had quite a life."

I bet she had.

"Now, Timothy, Ellie tells me that you're here in the city to do some research on the Titanic disaster for some kind of advertising campaign." I started to interrupt her. "I did survive that incident," she said. "I was twelve years old at the time, and I suppose it did have some kind of impact on the rest of my rebellious life." She leaned down, pulled what looked like an old photo album from a drawer in the desk and handed it to me. Then she poured us each a cup of tea.

As Fran spoke, my interest in the Titanic stories was suddenly rekindled. I was in awe that this woman had been on the ill-fated ship all those years ago. Then I opened the album, and the first photo I saw was of a young woman—perhaps fifteen or so—in a grainy, formal portrait that looked very early twentieth century and slightly familiar. I lifted the album and pointed to it. "Is this you, Mrs. Phillips?"

"Fran, please, as I mentioned, and yes, it is. I believe it was around 1915 when my father insisted that I sit for some formal portraits. My parents wished me to become the very epitome of the proper young lady, and I think they were planning on using them to entice potential suitors."

"Did it work?"

Fran snorted in a most unladylike way. "No on both counts, I'm afraid." I could hear a slight British accent creep into her speech patterns as she spoke about her parents. "They neither turned me into a lady nor did they find a husband for me. All to my benefit, I might add. Being a proper English lady was not something I ever aspired to become. Nor did I wish to be married."

"Pardon my impertinence, Fran, but were you ever married?"

"Briefly, many years later, which is how I ended up in Canada. But I left home early and spent those wonderful 1920s in Paris."

I slid a small sketchpad from the satchel I was carrying and asked her if I could make a few sketches based on the photos in the album. She had no objections, so I did a few quick drawings.

"Will you use those for your advertising campaign?"

"I'm not sure. I also do some artwork of my own."

"So, you're an artist. Why are you not devoting your life to your art rather than this advertising?" Fran said, frowning. "I cannot comprehend young people who are gifted choosing to spend their lives on mundane pursuits. My granddaughter, Katherine, almost fell into that trap until she could find her way back to her fashion design gifts."

"Fashion design?" I had heard endless stories about fashion designers in New York from Antonia over the years. She was an inveterate label hound. I was curious. "Would I know her work?"

"Have you ever heard of *Kosmic Kat Designs*?" I had indeed. Antonia raved about them. Fran continued. "My granddaughter Katherine—Kat to her friends—is the genius behind that company. I only hope her daughters—my tiny great-granddaughters—will be able to follow their own gifts."

I was impressed by everything about this woman. I madly finished my rough sketches, making sure to get down the contours of Fran's face as well. I didn't know what I would do with them, but I was inspired, nonetheless.

"And now, Timothy, I want to talk to you about something else."

I could not imagine what this woman I had just met would want to talk to me about—unless Ellie had been telling stories out of school.

"I am writing a new book," she said. "It is very different from any other book I have ever written, and I hope it will be something of a legacy to leave to my great-granddaughters and their children. It is something of a romance. I hope it will be the romance story of the century, but I don't know how it ends." Fran sipped her tea. "Are you familiar with Ellie's romance?"

"She did share a bit of her story with me." I started to squirm.

"Ah, yes, she would have done. You see, I am using it as the basis for my romance novel."

"Then you do know how it ends," I said, unsure of how this involved me.

"No, Timothy, I do not. Not quite. But you might." Just then, she began to look quite faint. "Dear Timothy, would you please go and find Gladys and tell her that I am feeling unwell." She placed her palm in the middle of her chest and cleared her throat. "I am afraid we will have to continue this on another day. But I would like to continue our chat. Perhaps when I return from Paris. I'll be gone a few weeks."

I wanted nothing more than to comply. But it never happened. Fran Phillips died before we had a chance to speak again. I wondered what happened to her novel.

TWENTY-SIX

EVERY FOUR WEEKS SINCE I'D ARRIVED in Nova Scotia, like clockwork, my landlord George showed up at my door with a bottle of rum. Every time he came, I welcomed him in, and he wordlessly handed me the bottle. I ran to the kitchen for two juice glasses—I'd learned that this was his favoured vessel for consuming rum. George then poured two fingers of the amber liquid into each glass and handed me one. Before I met George, it had never occurred to me that anyone drank rum straight—without even ice—but this was how it was done, evidently, and I complied.

The first time I had a glass of rum this way, I was reminded of Antonia and how gauche she would consider this—she of the dry martinis and expensive French wine brigade. I could picture the displeasure on her face if she could see me, and I have to admit this image made me smile every time George and I clinked glasses.

That rum ritual out of the way, George inevitably began the conversation the same way every time. "How's it going, Tim? Got everything you need? Staying another month?"

He never waited between questions for an answer, but each time, I said, "Everything's great. Got everything I need. Another month sounds terrific if you'll have me."

He always nodded and shook my hand. And he always left the bottle.

This month, George's visit began just like the previous two. But this time, when he said, "Staying another month?" I said, "How would a year sound?"

George smiled his half-smile that I realized meant he was ecstatic and held out his hand to shake mine. "I always knew you'd stay." As he left that day, he turned around on the porch and looked back. "Okay if I still come over once a month to see how you are?"

"I wouldn't have it any other way," I said, grinning.

"Turning into a real Bluenoser, you are," he said as he opened the door of his van.

"Bluenoser?" That was a confusing one, and I'd come across many confusing terms since I'd been here.

George laughed. "That's what we call real Nova Scotians." His face darkened for a moment. "You mind what I said about Megan. She's a darling girl and like my daughter."

I did remember. I just wondered what he'd heard. Nothing, I hoped.

~

It's funny how big life decisions come to you. I don't know about you, but it seems that one day when I'm least expecting it, I realize that the decision is already there—as if it has always been there just outside my consciousness. It's as if I made it at some point and didn't quite grasp that it was complete. But there I was. Decision made. I wasn't returning to New York or the advertising business. Not now. Not ever. That felt so right, but there was one huge unanswered question. How was I going to make a living? The decision might have felt right, but it was equally terrifying. It was so terrifying that I decided to ignore the cause of the terror. Maybe it would go away.

I spent the entire month of September wondering how I could make my way back to Megan and my painting. By the end of the month, I felt I was ready, but there was something I had to do first.

I got into the car—my still prized possession—and drove along the Peggy's Cove Road that wound along the shore of St. Margaret's Bay and around through places with names like Blind Bay and Shad Bay and Prospect Bay, all the way into the city. Driving the Supra around the hairpin turns was exhilarating, and I relished every second of that drive. I finally arrived on Lady Hammond Road in the city (I wondered briefly who Lady Hammond had been), pulled into a car lot, and parked among the vans, pick-up trucks, and 4X4s. I started walking up and down the rows of vehicles.

I must have looked a bit lost. The truth is that I did feel a bit out of my depth. A car had always been a toy for me, but now I was beginning to think differently about it. After about ten minutes, a salesperson opened the door of the sales hut and walked over to me.

I had walked around in a circle and was now back, standing beside my car.

"That's quite an automobile, son," he said, walking around the Supra. "By the way, I'm Hal."

"Yeah, well, I guess it is," I said. I had to get to the point quickly, or I might lose my nerve. "Anyway, it's not what I need anymore."

Hal looked surprised. "We don't stock the kinds of cars you'd be looking for, son." He gestured around the parking lot. "We specialize in working vehicles. Take this Jeep, for instance. Makes quick work of a gravel road."

I walked around the Jeep. It was a red Cherokee with four doors and a back hatch. I opened the hatch, looked at the trunk space's flatbed, and mentally measured it. I turned to Hal. "I'll take this one."

Hal looked skeptical. "You sure you want to part with this one?" he said, running his hand over my Supra's sleek, shiny black hood.

I nodded and suddenly realized that I meant it. Then I remembered that Axel had been interested in buying it. I struck a deal with Hal to give Axel first refusal and act simply as the broker before offering it to any other customer. We shook hands, and I climbed into the driver's seat.

I drove away from the car lot in my new (only slightly used) red Jeep and headed to a framing shop. As expected, the trunk had no problem accommodating all the frame parts I needed. And I knew it would have no problem accommodating the paintings I intended to slide into it in due course.

~

A week later, I cleaned myself up, trying to look as much like a successful artist as I could (not really knowing what that might look like) and stacked a dozen or more paintings into the back of the Jeep. On top of them, I placed the large, black leather portfolio I'd bought recently to hold larger, unframed paintings. My destination was *The Kaufman Gallery* downtown on Lower Water Street.

I drove around for a while to find a parking space large enough to hold my new vehicle and got out of the car. I walked into the gallery and announced myself, taking the portfolio with me. I had an appointment, and Mr. Kaufman was waiting for me.

As we stood at his counter, my portfolio still closed in front of us, I could feel his skepticism. I had been expecting this and let it slide off me. I was used to this—I'd faced more than my share of suspicious clients who sat in board rooms wondering why they had spent their hard-earned cash on me. I had always relished that moment when I could see their doubt turning to amazement and then delight as I unveiled my ad campaign. That was what I was going for this morning.

I unsnapped the portfolio and began taking paintings out, lining them up on his long counter side-by-side. Then I stood back, said nothing, and watched his eyes.

First, Mr. Nigel Kaufman's eyes widened. Then he stepped close to take a better look. Then he lifted one of the paintings and held it up. Then he placed it against a wall and stood back. He slapped his hands on either side of his face, and the flamboyant impresario that his smart clothing and silk scarf suggested he was, began to emerge.

"Oh, my, my!" he said. He returned to the counter just as I took out another and placed it on top. "No! Please, may I?" he said, gesturing toward the painting I was about to cover up.

I handed him my impressionistic painting of Halifax Harbour. He took the piece, which was dry-mounted like the other unframed pieces I was carrying with me, over toward the plate glass window into the natural light. He held it up at arm's length and took a deep breath.

"I am entranced. You, sir, have a gift for capturing a certain essence of the inner being."

I was puzzled. "I do? But they're all landscape paintings."

"Indeed," Nigel said, taking the paintings out one at a time and setting them against the walls. "And what better metaphor is there for our inner beings. Oh, yes, yes." His voice sounded very excited. "They will do very nicely for both of us. Timothy, isn't it?" He stopped fiddling with the paintings and looked at me. "Would you be interested in a show?"

I was incredulous. I had hoped he might take a painting or two on consignment, but a show? I had not expected this.

"I know, I know. I'm far too kind to a young, unknown artist. But it's just my solicitous nature, I suppose."

I tried to hide a smile. I could almost see the wheels in his brain turning. Or perhaps it wasn't wheels so much as a cash register. Then I got serious. "But is there enough of a body of work here for a show?"

Nigel put his chin on his palm and held his elbow as he looked at the collection. "Do you have others in your studio?"

"My studio? Oh, yes, my studio. Well, there are others there and in my car, but they're a little different."

"If they are of the same quality as these, they will do very nicely," Nigel said. "We need to get to the arrangements." Nigel walked over to his desk in the corner of the gallery and started flipping through a large leather-bound calendar. "I'll arrange for my framer to come in tomorrow."

"I have a few already framed," I said.

"Good, bring those as well. Can you be here at nine tomorrow morning to meet him? I know he'll be free for this project."

"Sure. I don't see why not," I said, realizing I had nothing else on my calendar.

Nigel looked carefully at me. "And bring everything, Timothy. I mean everything."

I nodded.

"I feel this is the start of a long and mutually beneficial relationship," Nigel said, then he smiled, and we shook hands.

My first art show was a go!

~

Nigel was true to his word. I met with him and his framer, Gordon, the following day. Gordon said he could have them all done in three weeks, so Nigel set the date for the opening four weeks hence. It seemed faster than I could ever have imagined them getting it together. There would have been innumerable obstacles to arranging everything if this had been New York. In Halifax, it didn't seem to be a problem at all. When I stopped by the gallery the following week, Nigel presented me with several tickets for the opening—printed already. The speed at which he got things done took my breath away.

"For your nearest and dearest," he said, handing me the gilt-edged envelopes.

My nearest and dearest? I wasn't sure I had such people in my life. Or did I?

The next afternoon, I found myself standing on Ellie's porch, a bouquet of yellow and orange autumn flowers in my arm and two of the gilt-edged envelopes in my sweating hands. I couldn't remember ever being so nervous about anything in my life. I rang the bell.

"Timothy," Ellie said, opening the door. "How lovely it is to see you. I had hoped you'd visit again."

"I apologize for not calling first, Ellie, but I wanted to surprise you." What I didn't tell her was that it occurred to me that she might refuse to see me entirely, but she seemed genuinely pleased. I

continued. "I have some terrific news I wanted to share with you."
I looked down at the flowers in my arm. "Oh, and these are for you."

Ellie took the armful of flowers from me and smelled them.
"These are lovely, Timothy. I do love to have flowers in the house.
Thank you so much."

I looked down at the envelopes still in my hand and offered
them to her. "One of these is for you," I said. "And the other is for
Meg."

Ellie took them from me, frowning. "I think you better come in,
Timothy." She led me into the living room, where she rummaged in
a cabinet for a vase. "I'll just put these in water," she said, heading
toward the kitchen. "When I come back, you can tell me what this is
all about."

I sat down tensely, clasping and unclasping my hands like a
nervous schoolboy. What was wrong with me? I gazed toward the
window where the Erté prints hung on the wall and noticed a piece
of sculpture that hadn't been there before. It was extraordinary. I got
up to take a closer look.

It was about five feet high and appeared to be a formal gown
without a body, yet it was formed as if there were a body in it. It was
a one-shoulder gossamer, peach-coloured gown with a slit that
would have exposed a lot of leg if it had been worn. It seemed to be
fabricated from an actual dress that had been stiffened somehow to
make it stand alone on its pedestal. It shimmered and shone with
the backlight from the window. I wondered where Ellie had gotten
this remarkable piece of art.

"Ah, I see you've discovered Opal," Ellie said as she returned
to the living room with the bouquet now safely immersed in water.
She placed the vase on the coffee table and came over beside me.

"Opal," I said. "Yes, it does look like an opal."

Ellie laughed. "Her name is Opal, Timothy. All the sculptures
have names."

"All the sculptures? You have more?" She nodded. "Who's the
artist?"

177

Ellie smiled enigmatically. I couldn't quite figure her out. "Timothy, it seems we all have dimensions to our lives that we only discover after we let ourselves." I still wasn't quite getting it. She continued. "I am the artist," she said.

"You? *You're* the artist? I thought you were a doctor."

"You disappoint me, Timothy," she said, pouting slightly. "Are we not permitted to be more than one thing?"

She had me there.

"Yes, my dear boy, I am an artist." She looked Opal up and down. "And a pretty good one, if I do say so myself."

I had to agree with her on that count.

"Anyway, Timothy, let's sit down and perhaps you can tell me what this visit is all about. I don't flatter myself to think that you have come just because you wanted to enjoy my company," she said, "Although that would be charming in its own way."

I sat down on the couch, and Ellie sat in an oversized chair across from me. "I'm having a gallery opening," I said.

"A gallery opening?" Ellie picked up one of the envelopes from where she'd placed it on the coffee table on her way to the kitchen. "You mean like a real artist?"

I deserved that. "Yes," I said sheepishly, "like a real artist."

Ellie opened the envelope and slid out the invitation. "*The Kaufman Gallery*," she said, reading the invitation. "That's just about the nicest one in the city." Ellie turned to me. "And that Nigel Kaufman. He's quite a character, don't you think?" She was smiling broadly now.

I did have to admit I thought he was an original. "Do you know him?"

"Oh, yes," she said. "This is a small city, Timothy. *Anyone* in the art world knows *everyone* in the art world here. I've known Nigel for years. I've bought several pieces from him over the years." She stopped for a moment. "I've also sold a few."

I was impressed but not surprised after seeing her work. "So, will you come?"

"To your opening? Well, of course. I wouldn't miss it for the world."

"What about Megan?"

She cocked her head to the side and looked carefully at my face. "What exactly do you mean?"

"Well, it's important to me that she be there. Do you think that's possible? She is back in town, isn't she?"

"She's been back for some time. She was only away for a few weeks. But Timothy," Ellie said, "we will have some work to do if we want to bring her around."

I was afraid of that.

Just then, the front door banged open loudly. "Gran! Gran, where are you?"

"In here, darling."

"Who owns that red Jeep parked in my spot in front of the house?"

TWENTY-SEVEN
MEGAN, 1989

SINCE I'D RETURNED FROM TORONTO, I had spent almost every waking hour with my nose to the grindstone. I'd taken Fumiko's words to heart and worked feverishly on the final draft of my dissertation. I wanted to have it ready to present my public defence and get my Ph.D., but I also wanted to complete it so I could deliver a paper at a conference coming up in February in New York. It would be my chance to impress academics from around the world. I had to start building my reputation if I wanted a serious career—if I wanted to make a difference in the world. But whenever I lifted my head from my work, my mind was filled with nothing but Tim—or so it seemed.

My visit to see Patrick hadn't gone as I'd hoped it might. To be honest, I'd expected him to take my side, and I was a bit peeved. Now, as I thought about it, I wondered what sides there were in this situation. Tim's? Mine? Or were there no sides? I was thinking about Patrick's quote as I got out of my car on that late September afternoon. *The love that you withhold is the pain that you carry.*

I pulled in behind a mysterious red Jeep parked in the spot directly in front of Gran's walkway that I always considered mine. I grumbled a bit and got as close to its bumper as I could without touching it. I hadn't been to visit Gran in weeks because of my self-imposed work schedule, but I'd been hoping to spend a bit of time with her today. Darn, now it looked as if she had a visitor. Perhaps I should have called first.

I called out to Gran as I opened the door, which slammed behind me. Her voice came from the living room.

"Who owns that red Jeep parked in my spot in front of the house?" The words were out of my mouth before I could even think about how rude they might sound if she did, indeed, have a visitor.
180

I clapped my hand over my mouth to stifle any further rudeness, dropped my purse on a chair in the hallway and followed Gran's voice into the living room. I stopped, frozen in my tracks as I rounded the archway and saw Gran—and Tim.

"What are *you* doing here?" I said, unexpectedly incensed to be usurped by an intruder with my own grandmother. "Don't you have some whales to help your clients kill?" I could not help myself. The words just spilled out.

"Megan, please," Gran said. "Timothy is a guest."

I took a deep breath. "Sorry, Gran. I shouldn't have just dropped in like this. I'll leave and come back when you're not so busy." Even I could hear the petulance in my voice—like a spoiled child.

As I turned to leave, Tim got up. "It's okay. I was just leaving. It's nice to see you, Meg. I'd really like to have a chance to explain a few things."

"Yeah, sure," I said, not even able to look him in the eye. I crossed my arms as if to protect myself.

"I'll just be going, Ellie. Thank you so much for your hospitality." He glanced at something on the coffee table. "I hope to see you again very soon." As he passed me in the archway, he said, "You, too, Meg." Then I heard the front door open and then close behind him. The silence was deafening.

I walked into the room and sat down across from Gran in the chair Tim had just vacated. I looked at her face and couldn't get a reading at all. She was implacable, sitting in her chair, her hands gently resting in her lap. She seemed to be waiting for me to say something.

"What was he doing here, Gran? And why did it seem as if you two know each other? It hasn't been that long since I've been over to visit. When did you and Tim become so chummy?"

"Are you finished, Megan?"

I was near tears and didn't want to have to speak at that point, so I simply nodded.

"You do realize how rude you were, I presume." Gran continued to sit in her kind of Zen-like position. "What is really the matter, darling?"

"It's that damn man!" A tear slid from one eye, and I could feel it tickle my cheek as it slid down, depositing that familiar saltiness in the corner of my mouth. "I think you know that, Gran." I wiped away the tear with the back of my hand. "Why does he have to be who he is?"

Gran took a deep breath. "I don't think you know very much at all about who he is, young lady."

"Gran, I—"

"You and I need to have a talk, Megan. You look like you could use a cup of tea. I'll be right back."

Gran headed toward the kitchen as I threw myself back against the soft cushions of her couch. I grabbed one of them, hugging it tightly to myself. I looked at the massive bouquet of flowers and wondered if Tim had brought them. *Now, why would I think that?* I thought. Then I noticed the gilt-edged envelope on the coffee table beside the vase. It had my name on it.

I put the cushion aside and picked up the envelope, running my finger across the gold edge, willing myself to open it. I turned it over and wondered what I was looking for. A clue as to its content? That was so absurd. If I wanted to know what was in the envelope, all I had to do was open it. After all, it did have my name on it. I put my finger under the flap and tore it open.

I slid the card out of the envelope and registered that it looked like an invitation of some kind. I recognized the *Kaufman Gallery's* logo at the top. Reading down, I could determine only that it was an invitation to an opening at the gallery. I shook my head. It didn't make any sense.

Gran came back into the room and handed me a mug of tea. Gran must have been in a hurry—she usually brought a tray with a bone china teapot and matching cups and saucers. Today warranted only a mug. "I see you've opened your invitation," she said as she sat down in her chair once again.

"What do you know about this, Gran?"

"That's one of the things we need to talk about, but we'll get to that eventually. First, I want to tell you an old story about your grandmother."

"About you?"

"Well," Gran said, sipping her tea as I watched the steam encircle her head like a halo, "at the very least, it's about someone I used to be. You know, we all become something different than we were as the result of circumstances. And the people we meet can have a remarkable effect on who we become. Anyway, darling Megan, it's a very old story, but I think it's time you heard it."

Gran began describing an evening in 1942. As the war raged in Europe, young Ellen McMaster was a singer with a local band—a singer who wanted to become a doctor like her father. She described meeting a young American naval officer who was in Halifax for a few days before his convoy set sail for Europe. As she started speaking about the American, I could feel my neck tense. I had heard this story before. What did she mean when she said it was time I heard the story? Gran had been left bereft and broken by a visiting American who simply used her and left her. At least, that's the story I'd told myself for my entire life. That's the story I heard whenever it came up during my childhood. But Gran's story felt different—so different that it made me wonder if I'd ever truly listened to her before.

I watched her face as she recounted the story of that night at the *Jubilee Boat Club*. I could see in her eyes that she remembered it as if it were happening right before her eyes. Her recollection was so vivid. Then she described four days of what sounded like—and now felt like—bliss, and I was ashamed that I'd never considered that my grandmother had once been a young woman. I could see that the young woman was still there behind the older eyes.

"On that last evening," she said, tears falling from her eyes, "I took to the stage as Bill watched. And I sang for him."

"His name was Bill?" I said.

"Yes. Bill. William Sinclair."

Something twigged in my brain. "Sinclair? Gran," I began, "what are you saying?"

"I'm saying that the American naval officer I met during the war was called William Sinclair."

My head was spinning. I could hardly concentrate on what Gran was saying—it made no sense to me. Now, she was telling me that she was pregnant when she left Halifax to go to Montreal, which meant that my mother must have been five or six years old when Gran married. I had been only ten when my parents died, so, like most other young children, I'd never really been aware of my parents' ages—and I'd never asked. But she was now telling me that my mother's father was—was what? The American sailor? That William Sinclair was my mother's real father? That my grandfather, Gran's husband, wasn't really my grandfather? Then she pulled a photo from a drawer on a side table and passed it to me before going to her bar and pouring two glasses of sherry.

I didn't know what I was looking at. It was me—and Tim. Yet, it wasn't.

"Oh my god, Gran. It can't be!"

"It can, and it is, Megan, darling. That picture was taken that weekend in 1942 at Lawrencetown Beach. Bill had his little Kodak camera with him and asked a passer-by to take it. The picture arrived in the mail three months later. He must have been able to have the film developed in England, where the ship was scheduled to stop. It came with a letter—the first of several letters he sent me over the next few years."

"Did you ever see him again?" Gran shook her head. "And you never told him?"

Gran spoke softly. "I never even answered his letters. I am ashamed when I think about how that must have made him feel. He

184

must have been heartbroken, but I knew he was married. I think I'd known from the moment I met him, although he described his situation in his letters. I didn't want to be the reason his family broke up, especially because he already had a young son by the time I met him." She sipped her sherry and sat up straight.

"And in case you're wondering, I have no regrets, Megan. None. I did what I wanted to do, then what I had to do, and never looked back. I have always taken responsibility for my actions, and this situation was no different. It taught me valuable lessons about love and commitment. I was fully committed to your mother, and when your grandfather came along, he was more than willing to be Anne's father. He truly was your grandfather." She put her sherry glass down and looked at me. "But Timothy is another matter. Look at that photograph and tell me there isn't a reason he's here. Tell me he didn't come here because he was compelled to do so. Tell me that he doesn't embody his grandfather."

I looked at the picture I was still holding and felt a ghost walk through me. "Gran, I don't know what to say. Are you telling me that Tim is like the reincarnation of his grandfather, and he's come back to set things straight?"

"I don't think I'd go that far. It isn't as literal as that, Megan. And just remember that William Sinclair was *your* grandfather, too."

I was having great difficulty getting my head around that piece of information.

Gran continued. "I just know that everything in life happens for a reason. I believe Timothy is here for several reasons—one for you and I believe one for himself."

I was so confused and still very suspicious. "I can believe that there's a reason for him, but I'm not so sure there's one for me. And the very thought that we're somehow related—"

"Megan, I don't think you've been listening to me. Timothy was supposed to be here so he could meet you and see where he's going with his life. You may disapprove entirely of the life he left behind in New York—"

"He hasn't left it behind. He's just taking a break."

"As I was saying, you may not approve of the life he's left behind—which if you would just listen to someone outside your own head, you would understand—but I think you'll now find a young man who has changed since he arrived here in the spring." I started to interject, but Gran stopped me. "And another thing. You're a little too self-righteous yourself sometimes, you know."

"What? Of all people, Gran, I thought you believed in my work."

"Of course, I do. That's not what I mean. I mean that you always seem to take the moral high ground. No one—not even you, my dear—is always on the higher moral ground than anyone else."

"What am I supposed to do now?" I was more bewildered and miserable with every passing moment.

"That, my darling granddaughter, is entirely up to you. You have to figure it out. No one can figure it out for you."

~

No one could figure it out for me. Gran was right. I knew she was right the minute she said the words, but I wasn't ready to figure it out yet. I wasn't sure I would like where it led me. But isn't that the thing about life? You don't always like where it leads you, but you have to figure out how to make it work anyway.

The day after my visit with Gran—and my run-in with Tim—I sat in my study carrel in the library staring into space. The cubicle was tiny by office standards, with a slatted door that I could lock to keep my books and papers private. Graduate students applied for a library carrel each September and could have it as their own dedicated study space for the entire academic year. I had only recently settled into this one, and I was hoping that I'd only need it until December. That was my self-imposed deadline for finishing the work required on my dissertation.

I usually loved the library. I loved how I felt each time I pushed open the heavy glass door and entered the hushed space. I loved how it felt to walk up and down the narrow aisles with books as far as the eye could see. I loved how the books smelled. And I especially loved the Zen-like feeling I had when I settled into my own little space, surrounded by the books I'd selected and the pages and pages of notes I'd taken from them. Today, try as I might, I could not conjure that meditative feeling. All I could feel was my heart beating faster than it should as I sat there staring at the invitation to Tim's gallery opening that I had pinned to the bulletin board on the wall directly in front of me at the back of the desk. I don't know why I'd pinned it there.

No matter how hard I tried, I could not reconcile my feelings about Tim's work at the advertising agency with my feelings—feelings that seemed even more outrageous now that I knew he and I were related, no matter how distantly. Gran seemed to think that I needed to work this out somehow. I just didn't know how I ever could.

Before I left her house the day before, Gran asked me if I'd consider attending the opening with her as her date. I told her I'd think about it, but I didn't dare contemplate how I'd feel when I'd inevitably encounter Tim. I put the entire situation out of my mind as much as possible and got back to work for the next couple of weeks—until the day before the opening. I woke up that morning with a deep sense of curiosity. What was Tim's art like? I'd seen his works-in-progress and knew he was a talented watercolourist, but I'd never seen much finished work other than that outrageous Titanic ad he'd done for the oil company. I still hadn't told Gran if I'd accompany her to the opening, but my curiosity got the better of me. That's how I came to find myself standing on the sidewalk peering into the windows of the *Kaufman Gallery* later that morning.

I was trying to see the paintings that had already been hung around the gallery when I noticed a figure crouched over a large cardboard box on the floor. He seemed to be trying to slide a large, framed picture from the box. I jumped back quickly when I realized it was Tim.

My heart started racing, although I couldn't imagine why. I had chosen to come here today, after all. What did I expect to see on the day of an artist's opening? Of course, he was likely to be here. And I knew that. I stood back from the door, took a deep breath and pulled it open.

As I entered the gallery, I was overcome by the feeling that I was surrounded by the sky, the ocean, and the breeze. The paintings seemed to be dynamic beings that breathed their story into the air. I gasped. It was unexpected and exhilarating. Was this Tim's work?

"A gracious good morning, mademoiselle. How might I assist you on this lovely day?"

I knew the speaker was the gallery's proprietor, Nigel Kaufman himself. I'd met him once or twice when I'd been here to see a few of Gran's pieces on display before local art collectors snapped them up.

He suddenly recognized me. "Miss McMaster, isn't it?" he said, smiling widely. "How is your dear grandmother, Ellen?"

"She's marvellous as always," I said, looking around. Tim was near the back wall arranging the large painting he'd removed from the box. He had his back to me and hadn't seen me yet. My eye was drawn to the picture Tim was now hanging. Perhaps my eyes were not so much drawn as wrenched and mesmerized.

Nigel followed my line of vision to the painting on the far wall. "Beautiful, isn't it?" Nigel clasped his hands behind his back and cocked his head slightly. He stared at the painting, then at me.

Just then, Tim turned around, surprise registering on his face. I walked slowly toward him, my eyes riveted to the painting. He watched me approach him but said nothing. Finally, I stopped directly in front of the image.

Tim, who seemed to have been holding his breath, whispered, "Do you like it?"

"I...I don't know what to say. No one has ever painted me before." I couldn't take my eyes off it. The painting was a gentle watercolour of me lounging in front of a bay window, my hair wild and free, my face in a relaxed, contemplative pose. I looked...beautiful. And yet, I looked like me.

I could feel rather than see Nigel come up behind me. He inserted himself between me and the painting for a moment, clasping his hands in what appeared to be nothing short of glee. He looked at the painting, then at me.

"My, my! Isn't it fabulous! Subject meets herself! It's too much. Don't move a muscle." Nigel sprinted toward his desk and began rummaging in drawers.

"I wanted to be sure that even if I never saw you again, I'd always see you," Tim said when Nigel was out of earshot.

"Tim, I...I...Tim, I think I owe you an apology." I looked down at my feet. "My behaviour—"

"It's okay, Meg. Perhaps we can start over?"

"I don't know. I'm still having a lot of trouble with the work you do," I said.

Tim swept his arm around the space. "Meg, this is my work. If it hadn't been for you, I would never have understood that this is me—that this is what I'm supposed to be doing with my life. I would never have come to know people like you who are trying to make the world a better place. I would never have started to feel ashamed of how I was wasting my life—and talent. Even if you never get to change the whole world's attitude toward the environment, you've changed mine."

Before I had a chance to say a word, Nigel rushed back. Suddenly, I was almost blinded by the flash as he clicked the shutter of the camera he was now holding.

"For the gallery's memoirs, you know. Perhaps even the local paper!" Nigel said. "May I take another?"

Before I could say yes, he took two more before rushing away to his desk with a broad smile. I could tell he was elated.

"Where were we?" Tim said. I could tell he was trying not to smile, but it was difficult to avoid smiling at Nigel's antics.

"You were telling me about meeting people like me."

"Yeah. I guess I've spent my whole life in big cities where no one seems to be connected to anything but themselves and the concrete jungle. And they seem okay with that. People here are so much more connected to nature and themselves."

"I'm not so sure about that," I mumbled more to myself than Tim.

"What was that?"

I shrugged. "Aren't you going back to the ad agency?" I hoped to point the conversation back in his direction. I didn't want him dwelling on the idea that I might be one of those people he thought were connected to themselves—presumably having it all together, as they say. "And what about that revolting Antonia?" I clapped my hand over my mouth. "I'm sorry. I shouldn't have said that."

But my question elicited a smile from Tim. "It's okay. I deserved that, and she probably did seem a little revolting."

"A little?" Again, I couldn't help myself, or so it seemed.

"Well, maybe a lot. Anyway, my time here has given me a lot to think about, and I've figured out a few things."

I was still grappling with Tim's apparent about-face in his work. I wanted to believe that the last few months (and knowing me) had given him a new way of seeing the world —and himself—but I still had misgivings. My mind and my heart were torn. However, there was still another problem—and it was a big one. I could feel the big elephant in the room losing its footing. I could almost see it crushing me if I didn't get it out of the way. "What have you figured out about the fact that we're…related?"

"Oh, that," Tim said, thrusting his hands deep into the pockets of his jeans. "What are we? Cousins three times removed, or something?" We looked at one another and started laughing. "It hardly seems worth considering—except for the shared history bit."

I wasn't as sure about that as he was, but it was something for another day. At that point, I had no idea where we'd go from here anyway. "You must be excited for tonight," I said. "And proud of yourself."

Tim looked around at his work. "You know, Meg, I am proud. I'm prouder of this than of anything I've ever done in my life." He looked back at me. "Will you be here tonight for the opening?"

"Gran and I wouldn't miss it." I meant it sincerely. At that moment, there was nothing that would keep me away from this evening's party. "Besides, she gets a real kick out of Nigel. Gran says he has an eye for young talent. By the way, you still haven't taken me dancing, Mr. Sinclair. Saturday night at *The Old Jube*, maybe?" I watched as a goofy grin spread across Tim's face.

TWENTY-EIGHT
TIM, 1989

WHEN MEG LEFT THAT GALLERY THAT MORNING, I held my breath, waiting for the next shoe to fall. I could tell she wanted to believe me—and I hoped she did. But I realized it would be a big leap for her to get her head around the fact that people don't change so much as they evolve when they begin to figure themselves out. I'd never had any reason to consider this possibility before, but I sure understood it now. I guess I'd expected to live my whole life in New York, clawing my way to the top of the advertising executive pile, perhaps winning a few Clios along the way. The one thing that could be said for the marketing and advertising world: they really did love to give themselves awards—more than any other industry, except perhaps actors. I had begun to realize that the awards were for the creativity and cleverness of the ads. It had nothing to do with whether or not they actually worked. I guess that's what interested me the most: the creative part. So, here I was now—on the verge of my first gallery opening as an artist.

I arrived at the gallery an hour before the invited guests were expected to begin filtering in. The caterers were setting up little *hors d'oeuvre* stations and a bar. When Nigel made an announcement to the three or four servers who were already there that the artist had arrived, I was greeted with polite applause. You could tell they couldn't have cared less what event they were catering. They just wanted to get on with it. But one of the young servers—she must have been barely old enough to serve alcohol—came over to me with a glass of champagne.

"Mr. Sinclair," she said. "I think your work is glorious. I hope to be able to have this kind of event someday."

"So, you're an artist?"

192

She nodded vigorously. "A student at the College of Art and Design here. I'm just doing this to pay tuition."

I wished her luck and sipped my champagne, wondering if someone like her might just find herself doing the same thing I'm doing in the future—except in the opposite direction, moving away from art for art's sake to a more practical application of talent. I guess it's all about figuring out your purpose, but I was beginning to think that the purpose of life is to live—full stop. My thoughts then turned to what Meg had said about Antonia. I shivered with mortification when I remembered having a few drinks by myself a week or so earlier and calling Antonia to share the news of my gallery opening. Suffice it to say that I would never have done this if I hadn't been slightly inebriated. At least, I don't think I would have. Predictably, Antonia hadn't shared my enthusiasm. I could still hear her voice in my ear, becoming sharper and more petulant by the moment.

"Tim! What are you talking about? Art? What do you mean you're doing your art? You're a graphic designer! Graphic designers don't do art!" She had sounded almost desperate.

That really grated. I felt a wave of growing anger, but I knew it was anger at myself. I had never given Antonia a single reason to think I was a fine artist and not an artist-for-hire. I had never told her that I wanted to paint. Then again, even I didn't realize that's what I wanted to do. It was hardly her fault. We had shared a blind ambition to achieve as much financial success as possible. Before we hung up, she asked me if I was ever coming home. Much to my surprise, I could hear what sounded like pleading in her voice.

I didn't quite know how to answer this question because I felt as if I *were* home. But I knew what Antonia meant, and despite her fling with Nathan (if that's what it was), she deserved better closure. And besides, I was still a half-owner of the apartment in New York. There was that. I'd have to go back to tie up some loose ends and ship my "stuff" regardless of what else I wanted to do. I told her I'd be back within two weeks, and we could talk then.

193

I sat on a stool watching the caterers and Nigel as they flitted around. Nigel was putting large vases of flowers throughout the space, which made me hope he wasn't making it look like a wake. That's all I needed on my first outing as an artist.

I had never been much of a deep thinker when it came to my work. I knew I was good at what I did, and my promotions and paycheques over the past few years had supported that belief. This time things were different. I felt suddenly overcome with doubt. Would anyone come? Would they like my work? Would I be able to have thick enough skin to withstand the naysayers? Would anyone buy a piece of work this evening? Old habits die hard, I guess. I still equated success with money. I still felt that if I could make money from my art, I would be a success. I guess my purpose in life wasn't *just* to live.

At twenty-five minutes past seven, Nigel tapped my arm. "Showtime!"

Five minutes later, the first two guests arrived. Someone had really come! It was happening. Before I knew it, the place was filled. I started to circulate as anonymously as I could before Nigel began introducing me to everyone within his range of vision. I was trying to get a sense of the buzz of conversation. Did they like what they saw? Did they hate it? I noticed six or seven people standing in front of Meg's portrait, and I started to panic.

As quickly as I could, I sought out Nigel and hissed in his ear. "That one's not for sale."

He turned to me, seemingly unable to comprehend. I repeated myself. "The portrait of Meg—it's not for sale. I'm keeping it."

Nigel sighed in his most dramatic way and shrugged. He then made his way over to the knot of people still standing in front of the piece. He pointed to me, and, *en masse*, they all turned to look. Several of them nodded sadly. I didn't care how sad they were. Some things in our lives are not for sale. No one was more astounded by this realization than I was. I continued to circulate.

I almost missed Ellie and Meg's arrival as I stood, champagne flute in hand, discussing my painting of the Halifax Harbour with a couple of Nigel's regular customers. They were going to buy it!

Ellie came up behind me. "Timothy, this is wonderful. I'm going to buy that one." She pointed to my rendering of the Titanic gravesite at Fairview Lawn Cemetery. "It has such a feeling of melancholy about it." She looked at it sadly. "It reminds me of Fran."

Fran Phillips had died only three days before the opening. I would forever regret that I'd never had the opportunity to finish our conversation. I had barely known her, yet a wave of nostalgia washed over me. I shook it off and turned to Meg. "What do you think?"

"Oh, Tim," she said, looking around at the people and the paintings. There were tears in her eyes.

~

We finally went dancing. When we arrived at *The Old Jube* the following Saturday evening, we could hear the Allan Thomas Orchestra already in full swing. Meg and I got out of my Jeep and followed the sound. As we approached the entrance, I took her hand, and she let me. Ever since Ellie had told me her story about her romance with my grandfather, I'd had an odd feeling of connection to Meg. No, strike that. I'd felt the connection long before I heard the story. It was just that Ellie's story gave me a reason for it. Now, as we walked hand-in-hand through the door and into *The Old Jube*, where Ellie had met Bill, I had the distinct impression that I was falling through time. It seemed as if 1989 were slipping away, revealing 1942 before my eyes.

I could almost see the soldiers, sailors and airmen milling around, smartly turned out in their well-pressed uniforms. I could picture the beautiful young women in their twin sets and pearls, swishing skirts and heels. I could see the couples taking to the dance floor. The trumpet intro began, and the band swung into Benny Goodman's orchestration of "Sing, Sing, Sing."

Meg and I stopped a moment to look around. "I know you can sing," I said, "but can you dance?"

Meg smiled and started dragging me inside. We muddled our way to the middle of the dance floor, dodging flailing limbs everywhere we looked. By the time we made it to the centre of the floor, the first drum solo had started. Then the trumpets joined in—and so did we. I could barely keep up with her. I laughed, thinking about how "lame" Antonia had thought it was when I asked her to take some dance classes with me a few years back. Swing music was on an upsurge, and New Yorkers were flocking to dance classes. Antonia would not have been one of them without considerable pressure on my part. Now, here was this beautiful woman egging me on. I could not keep the smile off my face. I didn't want to anyway.

The music stopped, and the applause was deafening. Meg took my hand. "Let's find a table and a drink." She wasn't even winded. I, on the other hand, was a different story. I'd have to get back into shape if I wanted to keep up with Megan.

We found an empty table back near the bar. Megan looked around. "You know, Gran says the original *Jubilee Boat Club* didn't have tables."

"No tables?"

"No. She said there were just chairs around the walls. Can't you just picture what it must have been like—all those servicemen in their uniforms?"

I could picture them. I looked at Meg, who seemed to have drifted off into a dream. Suddenly she seemed to come back to the present. "When are you leaving?"

I had already told her I'd have to get back to New York—for a visit—but we hadn't discussed when that would be.

"Tomorrow morning," I said.

"Oh, tomorrow. So soon."

"I figure it's best to get it over with."

"Will you see Antonia?" Meg looked down at her hands clasped together, resting on the table.

Before I had a chance to answer, a server came by to ask us for our drinks order. No one could take up space at a table without ordering a drink. I ordered a beer for myself and a Singapore Sling for Meg. "I don't have a choice, Meg. Both our names are on the deed to the apartment, and it seems she has a buyer."

"Where are you going to live?"

I was seriously puzzled by this turn in the conversation. I thought that Meg knew very well that I planned to make Nova Scotia my permanent home—or at least as permanent as anything could be these days. "I thought you knew. I'm going to New York first to get some Canadian-American paperwork done as best I can, then I'm going to spend a week with my mother in Boston." I took her hands in mine across the table. "Then I'm coming back."

Our conversation was interrupted by applause. I looked over and saw Allan Thomas himself taking the microphone.

"Ladies and Gentlemen," he began. "Thanks so much. It's people like you who keep this music alive." He stopped and put his hand over his eyes as if trying to keep the light out so he could see better. "If I'm not mistaken, I think I may have a treat for you this evening. I see a special friend of mine in the audience—one many of you will know almost as well as I do." His eyes landed on Meg. He put the microphone back in its stand and walked down from the stage, heading directly for our table. The orchestra played a flourish as he arrived at the table. Allan looked at me. "Do you mind?"

"It would be my pleasure," I said. "Meg, what about you?"

I noticed a look pass between Allan and Meg. Meg smiled half a smile at me, then looked back at Allan. "I don't have a choice now, do I?"

Allan shook his head, took her hand and led her to the stage.

Meg stood in the spotlight, caressing the microphone, and I swear I could see her wearing a 1940s red silk dress and elbow-length gloves. Wait! She *was* wearing gloves. Allan had slipped them to her on their way up, and she donned them as she took the three steps up to the stage.

"This is for someone special," she said as the orchestra began a familiar intro. "Every time we say goodbye," she sang, and I swear I knew I'd die a little myself when I had to be away from her.

I knew I had to hurry back. Cousins—or whatever—or not, I wouldn't ever leave her again.

TWENTY-NINE
CHARLIE, 2022

I KNEW I WAS SITTING IN TIM'S OFFICE behind the gallery, but it felt like I was somewhere floating above, looking down on the three of us. I could feel the pricks of tears in my eyes as I listened to the ending of Tim's story. I glanced over at Ava, whose eyes were brimming with unshed tears, and I wondered if Tim had ever told her the whole story.

I dabbed at my eye to catch a falling tear and said, "So, that was the romance Fran wanted to tell. That was the story she wanted to have as her legacy."

"I think so. I mean, I don't know for sure. I thought it was Ellie's story that fascinated her. Wartime romances are a genre as far as I know, but that one time I met your great-grandmother, she seemed to think she had yet to figure out the end of the story even though she already knew how it ended for Ellie and William. She told me she thought I might know something more about the story's ending. I guess Meg's and my story does sound romantic now that I look back on it—at least it was for us—but it had only just begun."

"What happened when you went back to New York?" I said, hoping I wasn't pushing too hard.

Tim sighed heavily. "Things didn't go as smoothly as I had hoped."

"So, there was no happy ending?" I was desperate for there to be a happy ending to this romantic story.

"I didn't say that. It was just a bit more complicated than I had thought. When I got back to New York…well, let's just say Antonia was waiting for me as if nothing had happened. It was creepy, to say the least." He glanced at Ava.

Tim looked pensive as I willed him to continue his story. I had to know the ending. "Are you willing to tell me more? I mean, I don't want to overstep. You've only just met me."

Before Tim could answer, I heard a car horn outside on the street. Ava quickly picked up her purse and headed for the door, calling over her shoulder, "See you later, Dad. That's Lucas." And she was gone.

I noticed Tim sighing as if relieved as Ava left. It was probably tricky reliving ancient history with a daughter around, although I had no way of knowing how he was feeling telling a stranger his life story.

"Sure. I'll finish the story. Tell you what. Why don't we go out for a bite of lunch?" Tim checked his watch. "That is if you have the time."

"Mr. Sinclair...Tim," I said, "for some reason, this story was very important to my great-grandmother. I would love to hear the rest of it. But I can understand if you don't want to tell a stranger."

Tim looked at me thoughtfully. "I don't know why, Charlie—I'd never met you before an hour ago—but somehow, you don't feel like a stranger. I know my only connection to you is that one meeting I had with your great-grandmother, yet that meeting somehow affected me. I guess if I tell you the rest of the story, you'll just have to do with it whatever you think best. Lunch?" I nodded.

Tim put the "closed for lunch" sign on the door, and we walked two blocks down toward the harbour. We found an empty table at one of my favourite restaurants, *Salty's*, on the waterfront overlooking the ferry terminal. We settled into a booth by the window and watched the seagulls swooping overhead. Once we had placed our orders—fish and chips for both—Tim began talking again.

"Where were we?" Tim said as the server put a beer in front of him and a glass of Chablis in front of me. "Oh, yes, I was going to tell you what happened when I arrived in New York to settle my affairs with Antonia." He took a sip of beer as if for fortification.

"Let's put it this way. When I arrived in New York, I was greeted by rather unexpected news." Tim took a deep breath. "I should have known that something was up. She kept telling me that we had to talk. Well, let's just say that the moment I walked through our apartment door in New York, there was no need for her to say anything."

"I'm not following," I said.

"Antonia was pregnant. Seven months. It was quite obvious."

I think I gasped.

"And before you ask, yes, she did know when she visited me in Halifax and accosted Meg. But she thought I'd be home soon and decided to omit that little detail."

I'm sure he could see by the look on my face that this was much more information than I had expected to receive from a perfect stranger. I still wasn't sure why he was telling me all this in so much detail, but I wanted him to continue, so I kept quiet. Maybe he did want someone to finish writing the romance. He continued.

"I'm sure the first question on your mind is whether or not I was the father. The answer to that was yes."

"That must have been such a shock," I said. I had so many questions.

Tim plunged into the story.

He told me that Antonia was sitting in the apartment flipping through a magazine when he arrived. "She seemed to have arranged herself very precisely so that she looked calm, well-appointed, and pregnant. I had checked into a hotel and then called her to tell her I would be over in an hour. She'd been expecting me.

"I'd taken a moment to look around when I walked in to see if Nathan might be there. To my great relief, he wasn't there, but I was struck by how much I disliked our apartment, all white and clean and antiseptic. Her pregnancy was so obvious that she didn't have to say a word, and I think I knew before she opened her mouth that the baby was mine, although I have to admit, I hoped it was Nathan's. It had happened just before I left for Halifax in the spring.

"Anyway, Antonia and I talked around the subject for a while, and then she told me she didn't want the baby. What had I expected? That we'd suddenly become a family? That Nathan would disappear into thin air, I'd move back to New York and play breadwinner while this ambitious, single-minded businesswoman before me stayed home and changed diapers? Or that she'd uproot herself and move north with me? When I thought about her moving to Canada with me—well, it just made me laugh—almost out loud. But she was already seven months pregnant, which she confirmed by telling me her due date was in December, so it was far too late to end a pregnancy. I had no idea what she meant by not wanting the baby at that point.

"She also told me Nathan didn't want a baby in his life either. I demanded that she tell me what was going on with them. As I had suspected, they were a couple, and I was merely an appendage at this point—an appendage that needed to be removed. But this would be my baby, too, and that counted for something in my world."

Tim then told me about spending the next week cleaning up business and apartment-related legal issues before visiting his mother in Boston. "My mother had never warmed to Antonia on the few occasions I'd brought her to Boston. I have to give her credit, though. When she heard about my current dilemma, she didn't judge me. Instead, she gave me this piece of advice: *One of the greatest things a father can do for his children is to love their mother.*"

Tim gazed out the window at the water for a moment. I followed his gaze, and we both watched as the harbour ferry pulled out of the dock just next door to the restaurant and began its ten-minute journey to the other side of the harbour. We watched as it disappeared into the fog that had just now begun rolling into the harbour. Then Tim turned back to me and continued.

"You know, Charlie, I grappled with my mother's wise words on my flight back from Boston to Halifax. It was impossible, yet my mother seemed to think it was the one piece of advice I needed in this awful situation. I didn't love Antonia, so I felt I was a failure as a father, and my child hadn't even been born."

"What happened when you got back to Halifax?" I said.

Tim then told me how awful he'd felt when he finally saw Megan again. He told me he was terrified, and the depth of his dread was apparent on his face as he sat there remembering. He was afraid Megan might walk out the door the minute he told her Antonia's news. But he was determined there would be no more secrets.

"Meg's reaction was measured and thoughtful. There were no tears, no recriminations. She was pragmatic about it. She told me she realized this situation had happened before we met. She was also profoundly sad for the child that a mother wouldn't want to be a part of that new life. Then she asked me what I wanted from my own life. I told her I wanted her."

"Oh, Tim," I said. "It must have been so difficult."

"Charlie," I said, "I remember the look on her face. It was as if I were looking into the face of an angel. Meg told me she had a secret she needed to tell me, too. That's when I learned that she couldn't have children. I remember being both sad for her and relieved. Remember, Meg and I were related, even if distantly. Not having children was probably the best situation."

"That must have been so heartbreaking," I said, feeling peculiar that a stranger had let me so far inside his life.

"I suppose it was but only for a moment. That's when Meg told me she knew exactly what we would do. 'We'll be married,' she said. There was no equivocation. And there was no arguing with her—I couldn't have even if I wanted to, which I didn't. It was the best marriage proposal ever. She wanted us to get married in early December. Remember, it was already late October by this time. Then she said, 'We'll spend our honeymoon in New York. When the baby is born, we'll take that baby home and love it until the day we die.'"

I could feel my eyes beginning to well up again. "What an incredible woman."

"Yes," Tim said softly as if remembering Meg's determination.

"So, Ava was born in December of 1989?"

"Yes. And we brought her home—to love until the day we die."

"And Megan?" I tried to be as gentle as I could, not knowing where this was going.

Tim took his time answering. "She died when Ava was five," he said, and I could see him trying to swallow the lump in his throat. "Ovarian cancer. It moved so quickly, and then she was gone." He took a breath. "I've raised Ava with Ellie McMaster's help. Ellie was a wonderful great-grandmother. I'm happy Ava had the chance to know her—unlike you and your great-grandmother. As I said, I met Fran only once, but I think you would have had much in common with her." Tim picked at the few French fries left on his plate. "Oh, and that sculpture you were admiring in the front of the gallery?" I nodded. "It's one of Ellie's. Ava was her protégée. That piece was from a series of sculptures she created by fabricating copies of dresses in Erté designs from the early twentieth century. I remember visiting her when she was madly at work on her sewing machine, creating the dresses from silk and sequins before she started her process of making the fabric come alive as if it were on a ghost model. Ava was captivated by these dresses since she was a young child."

"Is that sculpture for sale, Tim?" I said.

Tim thought about this for a moment as if he might not be entirely sure. "Are you interested in buying it?"

"I absolutely am. I love the sculpture, and knowing its provenance makes it even more fascinating and beautiful. It would look amazing in our living room."

So, I bought Ellie's Opal. Tim then told me he would put one of Ava's sculptures in its place in the window. It was time, he said, and he knew she'd be thrilled.

Tim stood there as we were saying goodbye at the restaurant entrance, about to open the door. I looked at him and said, "Tim, I don't think you know how important it was for me to hear the whole story that fascinated my great-grandmother so much. I'm not sure why it intrigued her, but I do know she was writing it as a piece of fiction. I'm considering finishing it for her."

"Since the moment you mentioned that you're Fran Phillips's great-granddaughter and that Fran had been writing an unfinished romance, I realized that our story might have been the one Ellie had related to her back in 1989. She just had no idea how it would end."

"How do you feel about the possibility that I might finish the novel?" I asked.

Tim took a deep breath. "I'll have to give that some thought, Charlie. Tell you what. Why don't we plan to have dinner in a couple of weeks?"

"That would be wonderful," I said. "You and Ava are invited to my home. My husband, Tom, and I will make dinner for you."

"You don't have to do that," Tim said. "You hardly know us."

"Oh, I imagine I know more about you than most people at this point. Besides, I think I do owe you a dinner."

I drifted away from Tim out into the fog that enveloped the harbour as he disappeared into the mist in the opposite direction.

THIRTY

TIM AND MEGAN'S ROMANCE began to dominate my dreams, both awake and asleep. I would find myself standing in the shower, stock-still, water running down over me, just thinking. Sometimes I felt like a soul lost in a fog. At other times, I felt like I was trying to see through a frosted glass window. There were distinct shadows, but I could never really see what or who had cast them. Tom had to yell into the bathroom more than once to ask if I was all right. To tell you the truth, I wasn't sure. I thought about the romance, but I also thought about my great-grandmother, Frannie.

At one point, Tim had said, "You would have had much in common with her." Would I? Would I have had much in common with a woman who had lived an inscrutable life? A life that seemed to have begun with her surviving the Titanic disaster at age twelve? A life that revelled in rebellion and adventure and living life to the fullest? A life that had left such a legacy? I had done nothing to compare with any of this. Nothing whatsoever.

Since my mother had died almost three years earlier, I had first learned my mother's secrets. Then I had learned Frannie's secrets after discovering her dresses, her diary, and her Paris flat. What *did* we have in common?

Of course, there was the writing. Frannie could never have known that her tiny great-granddaughter—me—would have turned out to be a writer. At least I had written one book at this point. I had written a novel inspired by my mother's diaries and had been thinking about doing the same with Frannie's. That made me a writer, although I wasn't doing much writing these days. I spent most of my time teaching writing to high school students and trying to figure out what to do with the enormous sum of money Frannie had left to me. So, maybe I wasn't a writer so much. After all, writers write, don't they? So maybe we had a bit in common on the writing

206

front, but it didn't seem like much to me. Then there were the dresses.

Frannie had left behind the collection of couture dresses she had amassed throughout her incredible life, starting with the "Lucile" she'd hoped to wear aboard the Titanic but got left behind. More than once, I had mused that if she had taken it on the voyage, I would never have seen it. But it was more than a collection of dresses. I realized that the collection represented something more profound in my great-grandmother, and it might be part of the other things that we might share in common.

Frannie's early diaries had been clear on one point: she wanted desperately to be a dressmaker and designer, much as the great Lucile, whose dress (as I said) had never made it onto the Titanic. This obsession had taken her to Paris in the first place. Did we have that in common?

I thought about how I'd taught myself to sew with that dusty old sewing machine I'd found in my mother's basement after her death. It had ignited in me an obsession with learning to sew, and I'd made twelve dresses, each one more complicated than the one before—and each one, in one way or another, showed me a bit more about myself. I had then made my wedding dress, but the sewing seemed to have been put on the back burner. Should I explore that?

Then I remembered that Tom had mentioned something about Elizabeth—Miss Elizabeth Davies—my mother's friend from back in the 1960s, who had also been my junior high school sewing teacher. I had not exactly been a star pupil back then, but she and I had reconnected after Mom's death, and she had helped me out with some of the sewing.

Over dinner one evening a week or so after meeting with Tim Sinclair, I remembered Tom mentioning Elizabeth's phone call. "Do you remember what Elizabeth said when she called?"

"I wrote it down somewhere, but that was some weeks ago, Charlie. Haven't you called her back yet?"

I was embarrassed to say that I had not. Tom, who had finished his dinner and was just sitting at the table with me sipping on a glass of wine, got up and went out of the room for a moment. When he returned, he put a piece of paper in front of me beside my wine glass. I could barely make out his handwriting (like a true computer whiz), but it said, "Elizabeth called. Wants you to help with a project." That was all.

"I'll have to call her," I said.

"Yes, you will," Tom said. "Charlie, I think this obsession with what to do with your money is starting to cause you a problem."

"I'm not actually obsessing about the money," I said defensively.

"You sure?"

I wasn't. I tapped on the side of my wine glass. "Is this becoming a problem for you?"

"Not for me," Tom said. "I said it's becoming a problem for *you*. Maybe there isn't some big thing you're supposed to do with the money. Maybe you're just supposed to learn to live with it and use it to your best advantage over the course of a life."

That hadn't occurred to me. I wanted it to be some kind of grand gesture, I supposed. But why? Why did I need it to be a grand gesture? Was it because I needed the recognition? I shuddered at the possibility. I didn't want to be one of those people.

"I wonder what Elizabeth wanted." It occurred to me she might be looking for help with costumes for *Pointe Taken Dance Theatre*, a small, local ballet company she sewed costumes for.

"I suppose you'll have to call her to find out," Tom said.

"I'm going to call her tomorrow."

Tom, being Tom, said, "Why wait until tomorrow? Why not call her tonight?"

He was right again.

~

Elizabeth's phone rang four times before she picked it up. "Dear Charlie, how lovely to hear from you."

I might have expected this reaction to be a bit cynical coming from anyone else, given how long it had been since she called, but I knew that Elizabeth meant it. She would think it was lovely that I got back to her, no matter how belated.

I apologized to her for taking so long to return her call. She wasn't put off at all.

"Charlie," Elizabeth said, "I have a small project on the go—one I think might interest you. I wondered if I could discuss it with you."

"Of course, I'd love to hear about it. What kind of project?"

"Let's have lunch," Elizabeth said. "Why don't you come here next Wednesday, and we can talk about it comfortably."

It sounded a bit mysterious, but I agreed. It was a date.

~

I was sitting at my desk, staring at my computer screen, half asleep, when I heard a text ping on my phone. Tim and Ava would be delighted to accept my invitation to join Tom and me for dinner on Saturday evening. I suddenly realized I should probably do some research before they arrived. But I was so tired that I could barely keep my eyes open. I decided to take a short nap before I sat down to do some serious research. I don't know how long I slept, but it was getting dark when I woke up. I checked the time and realized I didn't have much time before dinner, so I got right at it.

So, I hunkered down at my computer to find out all I could about Ellen McMaster and Megan McMaster Sinclair. Tom and I had done only enough research for me to find Tim at this point. I needed more. So, I put my head down and got to work.

I expected to discover more about Ellen than Megan since she was something of a renowned artist in her later years. I actually didn't really expect to find anything about Megan, who had been dead for almost thirty years, so I started with Ellen.

I found very little about Ellen McMaster's career as a family physician—just a brief mention of it in her online bios—but I was astounded at the plethora of information on her artwork. How could I have been so oblivious to such an internationally recognized artist right here in my own community?

Ellen had spent the final twenty years of her life transforming herself from respected doctor to coveted fabric sculptor, with a ten-year overlap between the two roles. The reinvention was awe-inspiring. She had lived a very private life until the age of about sixty or so. After that, she was all over the art world—in magazines, blogs, and gallery websites. She seemed to have been very prolific. I paged through website after website, falling more deeply in love with her sculptures every time I saw a new one. They were difficult to describe.

Each piece was a sculptured couture dress. Ellen had copied a variety of designers from Erté, as Tim had noted, to Chanel to Halston to Christian Dior and everyone in between. The dresses were clearly recognizable, although they were primarily fabricated in finely woven, semi-transparent silk even if the originals hadn't been—at least according to a blog post I read on her process. The transparency permitted her to create pieces through which lights—which were part of the sculpture itself—could create a lit-from-within, ethereal quality. The substance she used to make the dresses stand up without the benefit of a form underneath was a well-guarded secret. I wondered if she had shared her secret with Ava, her protégée. I would make a note to ask her at dinner. When I sought out recent auction results, I was immediately alarmed that Tim had seemed to have given me too low a price for the sculpture he was arranging to have delivered to me before the weekend.

I thought about Dr. Ellen McMaster, who she was initially and who she became. I was reminded of that year I'd spent cleaning out my family home after Mom died unexpectedly and finding the sewing machine. My newfound obsession had led me to a fabric shop called *Sew Fine Things,* whose proprietor was what I began to think of as a fabric whisperer. Every time I went into the shop, he was there to help me in more ways than he could have imagined.

One day when I was in the shop searching for fabric, we had a conversation about whether sewing was a craft or an art. Al told me that my sewing was art because of what I put into it. Then he quoted Leo Tolstoy, who once said, *"Art is not a handicraft; it is the transmission of feeling the artist has experienced."* As a physician, Ellen McMaster must have experienced enough sadness and death to imbue her art with these feelings. I figured that this experience might have led to dark and cheerless art. But that wasn't the case at all, which made me think that she had experienced much lightness and delight in her life because her artwork made me breathe a little more easily every time I saw a piece.

Then I searched for her granddaughter, Tim's late wife, Megan.

Megan McMaster Ph.D. Tim had mentioned that Megan was in environmental science, so I started with a basic search. When I plugged her name into the search engine, I had a few hits. When I tried Google Scholar, there were at least twenty. I was impressed with the number of academic papers she had authored or co-authored in such a short career. Then I stumbled upon something very interesting—and unexpected.

Megan McMaster Sinclair had written a book. The book was called *Fashion Crisis: How to Dress for the Environment*. I clicked on the "look inside" function on the website to see that it had been published in 1997. That was odd. Megan had died in 1994. I did a bit more research and discovered it had been published posthumously. I was astounded by the name of the person who had finished the manuscript for her. Her name was Katherine Hudson. My mother.

THIRTY-ONE

I IMMEDIATELY WENT BACK TO THE WEBSITE where the book was posted. Of course, it was available only as a used book—after all, it had been published almost thirty years ago. I was surprised, though, that it seemed to be ahead of its time. It was only in recent years that I'd begun to see books and news articles about the environmental damage caused by fast fashion, among other aspects of the fashion industry. I would have to wait a few weeks to see if there was more information in the book itself about why Katherine Hudson, CEO of *Kosmic Kat Fashions*, finished this book for Megan. It occurred to me that Tim might know, and I would be seeing him in a few days.

I planned an afternoon of serious cooking to prepare for Saturday's dinner. On Friday afternoon, I got in the car and drove to my favourite gourmet grocery store downtown. I drove around for a while, trying to find a place to park, and finally had to surrender to one three blocks away on a side street. As I pulled my reusable grocery bags from the back seat, I realized I was only a block away from the street where *Sew Fine Things*, my go-to fabric store, used to be. Tucking the grocery bags under my arm, I decided to take a side trip and stroll past the old store.

I hadn't been down this street in almost a year. The last time I was here, I had been saddened by the news that the store and the building it was located within were both for sale. Now I wondered what kind of business had taken up residence here.

As I neared the building, I could see what appeared to be a brand-new red awning with black lettering. It said *Sew Fine Things*. What? That couldn't be, could it? The grocery store, all but forgotten, I headed straight for the door. I stopped to read a sign in the window. It said, "Grand Opening Sunday afternoon." The door was locked, so I couldn't get inside to see what appeared to be shelf after shelf of fabric bolts, all neatly stacked, so unlike the organized

SOMETHING I'M SUPPOSED TO DO

chaos that had been the state of its previous incarnation. Just the thought of this little store, though, gave me goosebumps. I could feel a tiny jot of adrenaline at the thought the store was reopening. I wondered why I hadn't stayed with my sewing. I guess I had gotten so busy with writing and teaching that I'd forgotten the feeling I had every time I walked into the space filled with colour and texture—but mostly, it had been filled with possibilities. Potential. Promise. For a fabric store was nothing if not a place for imagining what might be—for imagining what a skilled artisan could make of raw materials it held. I missed that feeling.

I took note of the time of the opening and planned to return.

~

Tom and I spent Saturday afternoon cooking up a storm. We had recently spent some time watching Masterclass, learning various types of cooking from several different chefs. This evening, we were making Gordon Ramsay's basil-crusted rack of lamb with glazed Thumbelina carrots and new potatoes. I set the table and then stretched out on the couch in the living room for a few moments to close my eyes. I awoke with a start an hour later. I'd have to hurry to be ready in time for guests.

They were prompt. I was surprised at the promptness of two artists. Perhaps, though, it hearkened back to when Tim had first been in the advertising business in New York.

The four of us—Tim, Ava, Tom and I—settled into drinks and dinner, which everyone said was the best lamb they had ever tasted. (I did have to admit that it was pretty good.) Then we had raspberry souffle for dessert. We talked about so many different things—my recent book, Tom's real estate business, Tim's gallery, Ava's artwork. We had yet to talk about the romance novel I was itching to finish. Finally, it was Ava who brought up the subject.

"Charlie, Dad told me you're writing a novel loosely based on his life with Mom."

"I'm not exactly writing it," I said. "My great-grandmother, Fran, who was a writer, began writing the book in 1989. She and Ellen were great friends and neighbours, and it seems that Ellen shared your father's story with her. Fran was inspired by that story and Ellen's own romance back in 1942 with your Dad's grandfather, William, an American naval officer she met here in Halifax during the war. It's really two romances, but she never finished it." I suddenly realized that Ava might not know the details. "Do you know the story?" I looked at Tim apologetically. He smiled and nodded.

"So, you're going to finish it," Ava said.

It was more a statement than the question I had anticipated.

"Yes," Tim said before I had a chance to answer. "Charlie's going to finish writing the novel. It's a good story—a real romance or two, don't you think?"

And I hadn't even had to ask the question.

Ava smiled. "I've always known that I was Mom's chosen daughter—that she could have chosen not to take me into her life. It's always made me feel special. Ellie made me feel special, too. I always knew she wasn't my biological grandmother, but that didn't matter to either of us. As far as I was concerned, she was my real grandmother. I can't even imagine not having had her in my life."

"Grandmother and artistic mentor," Tim said proudly, smiling at his daughter.

I turned to Ava. "Ava, that reminds me. Did Ellie ever share the secret to her sculpture's form before she died?"

Ava smiled enigmatically. "I shall never tell."

"If you won't tell me that, could someone tell me how it is that my mother, Kat Hudson, was credited with finishing Megan's book *Fashion Crisis*?

"I can answer that," Tim said. "A year before Megan was diagnosed with cancer, she started writing a book based on her doctoral research. She sent a proposal to the University of Toronto Press, and they were interested, but they were trying to break into the trade publishing business—they didn't want a book that would appeal only to other academics. They asked her to rework the material using a style the average reader would like, and they wanted her to incorporate some current, real-world people. Meg was stumped until she discussed it with her grandmother. Ellie reminded her that her friend and neighbour, Fran Phillips, had a granddaughter in the fashion business. Meg, of course, as you know, knew Fran, but she had only a vague idea about Fran's granddaughter. She hadn't been aware that she was the CEO of a fashion brand that concerned itself with how its fabrics were manufactured."

"And that granddaughter was my mother, Katherine Hudson," I said, marvelling at the interconnectedness of life.

"Wow! What an incredible coincidence," Tom said.

Ava looked at him thoughtfully. "*Coincidence is god's way of remaining anonymous.* Einstein said so."

"*Touché!*" Tom said, raising his glass to Ava.

"I was just thinking that I was only a bit younger than you are now, Ava, when I started seeing things that way," Tim said. "I figured things just happened randomly—until I met your mother. I had to almost lose her to figure out that things do happen for a reason and events are really interconnected. I now believe it's fundamental to our very existence on earth. It's how we achieve anything and everything."

I thought back about all the weirdness in my life over the past couple of years—and it had all started when Mom died. If she had lived, my life at this very moment would not exist as it did. I would probably not even have married Tom. I certainly would never have known about my great-grandmother. Her secrets would still be buried under a mound of real and imagined things in my mother's house and life, and the interconnectedness of these people and events would be out of reach. *Mom*, I thought, *thank you for letting me be there after you died. And thank you for leading me to this moment.*

These were my thoughts as I drifted off to sleep later that evening.

~

The following morning, I felt more invigorated than I had in months, or so it seemed. Tim's story was swirling around in my head, and I was excited about writing it. But I had other things to do as well.

That afternoon, I drove downtown again and parked as close as possible to *Sew Fine Things*. It was grand opening day, and I was beyond curious about how this fabric store—as different as it looked from the outside—was resurfacing.

When I arrived, the place was already full. People were milling around admiring the selection of what turned out to be Italian silks and wools. The store was no longer the hodge-podge of colours and fabric types I loved so much. It was colour-coordinated—all the blue fabrics together, all the red fabrics together etc. It was a feast for the eyes—especially for anyone who loved order. I kind of missed the chaos. Obviously, the new owner had a very different aesthetic than Al, my fabric whisperer and his mother, who had originally co-owned the store. I smiled when I saw the wallhanging behind the cash desk. It said: *Everyone sees what you appear to be; few experience what you really are. Machiavelli.* I remembered when Al and I had talked about it. I was delighted to see that the new owners had kept it. Then I saw her.

Standing behind the beautiful new, marble-topped cash desk with its state-of-the-art computer cash register (I wondered what they had done with the antique that had been there before), holding a cup of tea, was Mrs. Nassar—Mrs. Nasser, Al's mother and the owner of the original *Sew Fine Things*. She was wearing one of her signature flowing brocade caftans. This one was a spectacular red and gold brocade, the gold bringing out the deep gold of her earrings and her bangle bracelets.

I had been admiring (coveting actually) a very expensive piece of blue wool jersey but immediately put it down and turned to make my way through the crowd toward her. A hand on my shoulder stopped me. I turned. It was Al.

"Oh my god," I said, "Al, it's you! What are you and your mother doing here?"

"Dear Charlie," he said, his dark eyes lighting up. "I am delighted that you are still sewing."

I felt a bit chagrined at the thought that I hadn't been sewing, but I didn't share this with him since I had a feeling I was about to rectify that omission in my life. I intended to leave here with more than one piece of fabric under my arm.

"Are you liking the place?"

"It's wonderful, Al, but not as wonderful as it was when you and your mother owned it. I kind of miss the organized chaos." I turned to look at him. He was still a presence with penetrating dark eyes, his shiny black hair and his *café au lait* complexion. He wasn't overly tall, but he had always filled this space with his presence as well as his charm and wit and smooth, deep baritone voice. I noticed that he was still wearing those black-rimmed glasses that made him look so intelligent—which he was. "How's your medical residency going?"

When I first knew Al, I had been entirely oblivious to the fact that Al had graduated from medical school in Syria before his family fled to Canada until the day his mother told me he had finally been accepted to complete his residency training.

He smiled broadly, "Marvellously well, thank you."

I also knew that his mother had been the one to insist that she didn't need him to work in a fabric store just so that she could keep it while he missed the opportunity to complete his medical education and practice medicine, which was his passion.

"Do you know the new owners?" I said.

"As a matter of fact, I know them very well. I'll introduce you."

Al led me over toward the new cash desk where his mother was now standing beside a well-dressed older man who looked somewhere in his seventies. His full head of silver hair was neatly combed straight back, and his eyes were bright and alive as he looked around at the crowd. He was wearing a smart button-down shirt under a navy jacket with a red pocket square that looked suspiciously like the fabric in Al's mother's caftan.

"Mother," he said to Mrs. Nassar, "you remember Charlotte Hudson—Charlie?"

"Of course, I do," she said, putting down her teacup and extending her hand. "How lovely of you to come today."

Then Al turned toward the gentleman on her right. "And Tobias, please meet my friend Charlotte Hudson. Charlie, my stepfather, Tobias. He and Mom own the store."

THIRTY-TWO

TO SAY I WAS SURPRISED would be a colossal understatement. I wanted to know how this excellent news transpired, but Al's mother and new stepfather were very busy with their guests, so Al took me aside and told me the story.

After Al left for Ottawa to complete his medical residency, his mother closed the store and sold the building, but the new owner wanted to maintain a fabric store in the building. When widower Tobias Goldfarb (the new owner) arrived from Montreal to finalize the sale, he was taken with more than his new building and the city. He was smitten with Mrs. Nassar. Within a month, they jetted off to the Caribbean to board a cruise. When they returned three weeks later, they were engaged. Then, instead of Mrs. Nassar moving to Montreal with Tobias, he insisted that he preferred to let his son look after his two fabric shops on *Rue St. Hubert* in Montreal and that he and Mrs. Nassar (now, presumably, Mrs. Goldfarb) would open a new shop in Halifax. They were now newlyweds—married less than a month earlier. I was astonished by the romances flourishing all around me—past and present.

"Are you helping them set up the store?" I said when Al had finished bringing me up to date. "Your time must be taken up completely with your residency."

"It is, at that," he said with his familiar, slightly accented English. "But I have a week off and wanted to be here to help get things started. Besides, I do have another engagement while I am here." He didn't elaborate.

Al then showed me some fantastic Italian printed silk fabric, and I snapped it up without even looking at the price tag. There had been a time when I first encountered him in the organized chaos of the former shop that the price tag was top-of-mind when purchasing fabric. I thought about how wonderful it would be now, with my new circumstances, to cut into and sew with some finer fabrics.

"You should call this place Sew *Finer* Fabrics now," I said as I paid for the silk and a piece of wool jersey with an eye-watering price of eighty dollars a metre. I had never used anything over fifteen dollars a metre, and even that was stretching my budget when I first learned to sew. I smiled as I thought back about the recycled shower curtain I'd used for my first project. I wondered how I'd feel just before making the first cut. I also wondered what I'd make with it. I didn't care. It was such a beautiful piece of fabric that I thought I might just keep it to look at from time to time.

Al laughed as he took up his familiar position behind the cash desk and clicked the sale into the computer. I kind of missed the old cash register with its embossed nickel cover and its large, noisy keys. I also missed the sound of that ka-ching the monster made when it tallied up a sale as the drawer slid out. There was nothing quite like progress.

"What happened to the antique cash register?" I said as he passed me the bag, no longer a generic plastic bag. This one was a large, reusable bag emblazoned with the shop's name and new logo of a stylized mannequin.

"It's still in the back," Al said. "When I finally get settled, I will have it in my den. It will always remind me of my father and the opportunities we had when we first arrived in Canada as refugees just after the civil war started."

It was sad to think that Al and his family had to flee their home country, but I thought we were lucky to have them here.

I said goodbye and left the shop with my bag over my shoulder. I was thinking about Elizabeth Davies and my upcoming lunch with her. Since she had, after all, been the first person to introduce me to sewing back in seventh grade, she would likely be thrilled to hear of my plans for this fabric. I wondered if she'd visited the shop yet. If she hadn't, I'd offer to take her.

~

As arranged, I arrived at Elizabeth's lovely home on time for lunch on Wednesday. I remembered the first time I'd been here. I was apartment hunting, and I'd been surprised to see that she was the landlady of a fabulous studio apartment in the basement of this house that I'd made arrangements to view. I remembered her coming out the front door and leading me to the apartment's private entrance on the side. Now, Elizabeth opened the door and drew me into her arms, hugging me tightly. I must admit, I felt that I had missed her. I vowed that whatever little project she had in mind, I would be on board and help.

I walked into the hall that led to the living room and turned in under the archway. As I looked into the room with its cream-coloured damask drapes and sumptuously upholstered furniture, I was astonished to see Al standing there beside the coffee table, his hands clasped in front of him, grinning from ear to ear.

"Fancy meeting you again so soon," he said, extending his hand to me. "I would imagine that you are quite surprised to see me."

"Surprised would be an understatement," I said, warmly shaking his hand. "I would ask you what you're doing here, but that would be twice in one week. Probably rude."

Al laughed as Elizabeth joined us, carrying a silver tray with a bottle of what appeared to be champagne and three crystal flutes.

"I thought we'd start lunch with a celebration of being together again and," she winked at Al (was that possible?), "to toast what I hope will be a very successful new project."

Elizabeth was well into her seventies now, and I marvelled at how she seemed so excited about new projects even at this age. I hoped I'd be like her when I got to be that age.

This celebratory mood was all fascinating to me, but I was getting a bit impatient. I wanted to know what project Al could possibly be involved in with Elizabeth—and more importantly, I wanted to know how I fit into it. For the briefest of moments, I remembered something my sister Evelyn said to me after we learned that we were both left very wealthy women by our great-grandmother. Always the pragmatic lawyer, Evelyn immediately knew what she would do with her money. She also knew that her younger sister (me), the artistic personality, might not be quite so set on a course of action that led to financial security. She had given me a warning.

"Charlie," she had said, "money is to be enjoyed and protected to a degree. Beware of people who will inevitably come to you with asinine ideas. No matter how much you like the people involved, don't be reckless."

Okay, Evelyn, I listened. Then I listened to Elizabeth as she began to speak about her project. She planned to open a sewing school—but not just any sewing school. She had observed that many of the Syrian and other refugee women from the middle east had a great interest in sewing. She thought that if she could bring them together, they might learn a useful skill—or sharpen ones they already had—and be ready to integrate into their new country. The school would be upstairs in the building housing *Sew Fine Things*. Of course, Al's mother and Tobias were thrilled with the idea, so Mrs. Nassar had asked Al if he would meet with Elizabeth to get things going. They had both thought of me.

"I suppose you would like some financial support," I said before I even had a chance to think about what I was saying—or how they might react.

Elizabeth looked sad. "I suppose if you want to make a financial contribution, Charlotte, that would be wonderful. But I felt that you had skills beyond money." She shook her head. "Not everything is about money, my dear."

I was embarrassed for having brought it up.

Al said, "There is an old Polish proverb, Charlie. *When I had money, everyone called me brother*. I do understand how you must be feeling. Elizabeth told me of your great good fortune, and I expect

222

many people will ask you for money. But we need you for you and not for your money."

I wondered how Elizabeth had found out about my inheritance, but this was, after all, a small city. Word gets around. And I should have known better. These were not two people I should have expected had any wish to use me for my money. Who was I becoming? I didn't want to be like this or to have to think about money every time someone asked for my help. I didn't know how to get to that point, but I would have to try. Then Al started talking about how he would get some support from a local group that supported refugee women. I stopped thinking about myself for a moment and clicked back into the conversation.

"What was the name of that organization?" I said.

"It's called The Tara Group," Al said. "It's headquartered in Boston but just opened several Canadian offshoots. There's a new one just starting here. As it turns out, the organization was created by a former Syrian refugee. When she came to Ottawa, I met her to talk about the organization."

"Her name is Dr. Fatima Taylor-Jackson, isn't it?"

Al looked at me. "It is. Do you know her?" He sounded incredulous.

"She's married to my half-brother."

Al's eyes became as wide as saucers under the round, black-rimmed frames of his glasses. Elizabeth's mouth hung open, and no one said a word for a moment.

"Fatima is married to your half-brother?" Al said, sounding like he couldn't believe what he had heard.

I nodded.

Elizabeth put down her champagne flute she had been clutching by its stem. "Oh my god, Charlotte. I met Peter and Fatima at your wedding, but I didn't put two and two together. Now I understand." She got a faraway look in her eyes as if she had left us for some other world. Her voice became softer and softer. "Peter is Chuck's son."

Chuck had been a part of my mother's life some years before meeting my father. I had known nothing about Peter until more than a year after my mother died. As I listened to the tone of Elizabeth's voice when she mentioned Chuck's name, I remembered Mom's diary and that Chuck had meant something special to her, too.

I turned back to Al. "I think we should talk about the details of the project."

THIRTY-THREE

ELIZABETH'S IDEA TO OPEN A SEWING SCHOOL for refugee women seemed simple and powerful. I told her I'd be happy to help in any way I could, but I wasn't sure how I could contribute to the day-to-day operation other than simply providing financial support. Elizabeth seemed to think I'd interact well with the women. I thought about this as I sat in my office later that afternoon, staring at the computer screen with the unfinished manuscript in front of me on the desk. *I wonder what Megan or Ellie would have done*, I thought. I decided to go downtown and walk around for a while.

Forty minutes later, I found myself outside *Sew Fine Things* once again. I stopped to look in the window for a few minutes at the display of Italian woollen fabrics for the upcoming season. Then I crossed the street and looked back at the building. Yes, I could almost picture the sewing school upstairs. Then it was time for a coffee to give me time to sit and think for a while.

I walked down toward the harbour and found a spot at a coffee shop I knew was run by a refugee family. I'd seen a news story about them only a month before. The father had been an engineer back in Syria, but getting Canadian credentials was proving to be too complicated and time-consuming. Being an enterprising young man with a family to house and feed, he decided to take his savings and open this coffee shop with help from his wife, who had appeared with him on the news show. I remembered him talking about how difficult it was to integrate into the community but that he had it easier than many since he spoke perfect English. Sadly, his wife did not. She was having trouble with even the most basic everyday activities the rest of us took for granted—everything from navigating the grocery store to talking with her children's teachers. And she desperately wanted not to have to rely on her husband to do everything. That's when it hit me.

It wasn't so much about the skill set that a sewing school could teach. If that's all it accomplished, it was missing an opportunity. I ordered my coffee and took out my phone. I began composing an email to Fatima, hoping she might have some insight into how easy (or difficult) it would be for a woman arriving from some war-torn country to learn our language. Maybe it's because I'm a writer and words are so important to me, but I knew without a doubt that not knowing the language was the single most serious impediment for these women in their adopted homes. Sewing was nice. Language skills were priceless.

That evening, I asked Tom to work through an idea with me. He broke out the wine, and we sat at the dining room table with our computers in front of us, making notes and figuring out if my idea would work.

"Okay," Tom said, clicking his keyboard quickly, "you want this sewing school to teach English along with the sewing skills." I started to interrupt. He continued. "And you want it to have a daycare centre as well. For just the students or for other people as well?"

I wasn't sure about that, but Tom wasn't quite getting that I didn't want this to be just one school. I wanted a string of these schools across the country and in the U.S. I wanted the Tara Foundation to be a partner. And I wanted to fund them. I told him all this.

"That's ambitious, Charlie. Do you have any idea how complicated the logistics of getting even a few of these schools up and running might be? And you have no idea if the women you see as your students would be interested. I'm not saying it's impossible, but it might be close to it."

I knew he was right, but I felt like he was raining on my parade. "*Every noble work is at first impossible*," I said.

"The *great man theory*?" he said.

I nodded. "Thomas Carlyle. Great woman theory, too, as far as I'm concerned."

"Okay, Charlie. You asked me for my business advice. You know I've started up two successful businesses, but neither was focused on any kind of social good. That being said, I think I might have some insights for you. Would you be willing to start small? A kind of pilot project?"

"You mean open only a few schools to start?"

"I mean, open one school to start. Open it right here in the city so you can have complete oversight. Figure out how to recruit students, if they're interested at all. And by the way, there are some cultural barriers related to women's roles you might have to get over."

I knew what he was talking about. As much as I might see learning the language as the ticket to a family's financial and social success, women (and men) from other cultures might not see it the same way. I hoped Fatima might help me understand these issues and bridge them. But first, I had to talk to Elizabeth. This idea wouldn't work without her support—or at least I didn't want to carry on without it.

"And Charlie," Tom said, "this is going to be time-consuming. I know you, and you'll put your heart and soul into it. That might mean your writing will get put on the back burner, not to mention your teaching job."

I hadn't given that too much thought. I figured I could do it all and was slightly insulted that Tom seemed to think I had so many limitations. On the other hand, he might be right. I did have that book to finish, and I did have a job.

"Then there's us," Tom said. "Where do we fit into your plan?"

It had never occurred to me that *we* didn't fit in. I thought I could do it all. Suddenly I realized that I would have to set priorities. I had to know, without any doubt in my mind, what my number one priority would be. I looked at Tom. "I promise you, Tom, that you are my family and that my family will always be my first priority."

Tom smiled. "I know. I just wanted to check."

~

When I called her a few days later, Elizabeth was delighted that I was interested in helping with the project. I sensed some hesitation, though, when I began telling her about my idea for how it could be something more.

"I hope you don't feel that I'm horning in on your idea or wanting to take it over," I said. "It's just that I thought we could do more and do it together. But I won't do it without you since I'm really piggy-backing on you."

"Charlotte, I think it's a wonderful idea. It's bold and big, but I expected nothing less from you. You are your mother's daughter. It's just that…" She trailed off.

"Elizabeth, I'm sure whatever your concerns are, we can deal with them," I said. "I would sure like to give this idea a try."

"Charlotte, dear, as the old saying goes, it's not you. It's me." I could hear her intake of breath. "It's just that I might not be able to be a great deal of help in an enlarged project. I've just been diagnosed with cancer."

"Oh, Elizabeth, no!"

"It's quite fine, Charlotte. I'm of an age, as you know. Things happen. I don't expect to die any time soon, but I will need treatment, which will make me less of an asset to you. I had hoped to be relying on you."

I was devastated at Elizabeth's news. I had come to love her and look to her for advice on things I might have asked Mom about before she died. Now, to think that I might lose her as well! In any case, I wouldn't let her worry. She could count on me.

"Charlotte," Elizabeth continued, "cancer isn't always a death sentence these days, you know."

It sure sounded like one to me. Then Elizabeth said she was happy for us to explore the possibility of expanding the idea to encompass more than just sewing classes. My delight with this news was slightly diminished by Elizabeth's news, but I'd have to deal with it.

~

Fatima responded to my email within twenty-four hours, and we were on the phone the next day. She seemed as seized with the idea as I was, although her excitement was tempered with much fuller knowledge of the landscape than I had. Her main concern was that I would have to be able to fully express how my idea was different from all the other groups and resources that were already out there.

"I've been doing some research on that," I said. "I hadn't realized that so many groups and organizations in various cities offered help to women who came to North America as refugees."

"Then, you probably already know, Charlie, that there are places where services like employment support, coaching and even childcare are already offered. It probably isn't necessary to duplicate such services. But I think I hear you saying that you see this place as something different."

"Yes, Fatima, I do. I see it as a space where women could learn or relearn sewing skills, but most importantly, learn to speak English so that they have many more opportunities. I was thinking how much easier it would be for them if they could even just speak to their children's teachers."

"Okay," Fatima said. "If you can prepare a document describing your mission and vision along with an implementation plan, I can take it to my board. They will need that at a minimum. I think that having the backing of an established organization might help the project in the long run."

I could not have agreed more. There was one more person I needed to get on board with this project.

~

"Hello, little sister," Evelyn said when she picked up the phone the following evening. "How's everything going out there on the coast?"

I could hear crying in the background. I sounded like little Katherine might be demanding something.

"Everything's great here. How's your new house?" I hadn't yet visited Evelyn in her new accommodation—a five-thousand square-foot house in an area of Toronto called Rosedale—the same Rosedale where our great-grandmother Frannie had lived for a short time in the 1940s. Unlike me, Evelyn hadn't had any trouble deciding where to spend a big chunk of her inheritance.

We chatted about a few mundane things for a while—her law partners, her husband, my husband, my teaching job—then she asked me about Frannie's unfinished manuscript. I gave her the Coles notes version of the rest of the story as I understood it.

"Dear god, Charlie! Of course, you'll finish writing Frannie's book!" It sounded very much like a demand.

"I think I will."

"What do you mean you think you will? There should be no question whatsoever. This seems like something you simply have to do, or why are you even a writer?"

That was something I really didn't want to get into at this point. "Yeah, of course, Evelyn. I will get to it, but I'm not really a romance writer."

"Well, as far as I can tell, since you're not writing anything at the moment, you're not any kind of writer. What have you got to lose?"

Ouch! I had a sudden urge to slap her (as impossible since we were on the phone), but I knew she had a point, and I needed to get back to the reason I'd called her in the first place. "I'll think about it, Evelyn, but I need your help with something right now."

"My help? Sounds ominous, although I do love it when you need my help. What can I do?"

"I'm working on a new project," I said. "Do you still see Erica Flanagan socially?"

"Erica? Why?"

"Do you still see her?"

"Of course," Evelyn said. "Erica and I are great friends. We still have lunch once a month, and we occasionally take our husbands out to dinner together. Why?"

Erica Flanagan was one of those journalist-turned-TV-talk-show-hosts that seem to populate the daytime television airwaves. Along with three other equally charming (*cough*) and energetic women, she was a co-host of Canada's most popular daytime talk show. I'd recently read that it was even gaining traction in the very competitive American market.

"I think my project could be a great national story. I'm hoping you might help me get my project on Erica's show to garner some publicity."

"Don't you hate her?" Evelyn said, not even asking about the nature of the project. I will admit she had good reason to bring this up since I'd made it quite clear on the odd occasions when Erica's name came up that I was less than charmed by her—despite her well-documented, audience-poll-verified popularity quotient. Erica's on-air snarky persona might play well with her afternoon television audience, but it had never sat well with me. "In fact," Evelyn continued, "I seem to remember you referring to her as a sell-out hack with the personality of a viper."

I laughed. "My, my, Evelyn, motherhood hasn't diminished your perfect memory."

"Yes, and that time you met her at a cocktail party at our place once when you were visiting, you took such a dislike to her that you deliberately spilled your drink on her."

"That wasn't deliberate!"

"If you say so," Evelyn said. "Anyway, how do you expect me to get her to say yes to giving you some airtime, especially since you've been deliberately vague about this project?"

Evelyn knew me so well. Yes, I was being vague. "You don't have to land an interview. I only need you to get me connected with her."

"Do I need to know what this project is all about?"

"I'll tell you eventually. Does it matter?"

"Not really, I suppose," Evelyn said.

"Anyway," I continued, "I might not even be the one she has to interact with. So, you don't have to worry that I might disturb your chummy relationship."

"Oh, I'm not at all worried about that. But I do think I at least owe Erica the opportunity to snap at you a bit, so I'll set her up with *you*. After that, you can explore how to get it on the air and who will do it if she's interested. But remember, I can't promise anything. And I need to hear every detail of your meeting with her—verbatim!"

That was good enough for me.

~

I had almost forgotten, but there was one other person I wanted to discuss this with—Al. He and his mother knew the situation of newcomers to our country so much better than I could even imagine. They knew it even better than Fatima did since she had already been in the U.S. when the civil war in Syria started back in 2011.

I called *Sew Fine Things* and spoke with Tobias. He told me that Mrs. Nassar (I still didn't know her first name or if she was now Mrs. Goldfarb) would be in the shop the following afternoon and that I should come along.

When I arrived, Mrs. Nassar was with a customer, so I took advantage of the opportunity to look around the store. I still hadn't done anything with the fabrics I'd bought, but I wanted more. As I ran my hand over the wools and silks, I began to think about Megan McMaster and her idea that fashion harmed the environment, and then I thought about sewing. Surely that must be more environmentally friendly? But textile manufacturing was the same whether you made your own clothing or bought it. Then there was all that scrap material. I knew this from first-hand experience. I had always puzzled about what I should do with those scraps. Whenever I put them in the trash, I felt I might be missing something. I thought about Juliette back in Paris and wondered if she had any thoughts about this situation. I'd have to make a note to email her. She'd be wondering about the ending of the Sinclair story anyway. My thoughts were interrupted by Mrs. Nassar, who was gently tapping my arm to get my attention.

She ushered me into the back office, which was spotless and modern. I accepted the offered tea, and we settled in to chat about my project idea.

I had expected her to be wildly enthusiastic about it, but she seemed lukewarm. I didn't know her well enough to understand whether this was just her way or if she had issues with it.

"Mrs. Nassar," I began, "I would really appreciate your opinion on the need for such a project."

"Charlotte, my dear, I am impressed by your passion for helping women who come to this country. And I do agree that helping them helps their families in a major way. I am only cautious about…and you will pardon me, please. I mean no disrespect. But I am cautious about a privileged white woman as the face of such an enterprise. There is much to be disliked about those who do good works for their own self-aggrandizement."

I felt as if I had been punched in the stomach. "I am so sorry that this project comes across that way."

Mrs. Nassar shook her head. "You do not understand. It is not because I believe this to be the case. It is not that I believe you are doing this for the accolades that will surely come your way from the mainstream media. I am only concerned about how it looks from the newcomer community."

"I hadn't thought about that. I suppose it's because there are already certain types of organizations set up to provide support services, and they're running smoothly without anyone thinking they've been set up for the wrong reasons."

"Yes, that is true, my dear." She sat back and folded her hands elegantly in her lap.

I had been so enthusiastic that I had not considered the possibility that others would be more cautious or even have misgivings. Then it hit me.

"Mrs. Nassar, would you consider leading a board of directors to manage these schools and run the foundation?"

When she said yes (without even hesitating), that was the moment I knew that although this was something I wanted to do, I would have to get it started and then let it go—go to those who knew more about these things than I did.

Mrs. Nassar was true to her word and took over efficiently and capably. Within weeks, she had made contacts with people across the country and was organizing the first meeting. I put her in touch with Erica Flanagan's assistant, and they arranged for her to appear on the show in due course. I didn't even have to talk to Erica—a small relief, and there would be no need to report back to Evelyn on our encounter. I established a fund for the project, then stepped back and watched it begin.

What I was supposed to do with my life was still elusive.

THIRTY-FOUR

SIX MONTHS LATER, I WAS IN THE MIDDLE of a challenging semester at school. The students I had loved the first year I'd taught at Princess Margaret College now seemed less engaged and more flippant about their writing classes than when I began teaching and working as the writer-in-residence. I had been so impressed by their commitment to learning how to craft stories and had enjoyed every minute with them. Now it seemed that things had changed.

You might well ask if the problem was really so much that the students were less engaged or if I was. That would be a fair question, and the answer was probably a resounding yes. It was my problem if you'd asked my students. And the truth was that I hadn't written a single word in months. If a writer isn't writing, then she's not a writer. Isn't that what my dear sister had said? I had lost my writing motivation.

I was in a slump, and I had no reason to be. I had everything anyone could ever want in life. I had a wonderful husband who loved me, and we lived in a beautiful house. I had what used to be interesting work to do and good friends. We could take a vacation to anywhere in the world we chose and go first-class all the way. I had more money than I knew what to do with. And that was the problem. I still felt that money was somehow the primary determining factor in my life's purpose. The only smart thing I seemed to have done in recent months was rekindling a friendship with Al Nassar. We had begun regular email correspondence.

The year after Mom died, I had come to rely on my monthly visits to Al in the fabric store. He always seemed to have some words of wisdom for me—words that hit the target spot-on even when I didn't want them to. Now that he was back to being Dr. Alvero Nassar (something that had come as quite a shock to me), he

PATRICIA J. PARSONS

was no less forthright in countering my whining with his astuteness and vast knowledge of the world.

I had kept the depth of my listlessness to myself for months. Then finally, I just had to hear what Al thought about my situation. I feared that he'd see me as an over-privileged woman who couldn't get her act together, a characterization that was like fingernails on a chalkboard to my ego. To his credit, he was a bit gentler than I deserved.

"Dear Charlie. I am distressed to hear that you are still searching for that thing you are supposed to be doing with your life. I had thought that you were doing many wonderful things—being a wonderful partner to Tom, sharing your writing gift with the leaders of tomorrow, giving back through charitable means, generally making the planet a better place. I know you often feel that others have suffered so much more than you in your life, and perhaps you are undeserving of your privilege. Although that may be true on the surface, not everyone is meant to experience the same things.

We often spend much time in our lives searching for life's secret as if there might be only one and we are not privy to it. We look at others and think that they are the ones who have gained such knowledge. I do not believe that this is so. I do not believe that there is a single secret of life, despite what many wise people might have told us through the centuries.

One Indian swami has told us that the secret of life is to have no fear. An interesting consideration but hardly all-encompassing. Others have said, in so many ways, that the secret is to get up more times than you fall. Good advice, but not a panacea for all of life. Others say to choose your risks or to ask for what you want. None of these are secrets, by the way. Many people throughout the centuries have said much the same thing. I believe that if there is a secret, it is that there is no secret. You reach the top of the mountain to visit the enlightened one you believe will give you the secret you are missing. We all do this. Yet, when you arrive, you realize there is no secret.

What you need is inside yourself. It has always been there and will always be there. You will not find your happiness or success in what you accomplish or how others see you now or after death. You must look within.

Mark Twain wrote that you should give every day the chance to become the most beautiful day of your life. And Charlie, I believe that if you look inside yourself, you will see the potential for the beauty of every day. Your friend always, Al."

I sat for a long time, staring at the screen. Al's words began to shimmer and wobble until they swam before my eyes, each word, in turn, reaching out toward me and then receding like an ocean wave. I don't know how long I sat there trying to figure out what was inside me that I could reach in and find. What was that thing that made my life what it was supposed to be? But unlike in the movies, where the heroine suddenly awakens and knows without hesitation what comes next, I didn't have an epiphany. But what I did know was that Al was right. I think I'd known it all along.

~

The school year was finally over. I had now been at Princess Margaret College for two years doing a job I'd initially loved but not one I had ever intended to do. A month before the semester ended, my boss, Devin, the headmaster, asked me how things were going. I had wondered if he'd noticed that my enthusiasm had diminished. I was honest with him.

"I haven't been writing as much as I thought I would," I said to him that day as we chatted in his office. "I suspect I haven't been writing as much as you might have expected your writer-in-residence to do, either."

"Oh, my dear," he said in his northern-English-almost-Scottish accent, "you'd be surprised at how many writers-in-residence do no writing of substance while in the employ of schools such as ours. You did publish a book since you've been here, so that's something. But how are you really doing?"

I carefully told him that I seemed to be re-evaluating my career.

"Well, I suppose that's to be expected at your age. Let me know what you decide, Charlotte."

As soon as I knew myself, he'd be high on the list of people who needed a heads-up.

Around the same time I had this conversation with Devin, Evelyn had also called to ask how the work was going on finishing our great-grandmother's manuscript.

"About that," I said.

"Don't tell me you haven't been working on it," Evelyn said. "It's a half-finished book that was dropped in your lap like a gift. I would have thought any writer would swoon over that kind of opportunity. What more are you waiting for?"

I honestly didn't have an answer for her. What, indeed.

After my first week of summer holiday aimlessness, Tom came home one evening and sat me down. "Charlie, you know I love you." *Dear god*, I thought, *that's not an encouraging opening*. He continued. "I want nothing more than for you to be happy, but it seems that ever since you inherited that money from your great-grandmother, you've had this heavy burden sitting on you like a lead anvil. It seems to be pressing all the joy out of your life."

It was hard for me to argue with that depiction. I did feel like something was sitting on me heavily, and I wanted nothing more than to shake it off. I just didn't know where to look for inspiration.

"Look, Charlie," Tom said, "maybe you need a change of scenery. Why don't you go back to Paris for a few weeks and stay in your flat? You can visit Juliette, and I'll come over for a few days to see the city with you."

"Tom, would you come?"

He nodded enthusiastically. "Of course. I think I can get away for a few days in August, so we could have a mini-holiday in the city of love."

I called our travel agent the next day and booked the tickets. But I still had to get through the next two weeks.

~

For as long as I can remember, I have always loved a library. I remembered visiting the children's section of our local library with my mother and Evelyn before I was even old enough to go to school. Evelyn had to be dragged—I later wondered how she managed to be such a good student since she seemed to loathe reading—but I would be the first one outside the house, standing by the car waiting for our outing. I could have spent hours meandering in the book stacks, pulling one here and there, reading a page or two, putting it back, finding another. And on it went. As I got older, the library became my refuge. Whenever I had something on my mind, I took myself off to the university library to sit in a comfortable reading chair and enjoy the hushed atmosphere. I didn't even need to be reading a book. I could just sit there and enjoy being surrounded by the things that brought me the most joy in the world: books. So, I thought, I need to revisit that joy.

I made a date with myself to visit a couple of bookstores (I loved them almost as much as the library) and the main university library. I would spend the day among books.

The first bookstore I visited was one of those mega-bookstores where the company president had fully embraced the notion of diversification. I hadn't been in one for a very long time, but now I found myself standing in a section of the so-called bookstore that offered "lifestyle" items—there were cushions, candle holders, throws and even socks. There was a whole shelf of mugs with cutesy sayings.

I picked one up. It said, *"Please do not annoy the writer. She might put you in a book and kill you."* That made me smile. I put it back and picked up the next one. *"I may look like I'm listening to you, but in my head, I'm writing a novel."* I kind of liked that one.

"I think you might like this one."

I turned to see where the voice was coming from. The voice's owner was an older man with wild silver hair and a smile as wide as he was tall. He was holding a mug, which he offered to me. I took it from him and looked down at its message.

"When something in your life feels wrong, just yell 'Plot Twist!' and keep going."

I looked up to say thank you, but he was gone. I bought the mug and took it home. I poured a cup of coffee in it, yelled "Plot twist!" loudly into the empty house, headed to my office upstairs and sat down in front of the computer.

Frannie's unfinished, typewritten manuscript was still sitting in the middle of the desk in front of the computer screen. The pages were starting to get tattered around the edges since they had spent the trip from Paris last summer in my carry-on bag and been dragged back and forth to my writing group. I'd been moving it from one side of the desk to the other ever since. I had moved it back into the middle of the desk several times since I'd spoken with Evelyn a few months back. Her words about me not being any kind of a writer at all if I wasn't writing rang in my ears.

I had told Evelyn that I wasn't a romance writer. But what kind of writer was I? I looked at the mug sitting where I had placed it on a coaster my students had given me last Christmas. The coaster was emblazoned with a saying I had repeated to them more than once. They were making a point. The coaster said, *"Jump, and the net will appear."* It seemed it was time to take my own advice.

I opened a new file on my computer, took the elastic band off the manuscript and began writing.

Chapter 1
What the hell am I doing with my life? This was not the first time this thought had crossed my mind, and it wouldn't be the last.

THIRTY-FIVE

BY THE TIME I LEFT FOR PARIS, I had transcribed the entire first half of the book just as Frannie had written it. I had packed several notebooks and my laptop because I suddenly felt I had to get the rest of the story down on paper—or at least into a computer file. So much time had passed, though, that I was beginning to lose the details. The story was becoming increasingly hazy. Then it occurred to me that it didn't matter. Tim's story would only be my inspiration. It didn't have to be the literal story as it happened. I also wanted to spend some time sitting at Frannie's writing desk to do some revisions to the book's first half. When I arrived at the Paris apartment, I was so excited that I emailed Etienne and asked him if I could meet with him at his office. Frannie might have had trouble pitching this book to her publisher, but I was determined to pitch it successfully to her publisher's descendants. Then I made my way to a *boulangerie*, bought some wonderfully aromatic chocolate-filled croissants, and knocked on Juliette's door.

Juliette had been expecting me and met me at the door, leaning on her cane. I noticed that she seemed to have aged markedly since last summer. When she hugged me, she felt all skin and bones. I was alarmed.

"Juliette, how are you?" I'm sure my face was a mask of concern.

Juliette looked at me and frowned. "Not you too? *Pourquoi tout le monde est-il si préoccupé per ma santé*? Why is everyone so concerned about my health? I am good. I am merely old. It happens to all of us should we live so long." She chuckled, and I followed her inside.

Just as the first time I'd visited Juliette, I was immediately mesmerized by the modern décor—the creamy white walls and upholstery with those pops of turquoise and black. Juliette's housekeeper, Genevieve, was placing a large silver tray laden with

241

teacups, a large porcelain teapot, and champagne glasses on the coffee table. I could see a bottle of champagne chilling in a matching silver bucket beside Juliette's chair, where she sat down carefully, placing her cane close at hand.

"You remember Genevieve?" Juliette said by way of reintroduction.

"Of course. *Bon jour*, Genevieve. *Comment ça va?*"

"I stay well, madame," Genevieve said as she returned to the kitchen. "Please enjoy."

"Now, my dear," Juliette said as she picked up the champagne bottle, wrapped it in the snow-white linen napkin hanging on the side of the cooler, and passed it to me. "Would you do the honours, please?"

I was becoming something of an expert with champagne corks these days, so I was able to remove it with no more than a slight pop followed by a release of fine mist. I poured us each a glass.

"We must begin with a champagne toast. It is far more civilized than tea, do you not agree?" Juliette raised her glass. I raised mine as she continued. "We must drink a toast to your great-grandmother and my great friend, Fran. May her final story be her best one. And may her great-granddaughter know the pleasures of the writing life as she gives her own gift to the world."

I took a deep breath, and we gently clinked glasses. I found the sentiment a bit sobering under the circumstances. The pleasures of the writing life—there was something I had never considered. Pleasures, indeed. I would have to give that some thought.

When Juliette asked me how the work was going, I took another deep breath and told her I'd only just begun. "Every time I begin to think about it as a project, I seem to find myself up against an obstacle. Of course, I realize it's all in my head, as my mother used to say, but knowing that doesn't make the obstacle go away. And it isn't that I don't want to do it. At this point, there's nothing I want more. It's just that I've never thought of myself as a romance writer."

"What kind of writer are you, my dear?"

"I'm..." I was at a loss. I really didn't know.

"Oh, my dear girl," she said, "you have taken on a project begun by someone else. You need to make it your own. I knew Fran well, and I do not believe that your great-grandmother would have wanted you to feel as if you are taking on *her* project. It must be yours." Juliette tipped her champagne glass by its stem and sipped what remained in her glass. She retrieved the bottle from the ice bucket and poured herself another half glass. "Do you know of your great-grandmother's friendship with the famed Simone de Beauvoir?"

I nodded, remembering how astounded I'd been when I read in Fran's diary that she knew the great-grandmother of modern feminism. "Yes. As a matter of fact, Juliette, did you know that Ms. de Beauvoir sent Fran a signed first edition of her book *The Second Sex*?"

Juliette's eyebrows lifted toward her hairline. "*Mon dieu*, Charlotte, do you know how much that might be worth?"

"Priceless? Well, at least it is to me."

"But of course." She took another sip and then placed her glass on the coffee table. "I mention Simone only for the fact that she once wrote something that has stayed with me for all these years. I offer it to you. She said, *Capabilities are clearly manifested only when they have been realized.* You must recognize and use your aptitudes and gifts before you can see them."

I knew I was going to have to write that one down.

~

There must have been something about being in Paris, sitting in Fran's office, at her writing desk. I looked over at her old typewriter and pictured her bending over it, typing her manuscripts. Then I opened my laptop and started. I could feel my fingers flying over the keyboard, grasping for the story before it got away from me. Every time my fingers began to hesitate, and I started to edit myself, something seemed to propel me forward. It was as if someone or something was giving me a mystical nudge. I was enjoying the thought that it was great-grandmother Frannie herself, somewhere in the ether, propelling me onward. I kept writing.

After three hours of essentially non-stop writing, I sat back and looked at the computer file on the screen. I thought about Tim and Megan Sinclair and their great love story. But I realized that the story that was even more interesting to me was Ellie's—how she had a wartime, whirlwind romance that was never to be. Yet, it had an effect that continued and continues even now down through the generations that followed. Her romance with William Sinclair in 1942 meant that Megan existed, and although Megan never had any children of her own, her very existence was the key to bringing Ava, another budding artist, to where she was today. So much of what happened after that would never have occurred if Ellie had not met William and if she had not chosen to love and care for her daughter Anne and her granddaughter, Megan, the way she did. That seemed to me to be the truest definition of romance. Then it struck me.

Fran couldn't have known any of this when she stopped writing her manuscript. She knew only that the story began in wartime and that her friend Ellie sent Tim, a young man she was able to meet only once, to talk with her. Then she died. She had no way of knowing that her great-granddaughter would find the unfinished manuscript over thirty years later and wonder what she was supposed to do with it. Or did she?

I don't know how long I sat there at the desk, staring out the window. Fran didn't know I would find the people who inspired her characters and discover that their stories might let others see the world through different eyes. She could never have imagined how interconnected we all are. And my story—our story—would put these romantic ideas into a world in desperate need of romance in its truest form. Perhaps my idea of the romantic story would dwell on the impracticality of the quixotic dream, but a story—any story—could conjure ideas, for better or for worse. I only knew that

I wanted my stories to be for better. The moment this occurred to me was the moment I knew, without a doubt, that it was *my* story to tell.

It no longer had to be "our" story. I need not share it with Fran. She would probably never have wanted that anyway. It was mine. It was in that moment of absolute clarity, sitting as I was in a Paris apartment that was mine—not formerly my great-grandmother's, but mine—that I realized my problem. I realized what I'd been grappling with ever since the disposition of Fran's estate made me a wealthy woman. I was wealthy in the financial sense only. I was impoverished unless I chose to get out from under myself.

It was then that I realized the wellspring of my problem. I had been looking for something to prod me onward. I had been looking in the wrong place. I thought about something I'd read when I was studying for my M.F.A. in creative writing in grad school. Great writer Isak Dinesen had once said that *"to be a person is to have a story to tell."* I had a story to tell—perhaps many stories—and perhaps that's what made me a person. Some of these stories would become the books I wrote, but I suspected the most important one would be the one I chose to live. Either way, I knew my stories had to come from within me. No one—not even a long-dead great-grandmother—could nudge me onward if I hadn't the internal fortitude to do it for myself.

My mind was spinning with the possibilities. I had three more days until Tom would arrive in Paris, and I wanted to have my head sorted out by the time he got here. We would have so much to discuss. In the meantime, I kept writing, but I also made an appointment to see Etienne Lemieux. Although his predecessors might have passed on Fran's new book idea, I wasn't about to let this new generation of publishers let this one go.

~

Two days later, I found myself sitting in the stunning offices of *Éditions Lemieux*. Located in a mansion in the sixteenth *arrondissement*, the attached building looked as if it might have once been the home of a member of the Parisian aristocracy. From my research of Paris streets, I knew this was a prestigious address. Located at the end of a broad avenue lined with nineteenth-century homes equally as impressive, the publishing offices were only about five blocks from the *Arc de Triomphe*. I was also aware that this district was home to some of the most expensive real estate in the city—a city known for its eye-wateringly high prices.

I stood for a moment to take in the grandeur of the building, then walked up three steps where I expected to ring a bell. Instead of a bell, though, there was a camera, a screen and a keypad. I clicked the key that suggested it might be a doorbell of sorts. A moment later, the screen was filled with the smiling face of a young woman sporting Instagram-worthy eye makeup and a complexion so clear I wondered if her camera had a filter. She greeted me cheerfully, and after using my very best French to announce myself, she bid me enter. The lock clicked, and I opened the heavy door, entering a black-and-white tiled foyer not dissimilar to the one in my apartment building. She had told me to walk directly up the stairs with their black, wrought-iron railing.

I sank into the rich carpet with each step up and realized that this must be one of the ways they were able to dampen sound to the extent that one wondered if there was work of any sort going on. However, when I reached the top and opened the door to the inner chamber, I immediately found myself in a large, bright beehive of activity. And the complexion of the young woman whose face I'd seen downstairs on the screen? There was no filter.

After introducing herself as Agathe, Etienne's assistant, she led me to a room resembling a comfortable family dining room more than a board room. But I could see the telltale signs of modern technology in the computer screens and the overhead projector that were discreetly placed so that they didn't interfere with what I recognized as Louis XIV style architecture and furniture. The ornate features of the style were unmistakable, from the intricately inlaid wood of the large conference (dining?) table to the carved legs of the leather-upholstered chairs. Agathe invited me to take a seat and said she'd be back with espresso and Etienne momentarily.

Before I'd even had a chance to admire the room's details fully, Etienne appeared. He was carrying the tray of espressos and croissants, which he put on the table in front of where I was sitting.

"Ah, Ms. Hudson, what a delight to see you again! I trust all has gone well for you since we met last summer? Agathe did not indicate to me the nature of your visit, but I am happy to simply visit with you."

He offered me an espresso, which I gratefully accepted. "Thank you so much, Etienne. It's wonderful to see you, too. And these offices! They are magnificent!"

"Are they not?" he said proudly. "I am so grateful to my great-uncle that he had such good taste and rather deep pockets. There would be no way for a publishing firm these days to be able to afford the purchase price. *Mon dieu!* The prices in this neighbourhood—they are *scandaleux*!"

We laughed and chatted a bit about real estate in Paris. I happened to know that my own apartment on the Left Bank was well up into the seven-figures, as the realtors at home liked to say. (Being married to a real estate broker ensured I was up-to-date on my real estate holdings. Tom wouldn't have it any other way.) Still, I had no intention of selling it. That was one decision I'd made since I returned to Paris this week. Then, I set my empty espresso cup down and began my pitch.

When I was finished pitching the story of true romance across the decades, Etienne sat back against the high leather back of his chair and steepled his fingers. He said nothing for what seemed like several minutes, but I suspect it was only seconds. He pursed his lips and said, "That was a wonderful story, Charlotte. You are a true

247

storyteller. Is that not your great-grandmother's story that my predecessors rejected?"

I shook my head. "No, Etienne, it is not. It is *my* story inspired by Fran's plan for a book. What do you think?"

"I think you should send me a sample."

"Already done. I sent it this morning before I left. It should be in your email as we speak."

Etienne lifted his phone from a pocket and tapped into his email account. He pursed his lips again and sat back, reading for a moment or two. "I will say this, Charlotte, you have your great-grandmother's gift."

I said nothing. I suspected, however, that I didn't have her gift at all. I had my gift.

He read for a few more minutes before speaking again. "From what I read here and the pitch you have made, I believe this is a book that should be published."

I began to relax and even let myself start to become excited and immediately started picturing my name on the cover and inside, the gratitude and dedication to Frannie Phillips, aka F.E. de Plessis. It almost made me tingle.

Then Etienne said, "But we cannot publish this book."

My eyes widened in shock. "But I thought you said—"

Etienne waved his hand at me. "Wait, wait. I did say that it should be published, but I feel *Éditions Lemieux* would not do it justice."

My heart sank into my ankle booties, and I felt like I might start crying at any moment. This was going to be harder than I thought.

"But before you get too disappointed," Etienne said, reading my mind, or so it seemed, "know that I will facilitate this. We have a subsidiary in New York. Do you have an agent to negotiate on your behalf?"

I did not.

"Not a problem. I will set up a meeting for you with *The Leonard Group*. It might amuse you to know that this group of young literary agents began as *Priestley Benjamin,* your great-grandmother's literary agency."

I perked up at that thought.

"Yes, Margaret Priestley's protégée took it over when she retired, and it has gone on to have a life of yet another generation. I believe Leonard himself still goes into the office from time to time. I do not know how old he would be. In any case, you must go to New York."

~

My head was full of thoughts of New York when Tom arrived in Paris, pulling up in front of my apartment building in a taxi from the airport as I looked down from my window. I watched him as he stood there with luggage on the sidewalk beside him. Just as I had done the first time I had encountered this building, Tom stood there for several moments, gazing up, his eyes no doubt taking the measure of the building as any real estate magnate might do. He didn't see me waving in the window.

I stepped back to go to the door, wondering what he'd think of my next junket to New York. I hadn't told him anything about this yet—I thought it would be better to discuss it with him in person.

I was standing in the open door when he emerged from the tiny elevator. It was so good to see my wonderful husband, who had taken the time away from a busy summer of work to spend a few days with me. After we fell into each other's arms for a moment, he stood back and whistled as we stepped across the threshold into the apartment.

"Whew, Charlie," he said as he dropped his carry-on bag on the floor. "Even your photos didn't do this place justice. It's wonderful!"

"Isn't it?" I said, beaming. I was delighted that he seemed to love it as much as I did. "Let me show you around."

When we'd finished the tour, I whisked Tom off to my favourite neighbourhood patisserie, *Belle Vie,* the only one nearby with table service. I knew only too well that after an all-night flight, all you really want to do is eat a French pastry and drink coffee so that you can press on through the day to ward off jet lag. The biggest mistake in these situations was to take a nap. He'd fall into bed early tonight, but I'd give him a first-day tour of the Left Bank before that happened. So, we were off.

I kept him moving all through the day. When we finally sat down to a bottle of wine and a homemade *croc monsieur* (I'd learned a few quick and easy French recipes), I told him about my meeting with Etienne. Tom was delighted that I'd begun furiously writing and was concerned that his arrival might stop the creative flow. I assured him the story was not going anywhere and then asked him what he thought of my planned foray to New York to acquire a literary agent and potentially a publishing contract.

"Charlie, it's what you should do, but there is a slight problem."

I was all ears.

"The summer is moving along rapidly, and you still have a teaching job to get back to in September. You really need to think carefully about this. There are other people involved. Are you going to continue teaching?"

How could such a thing have slipped my mind? I was guessing it was because when I was in Paris, I almost felt like I was living someone else's life. Yet that was so wrong, given what I'd begun to realize about myself. No, it wasn't someone else's life. It was my life.

I wasn't sure what to say to Tom in answer to his very astute question and not because I didn't want to answer. I didn't know what the answer was. Did I want to return to my teaching job? It had seemed so important to me when I'd landed it. But that was partially because, at the time, I realized I needed to take a more practical approach to making a living other than simply living off the meagre avails of a part-time gig at the university library and the odd sale of a piece of writing. That was before I knew I didn't need the money. So, if I were being completely honest with myself, I had to answer the question: was I teaching just for the paycheque, or was it something I wanted or needed to do with my life?

I realized that the teaching job at Princess Margaret College was something I figured I should do when I took the position. I liked the idea of it, but I didn't ever think it was really me. The honest answer was that it was just for the money (and to have a real job as Evelyn, my ever-practical sister, said everyone should have). I suddenly realized that this wasn't fair to the school, and it certainly wasn't fair to the students. Perhaps it wasn't even fair to me. At that moment, I made my decision: I would give my notice immediately so that Devin, my boss, could start looking for someone else. I wondered if my truck driver-turned-romance-writer Karl from my writer's group (with his almost-Ph.D.—a story for another day) might be interested. The position also included being the writer-in-residence, a perfect fit for Karl. I would connect with him first, and if he showed any interest at all, I'd recommend him to Devin.

The next morning, I told Tom I'd made my decision.

"About time, Charlie, my love," he said, taking a large bite out of a *pain au chocolat* as we ate breakfast at home before starting out on a day of museum-hopping.

"What do you mean, about time?"

"What I mean, my darling wife, is that I've perceived for a long time that this job was just that for you: a job. You need so much more than a job. Look, I've spent all my adult life up until now doing exactly what I've been passionate about at the time. And, as you well know, that passion has changed. Lots of people seem to think that you choose one thing, and you have to keep at that for your whole life. They think that if you change gears—as I did—you're not committed. It's nonsense. Everyone evolves, and our passions often change. But for you, my love, your passion has never changed. You're a writer. It's just who you are."

"But you know I've been trying to figure out what I'm supposed to be doing with all that money—and my life for that matter."

"About that," Tom said as he poured himself another cup of coffee from my French press. "That money isn't *you*, Charlie. It's just something you have."

"But I have to do something with it."

"Do you?" he said. "When Jason and I were just starting out developing our business plan for our I.T. start-up, we did a lot of reading. I stumbled on Thoreau's work and liked how grounded it made me feel. I distinctly remember one particularly striking piece of wisdom. He once wrote that wealth is the ability to experience life fully. It isn't about the bank balance or even how much of it you give away or where you give it. You—and I—will only ever be as wealthy as our experiences are rich."

I put down my coffee cup and got up from my chair. I went around to the other side of the table and wrapped my arms around this wise man I'd married. "I think I must be the wisest woman in the world." Tom frowned. "I married you, didn't I?"

~

I can't tell you how far we walked that day because I didn't check my step-counter app, but we walked a distance. We visited the *Louvre* (as you do) to see the Mona Lisa, *the Musée d'Orsay* (my favourite in all of Paris) to see the Degas collection, *Galleries Lafayette* (I never said a retail mecca didn't count as a museum, did I?) to buy lingerie and ended at the Eiffel Tower (because every tourist needs *that* photo). By the time we arrived back at the apartment, we were exhausted, but we couldn't sit and put our feet up for too long. Juliette had invited us to dinner. I think she was dying to meet Tom.

Juliette's housekeeper Genevieve had the evening off, so she had hired her stand-in housekeeper—a young man named Alphonse. Alphonse was quite a character. He greeted us at the door with a bow and a dazzling smile that showed his vibrant white teeth. No more than about twenty-one or so years old by the look of him, he had a lock of dark hair hanging over one eye that looked a bit out of place with the crisp white shirt and black bow tie he sported. He seemed to be perpetually chuckling. I liked him on sight and wondered where in the world Juliette had found him.

When we found her, she was sitting comfortably beside the fireplace, which, oddly for the summer in Paris, was lit. She looked small and fragile, but her smile belied any underlying problem she might be having at her advanced age. Every time I thought about Paris, I wondered when I'd learn of her death. She seemed like the sort of woman who just might surprise me by outliving all of us.

Juliette welcomed us into the living room without getting up. "I see you have met my Alphonse," she said by way of introduction. "He studies to be a chef at the *Cordon Bleu* and does a bit of work for me from time to time when Genevieve is not able to be here. I do not tell her ever, but he is the better cook."

Alphonse beamed and nodded his thanks.

It transpired that Alphonse was not only a magnificent cook, creating a *classic coq au vin* like I'd never before tasted (he refused to divulge his secret) and apple *mille-feuille* for dessert. It was by far the best French meal I had ever had—and I'd thought that a few times recently. I asked him for his card—I was joking, but he was able to produce it from his back pocket—so that I could follow his career. I predicted he would be the most famous Michelin-starred chef in the world one day. He batted his eyes and excused himself to return to the kitchen. The three of us got up from the table and returned to the living room for cognac.

Juliette took both her cane and Tom's arm, which he offered to her the minute she mentioned getting up. When we were seated, Alphonse materialized with a tray of cognac accompanied by madeleines. I could not eat another bite, but I took the offered cognac and sipped slowly.

"Now, my dear Charlotte," Juliette said when we were settled, "tell me everything about Fran's book and how you have approached her old publisher. That Etienne. He is so marvellous, is he not? I do not doubt that he would see what his predecessors did not. They will publish her book, *non*?"

I explained to Juliette what would happen as I explored publication in New York. I also wanted to be sure she understood something else about the book.

"Juliette, I know we toasted to Fran's final story being her best one, but I have to make it mine. I feel deeply that the story is mine to tell."

Juliette sipped her cognac slowly, and I feared I might have insulted her—and her friend. She held her glass between her two hands in her lap, gently rotating it to warm up the amber liquid. Then she looked up and said, "I wondered how long it would be before you figured that out."

I was puzzled by her words. "Juliette, when I was here last summer, I asked you where Frannie's last manuscript might be hiding. You said, 'You will find it.' My question is this. How did you know I would find it?"

"*Ma chère*, I am afraid I was not entirely forthcoming with you when first we met last year. I did not tell you the entire story. The answer is yes. I did know where the manuscript was located. But it was Fran's wish that you find it yourself."

Now I was really puzzled. I looked at Tom, who seemed to be savouring his cognac. When I caught his eye, he simply shrugged (had he been watching all those Frenchmen?), smiled and sipped.

"But how could she have known that I'd grow up to be anyone who would be interested in this? How did she know the story would mean something to me, too? What if I hadn't come to Paris and just sold the apartment without even visiting? What if you had died before I found out?" I was breathless—and confused.

"*Mon dieu*," Juliette said, smiling enigmatically. "So many questions. First, you did not have the pleasure of knowing Frannie Phillips in her lifetime. Thus, you can only know her through her legacy. And I will tell you here and now that I do not know how she knew about you, but she did. She told me that she had no doubt. She was that kind of woman. And there is no doubt about the fact that you would find the manuscript even if I died."

"How is that possible?"

"Several weeks after Fran left here that last summer in 1989—and not long before she died," Juliette said, a tear forming in her eye, "she telephoned me. She told me she had forgotten the manuscript and where she had left it. She was bereft. She told me that I was to safeguard it until such time as you would be old enough to retrieve it." I started to interject, but Juliette shook her head and continued. "I wrote a letter to you. It is a letter that is left with my solicitor. In the event of my death, you were to receive the letter telling you where to find the manuscript. You see, my dear, Fran's last wish in her lifetime was that the story be finished."

As I sat there in Juliette's living room, I felt a warmth pass through me and momentarily wondered if Frannie might not be listening somewhere in the ether, breathing a sigh of relief. Her dense great-granddaughter might be starting to understand.

"Our dear Fran asked me to let you find it. But more importantly, she hoped the story one day would find an ending and that you should be encouraged to be the one to find that ending. Charlotte, your great-grandmother hoped that seeking the story's ending might somehow bring her closer to you."

I didn't know what to say. As I sat there now, thinking about my great-grandmother considering her tiny granddaughter, I realized that finding that manuscript had been the catalyst to changing my life. My problem had been that I'd been fighting it. "Thank you, Fran," I whispered.

"Charlotte, my dear girl, *this* is Fran's best story. What better story than her great-granddaughter learning who she is in the world? And making her own mark?"

THIRTY-SIX

THE MINUTE TOM AND I RETURNED home from Paris, I made arrangements to fly to New York. Etienne had been true to his word and set up an appointment for me with *The Leonard Group* and had given the agent a heads-up about the book and who I was. The minute he told me things were organized, I started to get nervous about upholding Fran's reputation. He assured me that wouldn't be a problem.

"Charlie, my dear," he said when he called me with the arrangements, "remember that this book is yours, not Fran's. And by the way, they are quite nervous to meet the great-granddaughter of the infamous and reclusive F.E. de Plessis or Peyton Winter—they now know these were one and the same. It is they who have reason to be anxious for this to go well—not you."

I was mollified to a degree. I'd published one book by this time, but it was a one-off work published by a mid-level Canadian publisher. It had been out for less than six months, so I didn't have a real sense of how it was received. I had hoped for better sales results, but that's just how things go when you're a writer these days—or so I'd been told by everyone from my writer's group colleagues to every online source. I felt this book was much more important for some reason, so I wanted things to go well in New York. This was the big time, and I didn't want to blow the opportunity—it might never come again. With the meetings set, I booked an airline ticket and then I had to think about accommodation. Etienne had offered to pay, but I had other ideas.

I called Evelyn to ask her if I could stay in her apartment in Manhattan—the apartment she had inherited from Fran. I thought it might be fun to be in another of Fran's homes, although I realized from reading her diaries that she'd never actually lived there. It was an investment that she visited only on the odd occasion.

SOMETHING I'M SUPPOSED TO DO

"Hey, Charlie, how was Paris?" Evelyn said when she picked up the phone.

"So wonderful, Evelyn. The apartment is fantastic. You must come to visit when I'm there someday. By the way, great-grandmother Fran's publisher has set me up with a literary agent in New York. Any chance I could stay in your New York apartment? Or do you have it rented out?"

"Rented out? I'm not Air-B-n-B, you know. Of course, it's not rented out. I leave my New York wardrobe there. We plan to take Katherine the moment I think she's old enough to appreciate *Bloomingdale's.*"

Well, I thought, *that might be eighteen or so years away. Or maybe it was thirteen these days. What did I know about kids?* Then I had another thought. *Maybe she'll turn out to be more like her aunt than her mother.* That made me smile. However, I did not voice this view to Evelyn.

"Anyway, little sister, I'll do you one better. How about we have a girls' trip to New York? Katherine is almost a year old now, and I'm sure Daddy can manage a few days without me with help from her nanny and her doting grandmother here in Toronto. And I'm desperate to get away. The practice has been wild lately."

Evelyn's work as a trial lawyer was always wild to hear her talk about it. But I was sure she could use a break. I just wasn't entirely convinced I needed to have her there—or, to be quite honest, that we could manage a trip away together and return home unscathed. Evelyn hadn't always been—how can I put this politely?—supportive of my life decisions. In the end, I agreed. After all, she was letting me stay in the apartment.

Over the next week, as the day of my trip neared, I started to get excited. I had never been to New York City.

~

Evelyn had already arrived at the apartment by the time my cab pulled up in front of the Upper-East side Manhattan building less than a block from Central Park. Her flight from Toronto had arrived several hours before mine, so I told her not to wait for me at La Guardia. She probably wouldn't have anyway.

I dragged my small case behind me as I walked under the inevitable canopy that led to the double doors at the entrance, where a doorman actually opened it for me and said, "You must be Ms. Hudson. The other Ms. Hudson is waiting for you. Take the elevator to the seventh floor, ma'am. Ms. Hudson's apartment is the one on the left."

I thanked him and made my way into the small but well-appointed lobby with its gilt-framed mirror covering an entire wall facing a small reception desk. I was already mesmerized by the New York noise and the traffic, but mainly by the mass of pedestrians who surged at every corner, waiting for the light to turn green. I couldn't figure out how anyone drove a car here with all those people looking just like horses at a racetrack the moment before the starting pistol sounded.

When I reached the apartment, Evelyn had already opened a bottle of wine, kicked off her impossibly high heels (I thought she might have eschewed them since the baby's birth, but I guess not) and was sitting back among a massive number of cushions that covered the twelve-foot sofa.

"Come and join me, Charlie." She sat forward and poured me a glass of wine as I dropped my purse on a nearby chair. Then I flopped into the deep chair across from her as I stared, open-mouthed, at the apartment.

"Wow, Evelyn, this place is amazing. And thank god for the air conditioning." It was beyond hot in New York that August. Evelyn, who had now lived in Toronto for many years, was far more used to this weather than I was. The weather on the Atlantic coast was generally cooler in the summer, with those ocean breezes, although lately, the summers seemed to be getting warmer.

We caught up on the news, and then I told Evelyn more about the manuscript and how I hoped to be able to sell this one to a big American publisher.

Later that evening, when we were finishing our divine meal at a wonderful Italian restaurant a few blocks south of the apartment, Evelyn sat back and looked at me.

"Do you ever think about how everything is so...what's the word? Connected? I mean, just think about it. If I hadn't insisted that you move into Mom's old house and empty it for sale, you would never have found her sewing machine and all those weird patterns. If it hadn't been for that, you would never have met Tom. And you'd still be single. Your whole life would be different." She drained her wine glass and patted her lips with the red-checkered napkin. "I've often thought how great that decision I made was, haven't you?"

Was Evelyn crediting herself with having been the catalyst to all the good things that recently happened in my life? I always thought she made that decision, as she put it, because she didn't have time to interrupt her life and career to work with me on Mom's clutter. I sighed. I guess she was. And maybe she was right.

~

The following day, I presented myself at *The Leonard Group* office on West 29th Street and 6th Avenue. Etienne had told me the office was still in the same place as its predecessor, *The Priestley and Benjamin Agency*, which, as he had mentioned, had represented my great-grandmother for decades. As I stood in front of the five-story red-brick building, I wondered what Fran had been thinking the first time she stood in this exact spot before meeting her first literary agent. I felt a frisson of excitement run up my spine.

I announced myself to the receptionist and was invited to wait in a plush chair for Anika Parker, one of their senior agents. I sipped coffee and listened to the hushed sounds of a busy office until Anika appeared.

When she appeared, she was as striking as the photo accompanying her bio that I'd read on the agency website. She was probably in her mid-fifties, with a white-blonde bob and large red-rimmed glasses. She looked like the quintessential New Yorker in her monochromatic cream-coloured suit and matching stilettos. I stood up to greet her and realized she was close to six-feet tall.

Anika smiled, introduced herself and led me to her immaculate office with its blonde wood walls and ceiling beams. Her online bio had told me she had grown up in the U.K. and had lived in Belgium and Italy before moving to the U.S. to attend university to study economics. I found it endlessly fascinating how people got to the careers they finally settled on. Anika had worked in investment banking and the fashion industry before discovering the literary agency field.

She sat down on a white-upholstered sofa and gestured for me to sit on its twin opposite her. "Charlotte, you have no idea how thrilled I was to hear from Etienne Lemieux that F.E. de Plessis's great-granddaughter was interested in having us represent her. But I think I was even more excited when he confirmed for me that de Plessis had been a woman. Of course, there had always been rumours, but no one had ever verified them. When our agency represented her, she used her American pseudonym Peyton Winter, and only a select few people at the agency knew that Peyton was a woman. Those who did know were sworn to secrecy. I understand from company lore that she chose to keep it that way even after it became obvious that it would no longer hamper her career. She must have been something. Did you know her?"

I explained to Anika that Fran had died the year I was born, so I never had the chance to know her, something I've always regretted. I told her about reading Fran's diaries.

"Her diaries! My god, Charlotte, that would make the basis for such an exciting book. We'll have to talk about it." I chose not to mention that I'd already started making notes about just such a book. She continued. "I think I've read every book she ever wrote and seen every movie based on her books. She was a master of storytelling." Anika picked up a page from a pile of papers in the middle of her desk. "And from what I can tell, Charlotte, you have her gift."

I bristled slightly. I was just beginning to acknowledge and accept that it was *my* gift, not Fran's, but I let it go. I had to admit, though, that having a New York literary agent tell me I had a gift for writing was pretty special.

"So, I take it you liked my book," I said. "And please call me Charlie. Everyone else does."

"Well, Charlie, as it happens, I do love it. As a matter of fact, I've already had preliminary chats about it with two publishing houses."

"Wow! I didn't know that's how it worked."

Anika laughed. "There's an old memoir written by a British literary agent called *They Read Books and Go to Cocktail Parties*. That's not quite all, but sometimes it's how I get things done."

We chatted for a few minutes about where I lived (she had never visited the east coast of Canada—only Toronto, as was to be expected), where I'd studied creative writing (she felt that an M.F.A. was often an impediment, but in my case, we could overcome it), my husband (another potential impediment, but what could you do?), my recent job (she applauded my resignation). Then she asked me about the story.

"Charlie, tell me about what inspired this story."

I chewed on the inside of my cheek, a habit I thought I had broken years ago. The inspiration was Fran's manuscript, of which Anika was already aware. Etienne had told her. He had also told her that Fran had been inspired by real-life people and their stories.

"Well, I guess you know I found that unfinished manuscript."

"Of course. And I think it's going to be a wonderful marketing hook. I mean, what could be better than a long-lost, unfinished manuscript by a famous author finished by her great-granddaughter. It's book marketing gold. I want to hear all about

261

how you were able to track down the real-life people all these years later."

I started to feel peculiar. I was thinking back to when Tom discovered the hand-written note on the back of the manuscript page, which started me on this journey to find the story's ending. But when I thought about Timothy Sinclair and Megan McMaster's love story and Ellie McMaster and her wartime romance, my thoughts began to take on a psychedelic quality that I had always associated with an acid trip—something I'd never experienced in all my sheltered life. Faces appeared, then blurred. Scenes faded in and out. I was just happy that I'd already written them down. I wasn't sure I could explain it to Anika—and I suddenly realized I didn't want to.

When my vision finally cleared, I said, "I guess it was just something that was supposed to happen. Anyway," I said, getting up, "I presume I'll be hearing from you with a contract?"

"As a matter of fact, Charlie, I have a copy of our standard contract right here, ready for you to sign. But perhaps you would like to have your attorney review it?"

I nodded as I accepted the file folder she offered, remembering Tom's last words to me before I left for the airport. Remember, he had said, don't sign anything until we have our lawyer review it. We bid one another goodbye, and she ushered me out. At the agency door, Anika stopped and placed a hand on my shoulder. "Charlotte Hudson, I predict a long and mutually beneficial relationship. Welcome to *The Leonard Group*."

I smiled and departed as quickly as I could. I was still feeling strange, and I had a contract that needed to be reviewed by my attorney—Evelyn.

~

"Just standard stuff," Evelyn said later that evening as she perused the legal document while we sat in the comfortable living room of her apartment drinking martinis and eating potato chips. "I'm not an expert in legal issues for writers, but it looks like it's all in order. So, you'll sign?" I nodded. "Now speak to me about all those people whose stories you're telling in the book."

A YEAR LATER

I HAD JUST FINISHED READING MY EMAIL and put my iPad down when Tom appeared in the doorway to my room, grinning from ear to ear.

"What a woman I'm married to," he said, waving what looked like a book. "Giving birth to two wonderful entities in the same week!"

I glanced over at the bassinette beside my bed and put my finger to my lips. "Not so loud. She just went to sleep!"

Tom feigned an apology and whispered, "Sorry, but I'm so excited for you."

He placed the book he'd been holding onto my lap as he sat down and gazed lovingly at the little bundle in the bassinette. We had named that little bundle Francesca Elizabeth—Frankie, for short. And, of course, F.E. for initials.

I had given birth, as Tom said, to Frankie only twenty-four hours earlier and was still in the hospital and would be for one more night because things had been a bit difficult—but the less said about that, the better. No one likes to hear horror stories about someone else's labour and delivery. Anyway, we were already in love with our little Frankie, and now Tom had given me something else to be proud of—an advance copy of my new book *Something I'm Supposed to Do*—hot off the press and already optioned for film. To say it had been a whirlwind year would be something of an understatement.

Anika was good at what she did—really good. Within a month of our meeting in New York, she found two publishers interested in the story and had managed an auction. The money was of little importance to me—I certainly didn't need any more money. But I was proud of my work. Anika had wanted to capitalize on my great-grandmother's legend, but I had asked her not to do that unless she thought we had a marketing crisis. It hadn't happened yet.

I studied the cover. It was black and vibrant yellow—a back-on illustration of a woman looking toward an urban horizon, wondering what she is supposed to do with her life. Or at least that's what it said to me. I had loved it from the moment my publisher sent it to me for review a few months earlier. Now, as I examined it more closely, it occurred to me that I liked it because it seemed to reflect my thoughts about the story—and especially the characters. I wondered if Tim and Ava would see themselves in the pages of the book. I hoped that if they did, it would make them happy.

"Tom," I whispered so I wouldn't wake the baby, "what do you think Tim would think about the book? Should I send him a copy?" I was trying to picture sending it to him, but I was having trouble capturing the thought.

Tom sat back from the bassinette and looked at me. He took my hand. "What do you mean? Send a copy to Tim Sinclair?"

I nodded.

Tom cocked his head slightly to one side and continued to stare at me. "But, Charlie, you know Tim is dead."

"Dead?" My thoughts began that odd swirling once again.

"Yeah. Remember when you went to the gallery to find him?" Of course, I remembered. "The proprietor told you Tim had been dead for ten years then."

I sat up straight in bed. What was Tom saying? He was wrong. "No, Tom, I met him that day in the gallery," I said. "I interviewed him. He shared his story with me, and you and I even had Tim and his daughter Ava over for dinner. How can you have forgotten? You were there."

Tom shook his head. "Wow, Charlie. It did seem vivid to you when you told me about it, but we certainly didn't have them over for dinner. Are you sure you're feeling all right?"

"What are you talking about? Of course, I'm feeling all right." I was having trouble keeping my voice low. I felt as if I had been ambushed.

Still holding my hand, Tom said gently, "Charlie, darling, the morning after you visited *The Sinclair Gallery* and found out about Tim and Megan being dead, you woke up and told me a story—down to the most minute detail. It was incredible. Then you started furiously making notes."

"Are you trying to tell me that I dreamed the story?"

"Of course." Tom shrugged.

I shook my head furiously. "But that's just not possible. How could I have dreamed something and felt so deeply that it was real? You have to be wrong."

"But, Charlie, isn't that exactly what great writers do? They dream up stories then put them together so the rest of us mortals can enjoy them."

I frowned as the pieces began to fall into place. After a moment, I said, "So, what you're saying is that it *is* my story."

Tom nodded. "It always was."

"I've spent so much time chasing something that isn't there, haven't I?" Tom didn't say anything, but I'm sure he understood that I wasn't talking just about characters and stories in a book. "You tried to tell me. Then Juliette tried." I shook my head as Frankie woke up and started gurgling. I looked over at the tiny bundle and smiled. Then I pressed Tom's hand, which was still holding mine.

"Now I finally get it. There isn't anything I am supposed to do. There is only something that I am supposed to be. Me."

AUTHOR'S NOTES & ACKNOWLEDGEMENTS

Something I'm Supposed to Do started life as a screenplay. I was inspired to write it by another true story—how my parents met at *The Jubilee Boat Club* (which really did exist) in 1941, mere months before my father was shipped overseas to fight for the next two-and-a-half years. My mother was eighteen years old.

However, once Charlie and her family invaded my writing some three books ago, I was grabbed by the notion that the story could embed itself within another story. And so, Frannie's manuscript began forming.

I never intended to write a series—it just happened because I couldn't shake Charlie. Each of the books in the series—*The Year I Made 12 Dresses* [book1], *Kat's Kosmic Blues* [book 2], *The Inscrutable Life of Frannie Phillips* [book 3] and this one [book 4]—stands alone as a story to be enjoyed. However, I believe the story is much richer if you read them in order. And you'll get to know Charlie much better!

Now, a few notes on the sources I consulted for this book.

First, apologies (sort of) to anyone of the CanLit ilk who bristled at my quotation of a (Canadian) writer who described CanLit in such disparaging terms. The writer was Douglas Coupland. I have taken artistic license with my quote since he didn't write that until 2006, some years after Frannie died.

Second, thank you to my ninety-nine-year-old mother, Gwen. She filled me in on the details of what *The Jubilee Boat Club* was like back when it was entertaining Canadian and visiting soldiers and sailors during World War II.

"One of the greatest things a father can do for his children is to love their mother." I have always subscribed to this belief and thought I had come up with it myself. It turns out it is attributed to several different people. I cannot take credit.

Every time I write a book, I have several important people in my life who provide input. Art and Ian, you both know how much your feedback means to me—now and forever. Love you both!

ABOUT THE AUTHOR

PATRICIA J. PARSONS has written nineteen books, including health and business books, a memoir, two historical novels, and women's fiction. She has been a fashion design and sewing fanatic for most of her life, a passion she writes about online at *The GG Files blog*. She lives, writes and sews in Toronto.

- Connect with her on Instagram at @patriciajparsons or @pjparsonswriter
- Join her on Facebook @patriciaparsonswriter and at facebook.com/groups/12 dresses
- Visit her on the web at www.patriciajparsons.com